SHIFTING WINDS

SHIFTER LORDS

S.E. BABIN

OLIVERHEBERBOOKS

CHAPTER

One

A strong, warm hand pressed against my abdomen, the rest of my body pressed against a hard chest. Hair tangled in my face, hiding the crimson glow of my cheeks when I remembered where I was.

And who I was pressed against.

A warm nose nudged the crook of my neck, followed by a hot kiss pressed against my shoulder blade. I arched against Caelan, his wicked chuckle ruffling my messy hair.

"I can feel you overthinking," he murmured against my skin.

We lay entangled in each other like vines, one of his heavy legs tossed over me. I was trapped but felt safer than I ever had. We'd been doing this for two months now, going back and forth to each other's homes, spending the night in each other's arms, and doing other more pleasurable things.

I'd fallen head over heels for him, and Caelan made no secret of how he felt about me. To him, I was his Lady, no matter there was no bond or ceremony or anything tying us together other than his actions. I shifted in his arms, turning so I could face him.

Large hands wrapped around my hips. All the stress and tension from the last few months had fallen away; his gray and golden eyes relaxed and languid, the haze of sleep still there. His full lips curled in a soft smile as he raised a hand to brush a stray strand of hair from my face.

"Beautiful," he murmured.

I shook my head, wishing he could see himself the way I saw him. "You," I whispered. "You're the most beautiful thing I've ever seen."

My words were true and heartfelt and dangerous. I pressed a kiss against his lips. "And," I said, gently pushing his hands away, "I have to get to work before the others vote to fire me."

Caelan groaned. "You're the entire operation, and we all know none of them would fire you. They technically can't."

"True." I wiggled from his grasp, laughing when Caelan's eyes lit up with interest. "But they can make me feel guilty about it. I've been taking too many vacation days, and we have events coming up."

The weight of responsibility the Shifter Lord carried each day had fallen away sometime over the last few weeks, allowing me to see the real man behind the tightly leashed violence. And that had been my death knell. I'd fallen head over heels for him once he let his mask fall away.

I was in big trouble.

With a groan, he released me, watching with glowing eyes as I snatched up his shirt from the chair and tugged it over my head. His eyes stayed on me until I stumbled into the bathroom and locked the door.

Pressed against the door, I squeezed my eyes shut and let out a slow breath. I had to figure this out. In no way, shape, or form was I equipped to rule over Caelan's wolves with him, and they didn't want me to. I could taste the hostility in the air anytime I was in the main part of the Keep. The only person who didn't want to eat me was Simone.

But even she had her doubts. I could see them when she thought I wasn't watching. Simone might be my friend, but her loyalty was to Caelan.

Not the woman he was sleeping with.

Some of the wolves were on board with me, but I'd put it at twenty-five percent. The other seventy-five were wary. With good reason.

I tugged on my underwear and the pants I found hanging over the shower rod, but my shirt was nowhere to be seen. After a quick face wash and a mouth rinse, I tried to do something about my hair but gave up when I realized it was hopeless.

Caelan was up and wearing pants when I came out, sitting shirtless on the edge of the bed, eyes glowing when he saw me. A predator lurked in those eyes, a hunger for me that both warmed me and terrified me. "Some of the pack refer to you as Lady," he said quietly. "I'd like to make it official at the next gathering."

I swallowed hard. He'd voiced his intentions that night I'd killed Finn and Rhona, but that was not the same as a formal mating and bonding ceremony. Those would solidify my place in Caelan's Keep and his Pack.

"I want you beside me, Evie. Always." His voice was low and soft and so sure.

Wonderful, beautiful words I always wanted to hear. The problem being I was an internal bundle of nerves. "It's only been a little while. We have plenty of time before we make any formal decisions." I smiled. "Besides, another pretty little wolf might catch your eye."

Power punched through the room. "The only person catching my eye is you. The moment you delivered that automaton to my Keep is the moment I knew I'd have you." He tilted his head and studied me. "Unless you don't want me. Is that it, Evangeline? Has another man or wolf caught your eye?"

I snorted, but when his power didn't let up, I froze. "Caelan. How can you ask me that? I haven't warmed anyone's bed in the seven years I've been here. Now you think I'm on the prowl?"

He rose, stalking toward me. I stood stock still, admiring his lethal grace and the play of muscles in his lean chest. Caelan planted his hands on either side of my head. I took a step back, my shoulders bumping into the wall.

"I don't share, flower girl."

I blinked up at him. "I didn't ask you to."

He bent his head, nipping at my neck. "What's wrong?"

"Nothing," I wheezed, his touch making my brain scramble.

"Don't lie to me." He tipped my chin up.

Our eyes met. "I don't want to," I whispered.

His brows furrowed. "Then don't."

I placed my hands on either side of his face, stroking my thumbs across the five o'clock shadow on his jaw. "I need more time. That's all."

He closed his eyes and inhaled. I braced for an argument, surprised when Caelan relaxed and nodded. "Fine. You are not used to a shifter's ways, and I know I've been...pushy."

My jaw dropped. "Er. Seriously?" Caelan was rarely this agreeable unless I was agreeing to something he wanted.

His face creased in a smile. "So disbelieving."

"Experience," I said and pressed one more kiss to his lips. "As wonderful as this is, I'm late."

Ducking under his arm, I scrambled for my shoes. "Can I borrow your shirt? I can't find mine."

"Everything I have is yours."

I stilled, the growly sound of his voice doing funny things to my insides. "I'll wash it and get it back to you."

"Keep it."

I glanced up at him from my crouch. My mouth went dry as my eyes went up, up, up, hitching and stalling on the golden beauty of his honed chest. Dear gods. The man was pretty.

"Keep looking at me like that, and you won't be at work until tomorrow."

I blinked, cheeks heating, and looked down. "Sorry."

He crouched down beside me, pressing my hands between his. "Again, do not apologize for staring at me like I'm dinner."

Caelan went to his knees and snagged my other sandal from far underneath the bed, waving me away when I reached for it. "Sit," he commanded.

I plopped onto my rear and wiggled my foot at him.

Caelan grinned and took my foot in his large hands, pressing his thumb against the middle and sending a delicious ache through the arch. "Mmm," I groaned.

He chuckled. "If you come back tonight, I'll show you more of these magic fingers."

Caelan gripped my ankle and fastened my sandals, first on the left, then on the right.

"My greenhouse and land need tending."

He rose and held out a hand to help me up. "Then I'll come to you."

I froze. Caelan, ever observant, slowly nodded. "Time. Right."

The Shifter Lord held out his arm. "I'll walk you out."

We said nothing as he walked me to my car, and just when I was about to get inside, Caelan bent and nuzzled my neck. "You won't escape me, Evangeline," he murmured against my skin.

I couldn't say a word. Caelan opened the door and waited until I buckled myself in before closing the door. He watched me until my vehicle was out of view.

That man was intense.

A single dark feather tinged with blue lay by the entrance to my greenhouse. I was bending to reach for it when a subtle shift in the air and a tinge of pine scent tickled my nose.

"Here to collect?" I asked my father, knowing it was him by the buckskin boots he wore and the smell of ancient forest.

"It's been a month."

I tucked the feather into my bag and faced Cernunnos. He wore a pair of leather breeches and no shirt today. His antlers rose high in the air, moss dripping and sparkling from the tines. Around his neck lay a leather necklace with a silver spiral charm.

Sometimes the Fae King showed up in joggers. Sometimes he showed up looking every inch the feral forest god. Today, he'd chosen the latter.

Meanwhile, I barely slept at all last night. I needed a shower and fourteen cups of coffee, and I was not in the mood to deal with Cernunnos.

My father.

Perish the thought.

"I never said yes." The greenhouse welcomed me when I stepped in, every plant in the vicinity of the door reaching out to brush my skin. I set my bag down and went straight to the work-table, needing to dig my fingers in the dirt for a little while before I showered and made my way to the shop.

I hadn't lied to Caelan. I was late to work, and my friends were getting frustrated with me, but the greenhouse sustained some of our shop's work, and I needed this time.

Preferably alone.

"You are my child." Cernunnos ducked as he followed me inside, his power tingling over my skin. Someone like him, no matter how tightly he cloaked his power, could never contain what he was. Even a human would realize there was something otherworldly about Cernunnos, even if they couldn't put their finger on why.

I pulled a flat of arugula seedlings over. The weather was cool enough to plant some of my favorite greens, and I'd overcompen-sated, planning on giving the others a bunch for their homes when they were ready.

"I wasn't your child until a month ago," I said in a cool tone. He might have offered the genetic material, but Cernunnos wasn't involved in my life until only a few months ago.

Cernunnos blinked in surprise, hurt flashing over his face. "Evie."

I held up my hand. "You can't not show up for eighteen years, pop in to help me a few times, refuse to answer my questions, then boom, all of a sudden hand me a damn crown and be like suuurrrprrriiiise!!"

He opened his mouth, frowned, and snapped it shut.

"And another thing, if you haven't noticed, I am completely ill-equipped to rule the fae. I wasn't raised with them, nor have I had any real contact with the fae unless you count my mother. Which I don't."

His expression grew thunderous. "Never?"

I slapped the trowel I held down. "How many times did you check up on me?"

If he had, he would have known humans raised me.

"I—" He scrubbed a hand over his jaw, a thoughtful look on his face.

I barreled through. "When Mom got tired of me, she dropped me off with two humans who raised me as their own. I had no friends, and Mom told me my father was human."

Cernunnos stared.

"There was no way for me to know what I was or what I was capable of. I figured some of it out on my own. Mom never bothered to teach me much, and I spent my entire childhood wishing I was special like her." My voice broke, and I swiped away a stray tear I didn't realize was there. I had never spoken about my life like this.

Moira and the others knew because I tried not to keep secrets from them, but standing here with my father had opened old wounds.

"So excuse me if I don't accept some destiny you want to thrust on me because you want to retire." I glared at the Fae King.

Cernunnos looked uncomfortable and sad. We stared at each other for a long moment before he turned and pulled up a stool, scooting it closer. "Tell me what you're doing," he said softly.

My hands trembled. "I'm separating and repotting the arugula so I can give it out to the people I work with. Caelan may want some, too."

He nodded. "And you don't use your magic to do so?"

"I use my magic to boost its health and growth. Potting plants allows me to know the soil I'm using and tells me what it needs." I lifted a shoulder in a shrug. "Plus, it's therapeutic."

"May I?" he asked, gesturing for the trowel.

My brow furrowed. I waited for the other shoe to drop, but Cernunnos sat there, one tanned hand resting on my workbench. "Fine."

I pushed the arugula and trowel over, handed him five pots, and scooted the large container of dirt closer. Then I pulled another tray of plants over for me to work on.

After I showed him how I repotted plants, Cernunnos got to work.

Half an hour later, the Fae King was happily potting other things at my direction, boosting some of my older plants with a soft touch of his fingers.

Eventually, the stress in my shoulders faded away, and I got into the rhythm of working with nature and my father's unusual presence. Magic saturated the air, mine and Cernunnos's natural power mingling together, different but similar.

Every plant in the greenhouse hummed with contentment, stretching and reaching for us both.

"You've never worked in a greenhouse like this?" I asked, breaking the long but comfortable silence.

A small smile. "The first thing you should learn about the fae is that most of us are old enough to forget about mundane work. Magic has become a catch all for us. If we can do something by barely lifting a finger, we will." His hands and forearms were coated in black dirt, a satisfied gleam in his eyes as he propagated a new type of pothos I'd accidentally created.

Interesting. "Have you ever used that against one of them?"

Cernunnos laughed. "Considering you had to show me how to pot a seedling, I'm going with no. I'm just as guilty as the rest, perhaps even more so." He carefully nudged dirt around the delicate cutting. "I'm older than everyone and never realized that perhaps I lean on my power more than I should."

Warmth filled me at his words. "Well, I'm the expert at getting by with a wing and a prayer."

Cernunnos stiffened. "Evangeline."

"Don't," I whispered. If he apologized, I might break. "What's done is done. I know you stayed away to keep me safe from Mom."

He inhaled a heavy breath. "And now I don't know if staying away was the right decision. But taking you back to my kingdom?" Cernunnos shook his head. "It is no place for a child."

I slid a look his way. "And yet you want me to take your

crown? What about me? What if I want children one day? Would you have me do as you did to me?"

My father's shoulders slumped. "You chastise me like a child." He shook his head and let out a short laugh. "And I deserve it. I should have known you wouldn't bow down to my demands. You've yet to do so with anything in your life. The fact remains, Evie. My kingdom needs an heir. You are my only child."

"Can you choose someone else? Does it have to be a child?"

Cernunnos pushed the pot away and took another, slowly filling it with dirt. "An heir is always a child, whether biological or adopted. But I would not trust anyone else to rule. You might not be human, but you live among humans. You understand them and think like them sometimes. The gods no longer inhabit the earth, but I am the land's steward."

I understood what he wanted and what he was saying, but I was barely equipped to take care of myself. "What about what I want?"

A thin smile. "Perhaps we can figure out a way for you to have the best of both worlds. There is always change when a new ruler arrives. The same will prove true for my kingdom."

"And children?"

He cocked his head and studied me. "Do you truly wish for children after growing up the way you did?"

"I don't often think about it," I admitted. "But Caelan knows what I am now."

His brows rose. "You wish for them with the wolf?"

"Not necessarily. No one has known what I am for many years. Who's to say I could even have children with him?" I shook my head. "And how can I have my life and my shop, Caelan and his Keep, and be queen of..." I waved my hand. "Your stuff, too?"

Amusement glimmered in his eyes. "My stuff might be a little more challenging."

I scoffed. "You know what I'm saying."

Cernunnos rose and dusted off his hands. "I am sorry for thrusting you into a position you don't want. While I do wish to retire soon, you've opened my eyes to the error of my ways. I still need someone to train, and I want that person to be you."

"Cernunnos—"

He exhaled. "It is your birthright, Evangeline. If there is anyone who can figure out a way to have it all, it's you."

"You have way too much faith in me."

Cernunnos shook his head. "You don't have enough faith in yourself. I will return once a month."

When I opened my mouth to protest, Cernunnos stepped forward and put his hands on my arms. "I will move the timeline to accommodate you as you learn our ways. You need to know who you're dealing with. Our people are powerful and complicated. Even if you decide not to accept what I'm offering, I'd like to make up for my past failures. Allow me to teach you about our people and my kingdom. At minimum, it will only serve to help you."

I frowned. "You're saying if I refuse you, you will let it lie?"

"I will move the timeline." His enigmatic smile and non-answer made me roll my eyes. "Thank you for teaching me this morning, daughter. I like learning with you."

With a wink, he disappeared in a flash of green and golden light.

I'd managed to move the goalpost but not the goal. If he wanted me to take his place as the fae ruler, he was going to have to wait a lot longer than a few months.

Maybe even forever.

oira, Tess, and Ash were gathered around my worktable when I finally made it in to work. An anticipatory silence hung in the air while all three grinned at me.

"Nope," I said by way of greeting. "We are not doing this."

Moira cackled. "Aw. Spoil sport. We know you've been up to some serious nonsense. Aren't we your besties?"

I rolled my eyes and set my purse behind the register. "We've been seeing each other for a couple of months now. Are you ever going to stop asking me?"

"Absolutely not," Ash said.

I gave him a look. "And here I thought Moira was the one corrupting you all."

"She's seventy-five percent of it." Ash winked and returned his attention to the small bonsai he was putting the final touches on.

I came over and nudged Moira over so I could take a look. "That's stunning," I breathed.

Ash was a dryad, and his knack was nature magic, most powerful with trees. His bonsai work took months and sometimes even years, but they sold for thousands. "Why is it blooming so late in the season?"

"Because I'm a dryad."

Moira laughed.

I shook my head ruefully. "Dumb question," I admitted. "But it's October. Azaleas are spring bloomers, so I'm curious why you forced it to bloom?"

"Much like you," Ash said as he snipped a tiny, almost microscopic piece from the bonsai, "I can coax flowers and trees into blooms." He smiled and straightened. "But this one has been happy from the moment I brought her into this shop. She's been blooming on and off for months now."

I reached a finger out and paused. "May I?"

Ash gestured to go ahead. "Be my guest. She's yours after all."

I gasped. "Mine?"

Ash told me a long time ago he was creating one for me, but after months had gone by, I'd forgotten about it.

He inclined his head. "A Satsuki azalea. She normally blooms in May, but as you can see, she's prone to express herself."

I pulled the rolling stool over and sat down, gently touching one of the blooms. Sending out the tiniest pulse of magic into the small trunk, I closed my eyes to get a read on her.

Gentle, feminine energy. Young. Happy.

A smile tipped my lips up. "She's ecstatic to receive so much attention."

Ash chuckled and stroked a finger down its trunk. "I think you should consider keeping her in the shop. She likes all the traffic and how much we're all together."

"Should I keep her in the window?"

Ash nodded. "Normally, these are outside plants, but this gal has the advantage of having two nature mages in close proximity. She'll be fine as long as we check her every few days."

"Thank you so much," I said, meeting Ash's eyes. "She's gorgeous."

"You're welcome." He jerked his head toward the window. "Want help carrying her over? The pot weighs a ton."

Together, we carefully lifted the new bonsai and made a place for her in the shop window, carefully rearranging some of the other flowers until we had her right in the middle. She looked a little odd with her soft pink flowers in the middle of all the oranges, reds, and yellows of our fall display, but it made me laugh. The bonsai was gorgeous and showy, and she'd bring in foot traffic just because people would be curious about her.

Tess floated over, stopping beside Ash. She hadn't said much this morning, but that was her way. The banshee rarely spoke unless she had something to say.

"Have you seen your mother?" she asked.

I blinked. Tess had a line on Cliona's location most of the time because my mother was Queen of the Banshees. "Not since that night on Caelan's land."

"You'll see her soon," Tess said before floating away.

"Alright," I said slowly. "Thanks for the warning, Tess."

The banshee passed right through one of the walls, headed to the break room, I assumed.

"Is she okay?" I whispered to Ash.

Green eyes met mine. "Her powers have been acting up some. I think she's gaining some new aspects of her magic she didn't expect. It's thrown her off a little."

"Does she need help?" Tess had a strange variety of powers, most pertaining to the dead, but she could do other things that didn't seem to fit in the banshee wheelhouse.

Much like my friend Moira, who was leaning against the register, watching us.

"I got it," Ash promised. "If we need you, we know where to find you."

"At Caelan's," Moira quipped.

I tossed a shed leaf at her, giving it a bit of extra oomph with my magic. It caught in her hair and stuck, the glimmer of orange bright against her dark tresses. Her grin widened as she plucked it out, turning it to and fro. "You've gotten control of your magic. Cool."

I had. A teeny tiny part of me wondered if all the extracurricular activities with Caelan had calmed my Chimera down so much it lay like a content cat inside me.

Moira's eyes glimmered. "You know what helps humans and paranormal alike when it comes to exerting extra energy?"

"Moira!"

"S-E-X," she spelled, grinning like a lunatic.

"I wish I had a bucket of leaves I could throw at you," I muttered.

"She's not wrong," Ash said.

"Et tu, Ash?"

He snorted. "Physical activity always helps when there's an excess of power built up. While Moira rightly assumes it's sex—"

"Can someone please kill me?" I whispered.

"Even a good workout regimen should help." He smiled. "So if things don't work out with Caelan and you don't have another boy toy to take his place, maybe you can take up running."

"I'm going to walk out the door and come back in again, and we're going to start the day over and pretend this never happened."

Moira came over and slung an arm around my shoulder. "Party pooper. There's no shame in a good, hard—"

I ducked under her arm and hurried toward the back doors, plugging my ears with my fingers. "La la la la la!" I cried.

Even through my plugged ears, I could hear their laughter.

A few hours later, I'd scratched a good portion of my to-do list off and had even managed to finish Hattie's weekly delivery. Setting the large bouquet of sunflowers and dahlias to the side, I pulled up the week's work orders and almost choked when I saw it.

"Yeah," Moira said, rightly assuming what I was looking at. "Your little romance with the Shifter Lord is good for business. We're booked solid for months."

"Shit," I whispered, my hands pressing on either side of my face.

Moira stilled. "Evie?" She leaned back and stared at me. "If you're thinking about breaking up with him, can you hold off until Christmas?"

I gaped at her.

Moira took a step back and held up her hands. "I'm just saying. We're bringing in a ton of money, and that hot barista I was telling you about invited me on a singles cruise. If we turn the faucet off now, my bonus will be lower, which means fewer drinks for me."

I counted to five in my head. "You're an immortal. You have more money than I do." My eye twitched. "You can afford to do a cruise every single month for ten years."

"Yes," Moira argued, "but I want to do this one, and it's twice as much." She laughed and poured herself another cup of tea. "But you didn't answer the question. Are you thinking of breaking up with Caelan?"

"No." I sighed. "But things are complicated."

"They always are," Ash said. "What's going on this time?"

This time. Six months ago, things were normal. I was a florist selling bouquets and floral arrangements, and things were great.

"Cernunnos has decided I'm his retirement plan."

A beat of silence before Ash let out a low whistle. "Queen of the Fae, Evie? That's a big promotion."

"An unwanted one. Things are already complicated if my relationship with Caelan progresses."

"Which it will," Moira chimed in. "That wolf would handcuff you and drag you to the altar if you allowed it."

He would. Caelan made no secret he wanted me for his own. I cringed internally every time I thought about what happened on his land. Not because of what we'd done. Never that.

After our tête-à-tête in the woods, I marched arm in arm with the Lord and butt-ass naked over to hundreds of his shifters and agreed with everything Caelan had said about me being their new

Lady. And if that wasn't bad enough, I somehow had commanded them because I wanted their Lord to myself for a little while longer.

I still had no idea why I'd done it. It felt like I was high or something, and after what Caelan and I had just shared, I had serious stars in my eyes for him. I would have said anything, done anything for him, and I would mean every word.

Then, of course, the real world came crashing back into our love nest.

And I, as usual, was internally freaking out. Again.

"What did you say?" Moira asked. She passed a fresh mug of coffee over, and I took it gratefully, wrapping my fingers around to soak up the heat.

"What I usually say before I get wrapped up in it anyway." I slumped against the desk. "Although, I think he came around to slowing things down."

"Really?" Ash sipped from a large water bottle. He might be in human form, but he drank water like an elephant. "I've never met a reasonable fae."

"Hey!"

"Present company excluded," he added with a wink. "Sometimes."

"Yes, it's not like he has a choice. If he wants someone of blood relation to take over, he has to wait for me." Not that I would. Dealing with my mother was bad enough. Thinking of dealing with all the fae made me want to close myself in a dark room and scream.

Moira's brows rose. "Are you thinking of doing it?"

I snorted. "Right now? No. Who's to say what the future holds, but I don't see myself ever leading an entire faction of people."

Moira's lips pursed. "And what about Caelan's people?"

"Even the shifters." I groaned. "Maybe I shouldn't have acted on my feelings." Doing so had opened a door I wasn't sure I could close. Or even wanted to. But just like me, Caelan came with complications. I didn't regret what we'd done, and I cared about the Shifter Lord more than I'd ever cared about anyone else.

"Don't apologize for following your heart." Moira topped off my mug. "Now, the store opens in twenty minutes, and you're on register duty because you've been slacking off the last few weeks."

She winked and tipped her mug at me. "We have an anniversary party in two weeks. I'll be in the back working on a few of the arrangements, but they specifically requested you to do the main centerpiece. They want one of those automatons like you did for Caelan the first time."

I gave her a dubious stare. "Hopefully not as involved as the others?"

"Nope. A simple scene, something romantic. I'll have to check my notes." She waved and headed to the back, leaving Ash and me alone in the front.

Ash had gone back to his own worktable and was occupied with scrutinizing the branching pattern on his newest project, a Japanese maple bonsai. A cool thread of green magic trickled from his fingers as he coaxed the bonsai to grow the way he thought it should.

I smiled and pulled the register over. Many things demanded my attention today. The least I could do was cross a few more things off the to-do list before I went home.

When I finally made it home, a letter wrapped in vines and divine magic lay tucked inside the screen door.

I set my bag down and opened it right away, not wanting the magic inside my house in case it was something unfriendly.

The parchment was thick and heavy, the ink the message was written with a deep, indigo blue.

The Court of Gods meets in two weeks' time.

Attendance is not optional.

It was unsigned.

CHAPTER
Four

I woke up the next morning, the damning letter still clutched in my hand. My eyes felt like sandpaper. Most of the night I stared at the ceiling wondering if I should have died on that field in Scotland. Things would be so much easier if I had.

And as soon as that thought crossed my mind, I mentally slapped myself and dragged my maudlin rear end out of bed. I wasn't the kind of fatalistic person who believed everything happened for a reason. I believed every decision you made led you to a certain path, and it's the choices that came after that drove your life.

Coffee first. Contemplation second.

Joy Springs had chilled considerably, the outside temperatures plunging into the forties overnight. I shrugged on a wool and cashmere blend oversized sweater, wiggled my feet into a pair of wool slippers, and took my coffee on the back porch.

A massive gray wolf peered at me through the forest cover. My heart skipped a beat until my brain unscrambled.

"Come up," I said quietly. "There are clothes in the top left drawer of my dresser. Want some coffee?"

The wolf trotted up the stairs and gently nudged me, careful not to spill my coffee. I gave him a healthy scratch under the neck and a gentle swat on the rear end. "I can't believe you're going to make me get up," I muttered.

Caelan huffed, stood on his hind legs, and got the front door open with no interference from me.

"Creepy," I said as I watched the wolf enter my house.

A couple minutes later, Caelan came out of the house wearing joggers and a t-shirt that fit and holding a steaming mug of coffee and a blanket from the back of the couch. He had a funny look on his face.

"Put your coffee down," he said in a snarly voice as he set his mug down on the other table by the loveseat.

I blinked and looked up at him.

His eyes had gone full gold.

I set my mug down.

Caelan bent and scooped me up in one arm. I wrapped my arms around his neck as he bent to get my coffee. He carried me over to the outdoor loveseat and sat down, settling me into his lap.

"Are you alright?"

"You bought me clothes." He handed me my mug and picked his up.

I had. It didn't seem right for him to wear my ex-husband's clothes, and they didn't fit him anyway. "Did I do something wrong?"

His hand cupped the back of my head, his fingers tightening in my hair.

My eyes closed. The damn man knew I loved it when he acted possessive like this.

Warm lips pressed against mine, the slide of his tongue against the seam of my lips dragging a moan from me. I opened, and Caelan kissed the breath right out of me.

"Well," I said when he drew back. "I guess you like them? It was only a few t-shirts and some joggers. Simone told me your size."

"You thought of me when I wasn't there." His eyes still blazed gold.

"I always think of you." Life would be easier if I didn't, but he'd wormed his way into my heart and my psyche, and I knew I'd never get him out.

Caelan's eyes narrowed. "Drink your coffee," he snarled.

The look in his eyes made my heart twist. The second I finished, he took the mug, slammed it down on the table, and rose, carrying me inside to the bedroom.

I didn't argue.

Not even a little bit.

I was on time, no thanks to Caelan, who kept trying to drag me back to bed. I'd left him rumpled and gorgeous in my bed with instructions to lock the place up. He gave me a wicked smile and asked me if I was sure I had to go in today.

Evil wolf.

Moira and Ash were already there. The vampire laughed out loud when she saw me.

"Morning loving? Damn, Evie. You're making us all jealous."

"Shuddup," I said, crimson heating my cheeks.

She grinned. "There's fresh coffee and some notes about the automaton on your worktable."

"I'll work on it today." I made a beeline for the coffee pot and got ready for the day, doing my best not to think about my morning with Caelan and failing miserably.

"Maybe we should add these to the website," Ash said. He crouched down to peer at the concept I'd spent hours working on. "You have a real gift."

A smile flashed over his face as he restarted the automaton. I'd created a forest scene with blooming flowers. A white swing, ropes entwined with vines and blooms, hung from an ancient oak tree, gently swinging as a fox lay curled up on the seat. Fog curled along the ground as a bright green snake slithered along the grass.

A second fox darted into the clearing. He ran in circles around the swing as the female cracked open an eye, pretending not to watch, then he skulked along the ground until the swing came back at the perfect angle.

In one lithe move, the fox hopped onto the same swing, quickly curling around the female. Hearts bubbled up over their heads as the female reached up to nuzzle the male's muzzle.

Tess popped into the room with a slight puff of air and a flash of light. Ash and I startled.

"New trick?" I eyed Ash.

"Yes. It's fun." His tone was clipped, and he gave Tess a dark look. "She's figuring things out as she goes along."

Uh oh. Trouble in paradise?

"So cute." Tess floated over to stand by Ash. "Those foxes are adorable."

"Thanks. I thought about putting a woman in the swing, but I couldn't figure out how to do it." I shrugged. "It's easier for me to use botanicals and forest scenes."

Tess's brow furrowed. "I could help you. Every time I send a soul on, I retain a tiny piece of their essence. You'll need it to animate something like this."

I'd been fussing with one of the blooms on the automaton when she spoke. My hands froze. "Why do I learn something new and unnerving about you every time you say something?"

Tess lifted a pale shoulder. "Maybe you don't ask me enough questions."

And with that the banshee floated away, leaving me completely perplexed. I sank into my chair and stared at Ash.

Neither of us said anything for a while. I finally laughed. "Is she like that at home?"

Ash rubbed the space between his brows. "Have you ever met someone you liked so much but just didn't get?"

"Pretty much every day."

A faint smile crossed his face. "She has such an effervescent, open joy sometimes, and it makes me feel..." He inhaled. "Glorious."

I sensed there was a big but coming and waited.

"But she's a banshee. Death is her purpose. It's anathema to someone like me." He rubbed a hand through his hair and slumped onto a chair next to me.

I slung an arm over his shoulder and drew him into a one-armed hug. "I'm not sure what to say. Love is complicated. Simple words, but they encompass the tangled morass of the heart, I think. If I can give you one piece of advice…"

He exhaled and gave me a short nod.

My heart broke for him. "If you can't see yourself with her for the long haul, you need to cut the cord sooner rather than later."

"And the shop?"

I'd been thinking about that the moment those two started making googly eyes at each other. "We're all friends. We've been together a long time. I think of this in two opposite ways. First, we're all adults and we love each other. If you're both mature about it, I don't see a reason why we can't all continue working together. Second, everything changes. Even when we don't want it to. As much as I'd hate for us to split up, I never expected us to be together forever. Even if I really want it that way."

He leaned his head on my shoulder. "I love her, you know."

"I know you do."

We sat that way for a while until Ash slid his chair away and stood. "Mind if we have the rest of the day off?"

I flicked my fingers at him. "As long as you bring us Brewtide Beans tomorrow."

"Done. I'll even throw in some muffins."

"Even better. Now go home." My face softened. "And Ash, be careful with Tess. As strong as she is, she's also fragile. You are her first…everything."

He swallowed. "Of course." Ash paused at the door. "But just so you know, it never went all the way. Maybe that will make this easier."

I highly doubted it. "I hope so," was all I said.

Moira left me to close the shop, and I was busy sweeping plant remnants from the floor when a soft knock on the window startled me.

Rowan stood there, holding a box and a tray of coffee. My spirits lifted as I hurried to open the door.

The Shifter Lord breezed in. I took the tray from him and watched as he went to the worktable and set the box down.

"I hope you brought me goodies," I said.

Rowan was insanely good looking. His hair was a little shaggier than the last time I'd seen him, and his hazel eyes were bright as he turned to smile at me.

"I'd never show up to a beautiful woman's abode without goodies," he said solemnly.

"Flirt," I accused with a laugh.

He took the coffee I offered him and gestured for me to stand beside him.

I peered into the box and gasped. "Is that a fuchsia?"

Bright purple and white blooms hung heavy from glossy green leaves. "What kind is it?"

Rowan lifted the plant from the box. "A kind no one else has."

I touched the soil, feeling Rowan's magical signature beating. He was like me, but also something completely different. "You created this?"

"An accidental experiment in the greenhouse."

I gasped. "It's triple bloomed!"

Rowan grinned. "That's the accident part."

"You could make a fortune off this!"

The Lord waved a hand. "I've got enough money. Trust me."

But I shook my head. "At minimum, you need to get this registered as a new variety. That way some asshat doesn't steal a cutting and take it for themselves."

"You think someone would steal from a Lord?"

The look on his face, so bewildered, made me laugh.

"There's always an idiot out there looking to make a buck. Trust me. You want to register this with the Ag department. I can show you how to do it."

Rowan grimaced. "I don't want anyone sniffing around my Keep. Especially not the human government."

"Hmm." I touched the silky soft petals. "How about I do it for you? I'll need to get some information from you about how you bred the new cultivar and probably some other things, but I can register it in your name."

He shook his head. "Register it in yours."

My jaw dropped. "Rowan. That's—"

"I insist. My name can't be tied to this, but you're right. I'd rather it belongs to someone I trust than someone looking to get rich."

I stared down at the plant. "Something this stunning deserves to be shared. What do you think about me carrying these in the shop?"

Something flashed in Rowan's eyes a moment before a smile tugged his lips up. "I wish we'd met first."

My heart did a little flip. "We do make a good team," I acknowledged.

Rowan tugged at a lock of my hair that had escaped my messy bun. "You think these would sell?"

I snorted. "Like frigging hotcakes."

He laughed. "Alright then. Let's do it. You take eighty percent."

My stomach lurched. "What? No. Absolutely not. This is your cultivar. I'll take five."

"Nope. You're doing all the legwork to get it registered and caring for all the cuttings and doing all the sales. Seventy."

"Rowan. No. You are terrible at business."

The Lord laughed. "I'm not, but I like you and never thought something like this would be worth anything. It's a hobby, after all. Fine. Fifty-fifty. Final offer."

My eyes narrowed. I hoped he met someone who understood just how giving and generous this man was. "How about I give you sixty percent, I take ten, and the other thirty goes into a scholarship fund for botany and horticultural students who maintain a B+ average in school?"

Rowan blinked in surprise. "I—Dammit, Evie. Think I could take Caelan in a fight?"

"Let's not find out. So how about it?" I held my hand out. Texas has a ton of good colleges, but so does your territory. Any preference on a college?"

"None." But he didn't shake my hand.

"Rowan," I groaned. "It's a good deal."

"It's a great deal, but I have a counteroffer. I take thirty, you take twenty, then we put fifty into that scholarship."

I wouldn't get a better deal. "Sold."

We shook, Rowan's callouses sliding over my equally work-roughened hands. I'd taken too much time off and my hands had paid the price.

"Deal." Rowan wandered over to the couch and sat down. "There are a couple more goodies in the box, but that's not the main reason I'm here."

I followed, laying a hand over my chest. "I'm wounded to my very soul that you didn't make a special trip from the PNW out to see little ol' me."

He grinned. "Sit, Miss Sassy Pants."

I settled opposite him. "Is the world ending? Because I just got back to work and that would be a real bummer."

"Not quite. I've just come from Caelan's, and he asked that I pop by here to warn you. He's caught up in meetings all day."

"Warn me about what?"

"The Council is pissed about Donovan, and I smelled your magic all over his territory. Want to tell me what went down?"

My cheeks colored. "Erm. How about the highlights?"

Rowan grinned. "From Caelan's preening, I take it things went well that night?"

"Shut it."

He threw his head back and let out a bark of delighted laughter. "About time."

I rolled my eyes and started the tale, leaving out all the things I couldn't tell him. When I finished, Rowan's eyes had narrowed, a hint of gold shining in his hazel irises. "You're leaving a lot out, aren't you?"

"I told you everything I could so I could leave it at PG-13."

"Hmm. You took out two Chimeras all by yourself?"

"With help."

He didn't say anything for a long moment. "And Donovan?"

I wasn't sure what Caelan had told Rowan, so I stayed mum.

"Evie," Rowan growled. "If the Council grills you, silence will sign your death warrant."

I snorted. "They can try."

The Lord sighed and dropped his head in his hands. "Why do I even try to reason with you?"

"I appreciate you trying," I said sweetly.

"Look. Caelan already accepted responsibility. He said you had nothing to do with it."

"Donovan was trespassing on his territory and betrayed his office by consorting with divinity in an effort to destabilize his rule."

Rowan's lips twitched. "How quickly you've caught onto politics."

I sipped my coffee. "It's because you lot won't leave me alone."

"That, my dear, is because Caelan won't leave you alone. His fascination with you tipped his hand."

I didn't agree with his assessment completely. "And yet, you Lords couldn't stay out of his business."

Rowan's grin was not wolfish. It was... My eyes narrowed. "You aren't a wolf, are you?"

"A man never tells his secrets," he said primly, eyes twinkling.

"Are any of you wolves?" I'd been around Soren, Rowan, and Caelan the most, but Caelan had never kept his animal a secret.

"I won't spill the other Lords' secrets, either."

"Dammit, Rowan. What good is a Lord friend if you won't gossip with me?"

He laughed and stood. "If it helps, Caelan has instituted strict rules about visitors, especially other Lords, coming into his territory."

"Does that mean you can't come see me at will anymore?" The thought of it made me sadder than I expected. I liked Rowan. A lot. While I wasn't as close to him as Moira and the others, I felt like we would be if we kept spending time together.

He reached over and cupped my chin. "Aw, Evie. You break my heart." Rowan shook his head. "You can come see me whenever you want. Caelan locked his territory down. Any time I want to visit, I have to jump through hoops." He grinned. "Though I will say he's made those hoops infinitely worse for the others."

"Maybe I will come see you."

"Good." Rowan went over and unloaded the rest of the box, tucking it under his arm. "Don't be surprised if the Council calls you as a witness after what happened with Donovan. Is there a way to undo what you did to his territory?"

I cringed. "If I knew how, I would." As it were, his territory was calling me, its tug something I found difficult to resist. Soon, I'd have to drive up there and walk Donovan's land, or mine, I should say, no doubt complicating Caelan's relationship with the other Lords.

His eyes widened. "Shit. You claimed it, didn't you?"

A pained expression crossed his face before he let out a bark of laughter. "No." He held up a hand. "Don't answer that."

I pressed my lips together.

"Does Caelan know?"

All I could offer was an awkward smile.

Rowan shook his head. "I'll say this about you. Caelan has never been on his toes this much since he stepped into this shop."

"I was happy living in floral obscurity," I said primly.

Rowan leaned over and brushed a kiss against my cheek. "Keep telling yourself that."

With a shake of his head, he opened the front door. "I'll hold you to your promise to visit." He winked and headed out.

I locked the door behind him and picked up the broom, thinking about Caelan and the complications I'd brought into his life.

"Ha," I muttered to myself. "Serves him right. I told him to leave me alone."

But even as I said it, I didn't believe it. Having him around felt like slipping my arms into a cozy shirt right out of the dryer.

Warm and comforting.

Except when it wasn't.

CHAPTER
Five

A blissful, normal week passed, and I was practicing changing forms when Cernunnos appeared in my back yard. This time, his presence didn't scare me. I'd become sensitive to his magic and felt the telltale swell of his power in the air before I saw him.

I'd just turned from a hawk into a lizard and back again. Cernunnos didn't disturb me, instead settling onto the rocking chair on the back porch. I had a few more things to try so I decided to keep going.

Twenty minutes later, I flew onto my father's knee and squawked at him, nudging him with my beak.

Cernunnos laughed and picked up the clothing I'd left on the small table by his chair. "I'll step inside. Call me when you're ready."

True to his word, he went into the house. I shifted into my human form and dressed quickly, shivering as the cold air hit my bare skin.

When I called out for the Fae King, he stepped outside carrying my fuzzy sweater. With a grateful smile, I tugged it on and curled up on the outdoor love seat. "Question," I said as he settled in. "Why do I get to keep my clothes when I shift into my wren form, but not when I use the Chimera magic?"

Cernunnos's brow furrowed. "I guess I never thought about it. Different magic, I suppose. Fae magic is much different from shifter magic. They don't keep their clothes, either. But Chimera magic is different from shifter magic, too, though it's similar. The changes are DNA deep. Fae magic is simply…magic. We are our other forms. I take the form of a stag, and you take the form of a wren."

"Shifters only have one form, too."

"Yes, but their changes are physical."

I blinked. "That makes no sense."

Cernunnos's teeth flashed. "It's DNA versus magic."

"But a shifter has magic."

He inclined his head. "Yes, but it's not the same as ours. Fae power is ingrained in the soil, the water, the air, everywhere around us. We are the world. Shifters are more earthbound. We are pure magic."

My brain hurt, but his explanation made me think of something else. "I don't feel any different now that I know I'm your daughter."

Amusement made his multicolored eyes swirl. "Why would you?"

"No idea." I tugged my sweater closer. "I guess I thought now that I'm the daughter of the Fae King, I'd suddenly be ripe with power."

"Do you want to be?"

"Ugh. No."

He laughed. "Your logic makes a good point. I still have a…" His eyes narrowed. "Block, I suppose is a good word, on your power signature. It keeps your heritage a secret."

"Is that why I don't feel anything?"

"Yes and no. Your magic has always been yours. If I remove the block, everyone will know who you are."

"Which means I'll be subject to requests for favors and people sucking up to me to get closer to you?"

Cernunnos grinned. "Clever girl. The choice is up to you. Your power will always be accessible, and that's why I'm here. I won't show you how to 'use it.' Magic is instinctive. I will show you your responsibilities and introduce you to the fae world."

"What if I screw it up?"

"Intent is everything, Evangeline." He stood. "Now come inside. I have a dress for you. We have an engagement this evening."

I blinked. "Erm. Tonight is Tuesday."

One eyebrow went up. "Time is a construct."

My lips thinned. "It means I have tacos. Taco Tuesday. Every week."

"Tacos?"

I rubbed my face. "You've never had tacos?"

"We're scheduled for dinner at ten."

I gawked. "Ten p.m.? Am I in hell?"

He gave me a dark look. "First lesson. You need to learn to measure your responses. The fae do not take well to glibness."

"And I do not take well to eating dinner past my bedtime!"

The Fae King sighed. "Fine. We have time for you to eat your tacos. If you make them now."

I huffed and uncurled myself from the couch. "You're eating with me."

"What if I don't like tacos?" My father held the door open for me.

"Then I denounce your claim as my father."

"Serious words for human foodstuff."

"Tacos are serious business, Pops."

The Fae King sighed again.

Cernunnos not only liked tacos, he stuffed a baker's dozen down his greedy gullet.

"You're lucky I made extra," I grumbled. "You have the appetite of a frat boy."

"I do not know what that means," he said with his mouth full, "but I approve of these meat shells."

"Yeah well, my grocery bill doesn't."

Cernunnos's hands paused in mid-air. A strange look crossed his face. "You are the heir to the throne. Money is no object."

I snorted. "Only if I take the crown."

Cernunnos's eyes narrowed. "When was the last time you checked your bank account?"

"I never check my bank account. Everything is set up for auto pay and direct deposit. I have no hobbies, and I don't go anywhere. As long as I have enough for groceries and the mortgage, I'm good."

Cernunnos looked like he was counting in his head. It took him a long moment to speak. "Even if you decide not to take the crown, you are still my daughter and, as such, will suffer for nothing."

I stared at him. "I don't want your money."

Cernunnos shoved the rest of his taco in his mouth. "I don't care," he said through a mouthful of meat.

I realized a while ago arguing with him would get me nowhere. "Can I buy a Lambo now?"

"Buy whatever you wish. Though I don't know why you'd want a lamb. They'll eat all your grass."

"A Lambo is a car—a really fast one."

He grunted. "Why would you need a car? You can turn into any animal you wish."

"Good point. But no animal can run two hundred miles per hour."

Cernunnos shook his head. "You have so much to learn, child. A Peregrine falcon can dive much faster than your lamb."

"Lies," I said hotly. "A falcon?"

"Almost two hundred and fifty miles."

"What about regular flight? I'm not going to be diving all the time."

The Fae King rolled his eyes, surprising a laugh out of me.

"You are fae and my daughter. If you want to go two hundred miles per hour, just do it. Save your money for a fortress in the sky or something."

My taco fell out of my hand. "Can I get one of those?"

His look held censure.

I held my hands up. "Fine. But don't get all weird when I get a floating castle."

We finished up the tacos, and after I cleaned the mess up, Cernunnos held up a fancy dry cleaning bag. "Wear this."

I frowned. "Is this a fancy dinner or something? What's wrong with what I have on?"

"Are you going to argue with me over every little detail?"

"Probably," I muttered.

Cernunnos closed his eyes and exhaled. "In this, I know best. Please wear this daughter before I strangle you."

I clicked my tongue. "That's not very kingly of you." But I took the bag and headed to the back.

Good gracious. I looked like a fae queen. As soon as I put the dress on, the damn crown appeared on my head again. I glared at it, but since it matched the dress, I didn't try to take it off. The dress was a slim fitting, glittering concoction strewn with blush pink living blooms and dark green ivy.

I looked good, though my hair was a different matter. If my father was correct, I could mojo it into submission, but doing so right before dinner seemed like a bad idea, so I settled for mundane means, i.e., a curling iron, what felt like a thousand pins, and a shit ton of hairspray.

"Shoes?" I called out. "I don't have anything to match."

A shimmer in the air and a pair of golden slippers appeared from nowhere. Thank the gods they were flat. They held the same flowers and ivy, but the straps wound around my ankles and calves.

After I put them on and added a few cosmetic touches, I stepped outside. Cernunnos waited for me, dressed in completely different attire. His pants were the same dark gold as mine, but he wore a crisp, white button up shirt with the first four buttons undone. His antlers were gone, but he wore a crown similar to mine.

"Dang, Dad. You look smoking hot." It was true. Cernunnos was the most beautiful being I'd ever seen, but where Caelan was warm, Cernunnos' features held an ancient coldness. Power cloaked his skin, held in check but evident inside the room. As it was, I'd have to trim my plants back. Every time he visited, I wound up with dozens of new cuttings, some of them I'd never seen in nature before.

Even if he hadn't given me money, I'd be rich just by virtue of all the cool new plant life he was giving me.

"Hot is not what I was going for," he said dryly, eyes narrowing on my appearance. His eyes dragged down my body in a cursory inspection, and he lifted his finger to zap the dress in certain areas where it didn't fit as perfectly as he felt it should.

The entire thing felt very much like I was a runway model about to step onto stage.

"Your hair," he murmured. "Wear it down, please."

My nose crinkled. "Really? I spent like fifteen minutes on this do."

"Evangeline," he groaned.

I pointed at my head. "A little help with the pins? Otherwise, it will take me all night to get them out."

As one, every single pin fell from my hair. "Cool." I shook the curls out, but he wasn't done.

The smell of fresh tuberose tickled my nose, and petals brushed my ear. I hurried over to peer in the mirror.

"I look like I stepped out of one of those Ren Faire photoshoots." Flowers bloomed all over my head, the stems wound into my curls. "Are you sure all of this is necessary?"

"Very." He held out his arm.

I hesitated. "One more question. If you don't want everyone to know who I am, why are you taking me to a fae dinner?"

"Because I trust everyone here tonight." He paused. "As much as one can trust the fae."

"They won't tell Mom?"

Cernunnos laughed. "Come. It's time to introduce you to your heritage."

I touched his arm, and the world swept out from under me.

CHAPTER
Six

My mother was considered one of the most beautiful fae alive today. As her daughter, I guess I wasn't too hard on the eyes either, but standing in this room full of insanely beautiful fae made me feel like one of Cinderella's stepsisters.

Gems and gold glittered everywhere, but even if every fae was dressed in rags, I couldn't ignore their splendor—my father included. We stood at the entrance to a grand ballroom filled with fae and creatures of all kinds. Women and men with bodies of goats. Shadows in dark robes that whispered across the room. Creatures with skin of bark and glittering blue eyes. Something too fast for the eye to catch swirled around the ceiling, trailing green and blue sparkles in its wake.

My heart pounded against my ribs.

"Easy," my father murmured. "Everyone can hear your panic. Slow your heart rate before they notice."

My fists clenched at my sides. I took a deep breath in and slowly blew it out, sending a small trickle of magic through my veins, the cooling sense of flora surrounding me.

"Good," Cernunnos said. "Are you ready?"

"No." I glanced up at him. My father's face was carefully blank, his gaze sweeping across the room. "Are you?"

His lips twitched. "I'd rather absorb myself into the ground and disappear in a gust of wind."

I blinked. "That's oddly specific."

"You'll see in a minute."

"I thought you said these people were your friends."

A faint smile. "They are."

Cernunnos nudged me into the room.

As soon as we stepped over the threshold, every eye in the room swung to us.

"By my side, Evangeline," he murmured.

I took a larger step, my fingers curling over his muscled forearm.

"Heart rate," he whispered.

"Shit," I muttered.

He placed a warm hand over mine. "Steady."

A woman glided over to us. Tall, regal, cold as ice. She wore a pale blue gown encrusted with diamonds across the bodice, sleeveless and mermaid cut. I'd fall flat on my face the moment I took a step in a dress like that. Her face was lineless and smooth, pale blue eyes resting for a brief second on my father before she bowed to him. When she straightened, her eyes landed on me.

The woman had the eyes of a predator, sharp and calculating. A shrewd intelligence glittered in her gaze. "You must be Evangeline." A slight dip of her head. "Charmed."

"This is Brigid," Cernunnos said.

My mother had mentioned her a couple of times in passing. For whatever reason, Cliona couldn't stand her. Unsurprising. Mom hated just about everyone. Sometimes she reminded me of the evil stepmother in the fairytale, asking the mirror who's the hottest.

Brigid was pretty enough to get under her skin.

"Hello," I said lamely. Brigid didn't look much like the

goddess of the hearth and home. She reminded me of old money, one of those rich white women who has the help put out specific china for important guests. When I thought of home, I thought of someone like Hazel. Warm, kind, maybe a little frazzled. Someone to offer you tea or coffee when you came over and maybe had warm cookies straight from the oven.

This woman was pure ice, a predator in a ballgown. She'd brag about the type of champagne she had and offer you caviar from some weird fish you've never heard of. If she was one of my father's friends, I'd hate to meet his enemies.

"Where has the king been hiding you for all these years?" She clicked her tongue. "Such pretty dark hair. You must take after your mother."

Cernunnos's muscle tightened under my hand, a minuscule motion I would have missed if I didn't know him. This woman didn't realize Cliona was my mother. Interesting.

Brigid was fishing. "I wouldn't know," I said sweetly. "I'm an orphan."

The goddess blinked, her eyes widening as she realized her apparent faux pas. "My apologies," she murmured. "I had no idea."

"Her mother is of no importance this night." He inclined his head the tiniest bit. "It was nice to see you again, Brigid."

"I'll save you a seat, sire."

"Mmm," Cernunnos said, edging his way past the goddess.

"Clever," he murmured.

"She doesn't know."

"Your mother is a viper. Our liaison was brief yet fruitful."

My nose wrinkled. "Eww."

Cernunnos chuckled. "Come. Let us make the rounds."

"Do we have to sit by Brigid?" I whispered.

He steered me toward the back window, where a long table was set up. "She is deeper than her surface beauty. Do not let her appearance lull you into false security."

"No worries there. You know who my mother is."

"Ah. Yes. I should have known you would not be fooled by someone's appearance."

No. I was more likely to distrust someone because they were pretty, thanks to dear ol' mom. Someone else approached, a tall, handsome man with dark skin and eyes the color of citrine.

He stopped before us and inclined his head. "Cernunnos. Who is this lovely creature you've brought this evening?"

My father relaxed. Whoever this man was, my father liked him.

"Conor," he said warmly. "This is my daughter, Evangeline."

"Charmed," I said.

"Same," Conor said. "You look a little bewildered. Is this your first foray into our society?"

The look he gave my father held a slight edge of disapproval. Cernunnos noticed.

"I had my reasons," he said before I could respond. Interesting, my father actually answered this man.

My mother never spoke of anyone named Conor, nor had anyone else I knew.

A sharp smile edged Conor's mouth. "Trust no one. Not even me."

Cernunnos sighed. "Good advice, but is it necessary?"

"You know our kind, Cer. I'm surprised you haven't already given her the same advice."

"Cer?"

My father rolled his eyes. "A childhood nickname. Right, Con?"

Conor laughed and slapped my father on the back. "May I take your daughter around and introduce her to a few of our kinder, gentler people while you charm your hangers on?"

A few dozen people had gathered around us, their eyes darting to us every few seconds, waiting for a lull in the conversation so they could jump in and gain Cernunnos's attention.

"You've been gone for weeks now, and they need the attention of their king." Another note of disapproval.

My father's jaw tightened. "Do not let her out of sight."

Conor gave a delicate snort. "In this hyena den?" he murmured. "Never."

He held his arm out and led me away. Conor smelled of wood smoke and the outdoors. Another nature god? Asking was a faux pas, so I stifled my curiosity and let him lead me across the room.

The back of my neck prickled. "Everyone is staring at me," I whispered.

"Yes," Conor agreed. "You are a new and shiny thing, and we both know how much the fae love new toys."

I stiffened. "Is that how they see me?"

Conor glanced down at me, a slight frown marring his perfect complexion. "You truly do not know anything about us," he murmured. "How fascinating." He paused for a moment. "Who was your mother?"

"No idea," I said, a smidge too quickly.

"A secret," Conor mused. "I so adore secrets."

A curious fae. Just what I needed. Conor patted me on the hand and smiled.

"No need to be frightened, dear. I have no intention of dragging your secrets from you."

I peered up at him. "Yet?"

He laughed out loud. "My hope is one day you will trust me enough to tell me."

My eyes narrowed. "Even though you just told me not to trust you?"

Conor's teeth flashed in a smile. "Beautiful and a good listener, too. Perhaps you will survive in this place after all."

"I don't plan to survive here at all," I muttered.

His brows flicked up. "Oh? You aren't here in the capacity of an heir?"

I stiffened in surprise.

"Your father and I are close friends, Evie. He trusts me with almost everything."

"Almost," I said. "Why not everything?"

"Because we are fae," he said, as if that explained everything.

A massive creature stepped before us, a thing of bark and limbs.

Conor stopped. "Hello, Birch."

The creature shrank down and down until a man about my height stood before us. He had nut brown hair, pale skin, and swirling green eyes. "Conor. Who is this delightful creature? She smells of flowers and mystery."

"Birch, please meet Evie, Cernunnos's daughter."

The tree man blinked. "Daughter, you say?" His eyes narrowed. "Are you sure? She looks nothing like the crabby king."

A bubble of laughter escaped me.

Conor sighed. "You'd best hold your tongue, Birch. Our liege is on edge tonight."

I glanced at him. "He is?"

"Few people bring their children around people like us, my dear," Birch said before Conor could speak. "Though you are no longer a child. Why has he kept you from us for so long?"

I didn't see the harm in telling the truth. "Humans raised me."

Birch frowned. "You're no changeling. Your blood leaks magic. Strange, interesting magic."

"You can smell blood?" I blurted. Did he sense my Chimera magic? Cernunnos hadn't said anything about the potential for someone sniffing out the secrets my blood held, and I hadn't thought to ask.

"One of his many, annoying talents." Conor's voice dripped with exasperation.

Birch's smile held an edge. "And a quite useful one."

He gave us a small bow. "I must be off, but I will see you soon, Evie. There is much we should discuss."

Birch disappeared, there one moment and gone the next. "He left the dinner entirely?"

Conor rolled his eyes. "Who knows. Birch is an enigma wrapped in tree bark."

"You don't like him?"

"I love the tree. Doesn't mean he doesn't aggravate the shit out of me."

And so it went, on and on. Dozens of introductions, numerous cryptic comments, and edged words. My head was spinning by the time Conor steered me toward the table and my father.

When Conor left me with a wink and a smile, Cernunnos leaned over. "How'd it go?"

"Everyone here is a silver-tongued liar," I whispered.

My father blinked before laughing out loud. "Yes," he said when he finally composed himself. "You've discovered a fae's universal talent."

"And you?" I asked, reaching for the napkin to spread it over my lap. "If everyone here has a silver tongue, is yours golden?"

Sadness touched his face. "When I have to be. But never to you."

My heart flipped over. "Is that why you don't answer my questions?"

He inclined his head. "Some questions I cannot answer for many reasons. But I would never lie to you."

"Good to know." Someone appeared at my shoulder and poured a golden, fizzy liquid into my wine glass. Just as I reached for it, Cernunnos snapped his fingers and the glass disappeared.

"No fairy wine," he cautioned.

"But I'm full fae," I argued.

"We introduce the beverage when our children are young, so it doesn't affect them like it does humans or changelings. You've never tried the beverage, and the side effects might be…unusual."

"What, you don't want me to get trashed and dance on the table?" My words were glib, but I was secretly glad he'd prevented me from getting myself into trouble.

"You've obviously never been to a true fae party. Table dancing sometimes begins before the wine starts flowing."

The sound of music started. My father stiffened and set his glass down. "Excuse me. I will be but a moment."

When he rose, my father was gone, and the Fae King stood in his place.

CHAPTER
Seven

I t was two in the morning. I was missing a shoe; I had a headache, and a handsome prince had not come chasing me down the steps with my missing sandal.

Fae balls sucked.

"I'm still hungry," I complained. "Is that how the fae eat all the time?" The dinner had more wine than anything: multiple courses, teeny tiny portions, copious amounts of wine. Everything tasted good, but there was no main course. Only nibbles.

Cernunnos snorted. "You know you don't have to eat, don't you?"

I flopped onto the couch and glared at him. "I do not see the point of living if I can't inhale a slice of chocolate cake when I get a hankering."

Cernunnos groaned as he sank into the seat.

"Do you not eat?" After his speech, he barely touched anything on his plate. A bite here and there, but most of his food went uneaten.

"I find my attention is on other things when I am among my own people. Eating does not hold the same joy for me as it does for you."

"So that's why you ate almost all the tacos."

"Human food is surprisingly delightful," he admitted.

"Amen to that."

"So…" His voice trailed off.

"What did I think of everything?"

"I know you were overwhelmed."

I thought about my words. These were my people. Technically. By blood but not by choice. But they were my father's, and I know he loved them. He promised me honesty, and I could do no less for him.

"I like knowing where I stand," I admitted. "I want my friends to feel comfortable enough to tell me I suck when I do stupid things, and that I'm awesome when I do great things. I want them to feel comfortable enough to come over to my house, kick their shoes off, and steal my food, but I also want to feel comfortable enough to do the same to them."

A smile tipped his lips up. "And you met no one like that tonight."

I shook my head. "Though I wonder if you feel that way about Conor."

"He is my oldest friend," he admitted, "but we are fae."

"I'm fae."

"Raised by humans."

"I dunno. If I'm fae and I can find friends like I have, why can't you?"

Cernunnos laughed. "You make it sound so easy."

"And you make it sound so hard." I flipped onto my side and studied him. "Did you love Mom?"

He stilled. "Such an abrupt change of subject."

"She seems so cold all the time. If I didn't know I was the product, I never would put you two together."

"I've already told you our time together was brief. Your mother is a…force."

"So just sex then?"

He looked pained. "Evie."

"It's cool. Sometimes the loins want what the loins want."

"I am rethinking this heir thing."

But I could hear the amusement in his voice. "Too bad. I'm going to come in and declare Taco Tuesdays and mandatory movie screenings in the throne room on Saturdays."

Cernunnos shook his head and rose. "Get some rest, daughter. I will visit again soon."

"Do we have to go back there?" I couldn't quite keep the whine out of my voice.

"They are not bad," he said after a moment. "Only complicated."

"And power hungry."

"Yes."

"And I should probably watch my back for assassination attempts?" My words were lighthearted, but some of the looks I received tonight got my hackles up.

His eyes swirled with fury. "No one would dare."

I tried not to laugh. "If someone thinks they won't get caught, they'll dare way more than we think they will."

"I will send a guard."

I held a hand up. "Absolutely not. If you get all protective on me, you'll regret it. I'm a grown woman. And if what you say is true, I have more power in my pinky than most people do in their entire body. I'll be fine."

With a groan, I hefted myself from the couch. "I'll hang the gown and give it to you next time I see you."

Cernunnos rolled his eyes and walked to the door, even though I knew he could disappear in a flash if he wanted to. He acted a little more human around me, which I appreciated.

"You will call me the instant something happens."

"I will," I promised, even though I had zero intentions of doing so. "Though I just want to make sure if someone does come after me, I can put them in the ground, right?"

His smile was all teeth. "I'd expect nothing less from my daughter."

We walked onto the porch. A swirl of magic surrounded me

before a heavy sweater lay across my shoulders. My fingers stroked the soft fabric.

"Cashmere?" I gasped.

"I spotted one tossed across your couch."

"It's so heavy."

Cernunnos pressed a burning kiss to my forehead. "Only the best for my child." He took my chin in his fingers and lifted my face. "Be careful, Evangeline. Violence swirls around you."

Before I could respond, he was gone in a wisp of golden light.

CHAPTER

Eight

CAELAN

Evie looked like a fae princess. I sank to my haunches and watched through a dense patch of forest. Her dark hair spiraled down her shoulders, and a glittering crown sat perched atop her head.

Wasn't that curious? It wasn't far-fetched for Evie to be considered a princess of the fae realm. Cernunnos was her father. But if she wore a crown, had she accepted that part of her heritage? And if she had, what did it mean for us?

She was hiding things from me, things I needed to know if we were to keep moving forward. Was it this?

Or something worse?

Their voices were too low for me to catch without giving myself away. Cernunnos bent to press a kiss to Evie's forehead, then disappeared. She waited for a moment before going inside, the gown dragging heavily behind her.

I could have gone home, put myself to sleep with a dozen questions swirling in my mind, but I was past that.

We were past that.

I dipped my head and let the go bag fall to the ground. A few moments later, dressed and angry, I slipped inside her home.

A vine reached out and slapped me in the face. "Caelan! I told you to knock!"

Evie had one hand in the air and the other planted over her chest. Her eyes were wide and her hair disheveled. She'd taken off the ballgown and wore a pair of sleep shorts and a tank top. Bare feet and bare legs.

Yum.

I grinned and wound the vine around my finger. "It's more fun when you attack me with plants."

She relinquished her magic, allowing the vine to slip back into its pot. But she didn't come to me. Instead, her eyes narrowed, and she watched me for a moment.

"You were spying on me, weren't you?"

I didn't deny it. "You've been acting weird."

She opened her mouth to argue but snapped it shut at my look.

Evie crossed her arms over her chest, the action boosting her cleavage and almost making me lose my train of thought.

"Cernunnos is being weird," she said after a moment. "He invited me to dinner tonight."

I thought about mentioning the crown but decided not to. This was Evie. She'd bring it up when she was ready, even if it was killing me to stay silent.

We stood several feet apart, the distance feeling like miles. "In the fae realm?"

She nodded. "They don't eat enough," she grumbled.

Her stomach chose to growl—loudly—just at that moment.

"Want me to make you something?"

She shook her head and sighed. A moment later, she closed the distance between us, resting her head on my chest. I wrapped my arms around her and inhaled her ever-changing scent. I'd noticed it a while ago. Depending on what magic Evie expended that day was how she smelled. Today, she smelled heavily of fae, a wild scent of metal and winter, with a tinge of greenery, probably from the magic she'd just used when I surprised her.

"It's too late to eat. I'm tired and need a couple hours of sleep. I have to work tomorrow."

I scooped her in my arms to her laughing protest. "Then let's go to bed."

She twined her fingers around my neck. "No funny business, wolf. I really am tired."

"My business is never funny. But I'm tired, too. And I sleep better wrapped up in you."

Her face softened, and she turned her head, pressing a warm kiss to my collarbone.

"Ditto," she said softly.

A moment later, I lay her underneath the blankets and slid in beside her, bringing her against my chest. Her palm rested over my heart.

I lay there until she fell asleep, her soft breath against my skin, and vowed to keep her, no matter what fate brought us. Evie was mine, even if she fought against the bond growing between us; I never planned to let her go.

CHAPTER
Nine

The room was full of vines and flowers. I blinked awake to the smell of jasmine and night-blooming tobacco, soft petals brushing against my cheeks.

"Oh shit," I whispered.

My bedroom looked like a jungle had exploded.

Caelan stirred against me, tightening his grip against my abdomen. He nuzzled my neck and placed a kiss against my shoulder.

I sensed the instant he opened his eyes. Caelan stiffened and inhaled deeply.

"Want to explain?" he murmured in my ear, his voice deep and rough with sleep.

It was nice being involved with a guy who didn't lose his shit over something like a random jungle in the bedroom after a sleepover. "I must have gotten too tired and didn't burn off enough magic yesterday."

I felt his grin against my skin. "I can help you burn off some excess energy."

His hand started seeking lower. I sucked in a gasp and pressed against him.

"Do jungles turn you on?"

He chuckled. "Only women who can make them."

I turned over and crawled on top of the Shifter Lord. "Hmm. I'm a little partial to wolves, too."

One dark eyebrow rose. "Oh? All wolves?"

I tapped my finger to my chin in mock thought.

Caelan growled and yanked me down, catching my lips in a bruising, claiming kiss.

Seconds later, there were no more words.

THE AUTOMATON WAS FINISHED, carefully placed in the walk-in fridge to await the anniversary dinner. We sat around my worktable, a mound of fresh flowers in the middle, making table centerpieces, smaller and more elegant than the ones we'd done for Caelan's get-togethers.

The walk-in traffic had been a little slow today, allowing us to catch up on orders. Rain pounded the pavement outside, only the bravest of tourists out and about. Tess seemed normal, and Ash wouldn't meet my gaze which told me he hadn't broken the news to Tess yet. Moira kept glancing at me and him, then at Tess, a small frown marring the perfection of her pale brow.

I hadn't said anything about what was going on. Getting involved in my employees' business was a fast way to lose said employee, so I interfered when I needed to (which was extremely rare) and gave advice the rest of the time. Whatever was going on between them had to be settled by them, not me or Moira.

"Alright," Moira blurted. "What's going on?"

I placed a white anemone in the bouquet and kept my mouth shut.

Tess frowned. "What do you mean? I'm trying to figure out if orange goes with green and it's messing with my head a little."

"If it's the flower stem, Tess, green goes with everything."

"Oh. I guess so." Her soft voice warbled.

My heart broke a little bit. I sent Ash a disapproving look.

Moira's lips thinned. "Oh Ash." She shook her head in disappointment and put the ranunculus down. "I'm going to get a head start on Hattie's bouquet. Maybe I'll draw something and see if you like it."

Our eyes met. She jerked her head slightly toward the left. I shook my head once.

No, we were not meeting in the freezer to gossip about our coworkers.

Not in front of them at least.

Ash's shoulders slumped. "Tess?"

She hummed a little tune as she put a salmon-colored rose in the foam. "Hmm?"

Ash sent me a desperate look.

I chewed on the side of my lip. "Why don't you two take a longer lunch? We aren't expecting much business today, and there's no reason for all of us to be in the shop."

Tess glanced up from her centerpiece. "It's only 10:30."

"Grab a coffee first. How about you two come back at 1?"

Tess blinked. "Are you sure?"

"Very," I assured her. The smile I gave was as reassuring as I could make it, but my heart hurt for them both. "Enjoy yourselves."

"Thank you," Ash mouthed. He helped Tess up, snagging her jacket by the door. Once they were both bundled up, they hurried outside to his car.

Moira and I watched them go.

"Is he breaking up with her?" she asked quietly.

"I think so. He was supposed to do it yesterday."

"That's why it was so awkward." Moira scrubbed a hand over her face. "Damn. Any chance of them working it out?"

My gut told me no, but I didn't want to put an absolute on something I only saw from the outside. "Maybe," I said instead.

She put her hand on my shoulder and gave it a light squeeze. "Things are changing."

"Yeah." I rubbed my eyes and sighed. "What about you? Anything new in your life?"

Moira laughed and sat back down at the table. I pushed a pile of flowers over. "Still single. Still trying to make the perfect cup of tea. Still trying to figure things out. So, the answer is…not really."

She smiled. "Whatever happens, we will all still love each other, Evie. You never have to worry about that."

"I'm more worried about us fading away from each other." Ash and Tess dating had made me pause and wonder if it was a good idea, but they'd liked each other so much I was hard pressed to stop them. If I was a more logical person, I would have extrapolated the data, come to the conclusions that statistically most relationships don't work out, and put a stop to the madness before it started.

But I wasn't an ice queen and had a soft spot for both Tess and Ash.

This was…human in a way. An ending. Maybe not a final one, but one for now.

"Tess is young, and Ash has been through heartbreak before. They'll be okay. Eventually." Moira sorted through the peonies for the best color. "And even if we go our separate ways, I don't think we'll ever fade." A faint smile tipped her lips up. "Though I think you're overreacting. None of us are going anywhere for a long time."

"That's what you say now," I grumbled. "But two of our people are out there breaking up."

Moira snorted. "Tess needs a job and Ash basically lives here. I don't think either of them will uproot their lives over this."

"I hope not."

"And if they do, you can guilt them into staying. You're great at that."

I tossed a pansy at her. She caught it, laughing.

"Now stop being so maudlin and let's finish this up before they get back." Moira stuck the pansy into her own arrangement.

Ash and Tess returned an hour and a half later. While Tess looked fine, Ash looked like he'd gotten hit by a train.

"Mind if I take off for the day?" Ash asked quietly as Tess returned to her spot behind the desk and checked the shop email.

"Sure." I touched his arm. "Are you alright?"

His jaw tightened. "Tess doesn't love like us. She's fine."

My brow furrowed. "Ash, I don't think anyone loves the same, nor do I think that assessment is fair. I'll check—"

"Don't." A sharp shake of his head. "Leave her be for now. I'll see you in the morning."

Without another word, he hurried out the door and back into the rain.

Moira and I exchanged glances. She rose from my worktable and went over to Tess, murmuring quietly.

I couldn't hear what was said, but Tess was here, and she seemed okay.

That was all I could ask for now.

CHAPTER
Ten

My stomach hurt. The ache started after Ash and Tess returned to the store, but as the day went along, the ache grew until I was having trouble walking. Immortals didn't get sick, unless the illness was magical in nature.

It could only be one thing.

Surprised it'd taken this long to start acting up, I rubbed the lower part of my stomach and grimaced when I shifted. I didn't want the others to worry, so I didn't move from my worktable for the rest of the day, except to get up and stretch, which caused a tearing pain in my stomach that made me gasp.

"Evie?" Moira said, eyeing me with a strange expression. "You alright?"

"Totally fine," I assured her. "I've been using more muscles than normal these days."

Moira grinned. "Caelan putting you through the wringer, is he?"

"I cannot wait until you get a boyfriend."

The vampire laughed. "You're going to be waiting quite a while. Boys are too much trouble, and I like my life just the way it is."

Tess's head popped up from the computer. "Ash broke up with me today."

"Oh honey," I said. "Are you alright?"

She shrugged. "Why wouldn't I be? Everything changes, doesn't it?"

I walked over, doing my best not to hunch over in agony. "It does," I agreed. "But that doesn't mean we want it to. Sometimes change takes us by surprise and it's difficult to adjust."

Her silvery eyes glimmered. "But he will still be here, won't he? I'll still see him every day."

Moira and I exchanged a glance. "You will, but things will be different now. At least a little."

Tess's face took on a contemplative look. "Like no kisses anymore?"

"Right. No kisses and probably no sleepovers if you ever had those."

Tess frowned. "I liked Ash's kisses."

Moira closed her eyes for a brief moment. "I hope you two can still be friends after this."

Tess let out a merry laugh. "Why wouldn't we?" She shook her head. "Ash is still my best friend."

Tears sprang to my eyes. Tess wasn't stupid, but she had a way of dealing with the world that wasn't always the healthiest. "Ash may need more time to think about things," I said gently. "Breakups are usually harder for men than they are for women, so it's important you respect his boundaries until he's ready to tell you how he wants to move forward."

The banshee looked at me, then Moira. "You don't think he'll want to be my friend anymore?"

"That isn't what I mean," I rushed to say. "You and Ash were still friends when you were boyfriend and girlfriend, but now you aren't anymore. He may need some time to get used to the fact that things are different."

Tess slumped. "They don't have to be," she said softly. "I can't help the way I am. It bothers Ash. I think he wanted me to be different. Not me anymore."

I picked up Tess's cool hands. "This is an important lesson. Our first love isn't usually our last, but every relationship teaches us something. If Ash can't accept you as you are, then good on you for not allowing him to try to change you. Eventually you will find someone who loves you exactly as you are."

"He loved me that way when we were friends. And you love me, don't you?"

I gathered her in a hug and took a shaky breath, ignoring the shards of glass feeling in my abdomen. "Yes, of course we do." I leaned back and took her face in my hands. "But a boyfriend or girl-friend or husband or wife should love you in a different way than we do. And if they can't, then they aren't the right one for you."

Tess nodded against my shoulder. "I understand."

"Good."

"Do you love the Lord that way?"

Leave it to Tess to aim a question like a dagger. "I am not sure how I feel about Caelan, but I know I care about him very much."

"Does he try to change you?" Tess's silver eyes glimmered with tears.

I thought about it. "No. He does other things that make me question the longevity of our relationship, but he's always accepted me." I shook my head. "More than accepted me and my quirks. I have no complaints in that department."

"Do you think he'll be your husband one day?"

I blinked.

Moira chuckled. "If it's up to Caelan, he'd marry Evie today."

"But you don't want to?" Tess asked.

"Things are complicated," was all I said. "If I marry someone, I want to ensure it's of my own volition, and I'm not pressured to make the decision."

"I think Ash wanted that," Tess said with a sigh. "But I'd leave him if I faded into the mist, and I don't want him to be sad."

I stilled. "The mist?"

"Your mother has been calling us home, back into the mounds behind the mist." Tess bowed her head and toyed with her fingers. "The shop wards help me resist."

That bitch. "She's calling all the banshees home?"

"I'm not sure. My friend in the graveyard doesn't hear the call, but I do."

That bitch. I seethed inside, anger like acid in my chest. "I'll talk to my mother."

"Evie—"

"No," I snapped at Moira. "I can handle her. Things are different from before. My mother knows I'm not someone she can slap down anymore."

Returning my attention to Tess, I spoke once more. "Keep resisting. How are the wards in your apartment?"

"Strong," she assured me. Tess had an ingrained talent with ward making, maybe even better than mine. "But I can't go out much anymore. If she senses me wandering, she strengthens her call."

Fury made my fingers tremble. "I'll talk to her tonight."

Tess's eyes widened. "I don't want you to get into trouble."

Her innocence made me smile. Tess's idea of trouble was vastly different than my mother's. If Cliona could get away with it, she'd probably kill me, even if I was her only child.

"Don't worry about me. Many things have changed over the years. My mother and I are on equal footing now." Or, at least, the footing was sloped in my favor these days.

"Thank you," she whispered.

"Of course." I checked my phone for the time. "Let's lock up and get out of here. We haven't had a customer in two hours."

The earlier I got out of here, the sooner I could confront my mother.

Hurting Tess wasn't on her radar unless it hurt me. But it was a message.

Cliona wanted to talk.

Never a good sign.

Much to Hazel's consternation, I'd never been great at spell work. At its heart, Floromancy was an intuitive magic, driven by the mage's heart and intent. But I wasn't just a Floromancer anymore, was I?

Before leaving the shop, Tess gave me a lock of her hair at my request. I carefully snipped off a bead at the very bottom of the gown my father had given me and dug deep into my closet to retrieve a box of childhood memories.

Once I had a dried petal from the only flower my mother had ever given me and the other materials I needed, I went into the greenhouse, where my power felt strongest, and set everything up.

My magic settled inside me, the pain from the seed lesser now for some reason. I set up four green taper candles at each cardinal point in the circle I'd drawn. A small silver bowl filled with purified water and graveyard dirt sat in the middle. I lit each candle, starting from the north and going in a clockwise direction. Once each taper burned, I touched the charcoal brick of incense with the lighter, holding it to the flame until it sparked and caught.

Once the brick began to smoke, I sprinkled a little incense on top and waited for the smell of rose and lavender to waft through the greenhouse. My plants grew curious. A few vines stretched from their pots and curled over my shoulder. Every time I performed magic now, the greenery became a little more sentient than it should. I wasn't concerned. Yet.

I sensed no danger, only a solid sense of comfort and curiosity, so I continued on.

Tess's hair went into the bowl first, followed by the bead. The petal was the last to go.

"Cliona," I whispered. "I heard your summons. I wish to speak with you."

No one had seen my mother since she left Caelan's Keep after I transformed into my Chimera form. She was, wisely, keeping a low profile. I didn't mind one bit, but her screwing with Tess was unacceptable.

The greenhouse shivered, a silvery, opaque portal opening a few feet away.

"You bitch," I whispered. Cliona was well protected in her own domain. I'd never been to the mounds and had no idea what to expect. My mother knew it and wanted to throw me off my game.

I watched the portal for a few moments deciding whether or not to go through.

"Fuck it," I snarled, snatching one of the plants from the table —a thorned ivy, one of my newer creations I hadn't tested out yet. I'd look like a crazy person stepping into the fae lands wielding a potted plant, but better safe than sorry.

I took a deep breath and stepped into the silvery beyond.

CHAPTER
Eleven

T he sharp scent of rain on stone hit me first. A moment of disorientation and I blinked away the dizziness to see a stunning, fertile land of green.

My Floromancy sang in my veins. Multiple small mounds rose in every direction, some covered in flowers, some covered in thorns. Birds of all shapes and colors flew through the air, their songs high and sweet. The sky above was a crisp, vivid blue, not a cloud to be found. I inhaled fresh, clean air, tears coming to my eyes at what I was denied.

My mother appeared on a flower covered mound, dressed in a silvery blue gown. Her hair streamed behind her. She made no move toward me but stayed silent and watchful.

I bit down my annoyance and started walking. Before I got very far, a wail in the distance made me freeze. Darts of silvery mist appeared in the distance, heading right for me. I watched, certain these were banshees. As far as I knew, I wasn't marked for death.

Tess, I hoped, would tell me. The thought made me laugh. It'd be just my luck if my ass was about to die a horrible death in front of my mother because my banshee friend forgot to tell me I was due to die today.

Five banshees landed before me. Some short, some tall. All female, all with long, flowing hair.

"Speak a memory you refuse to think or speak of," said the tallest banshee, "and you will be granted access to our queen's domain."

I exhaled. "Mom. You know this is bullshit, right?"

No one said a word. "I'm your daughter, and you're the one who opened the stupid portal."

Cliona didn't even blink.

"I swear to the gods, you are off my Christmas list."

"What kind of memory?" I said to the creepy banshee. They were pale imitations of Tess, washed out visages of once living women. I was half convinced my hand would pass right through them if I reached out.

"A memory you refuse to think or speak of," the banshee repeated.

"Helpful," I drawled. My brain was full of memories I refused to do either of, but would any of them work? Was my mother searching for information to use against me, or was she just being a bitch?

Both could be true. I racked my brain, keeping my mother in my peripheral vision, trying to come up with something good enough to let me through.

"Does it matter when the memory was?" I asked the banshee.

"No."

Chatty, this one. "Who decides if the memory is good enough?"

"The magic will decide," the banshee said.

Hmm. I'd told few people about Scotland, but never how I felt lying on the ground, dying. My mother didn't deserve that memory. I thought of Caelan and how I never voiced how he made me want for something I may never be able to have. Cernunnos came to mind—how angry I was at him for abandoning me and trying to reckon with knowing he'd done it to keep me alive. I thought of Moira and Tess and Ash and my shop and land. Joy surrounded me. All I had to do was reach out for it.

Even so, a well of grief and anger lay deep and endless inside me.

And then…I had the memory. A soft, tender memory, layered underneath years of confusion and horror.

I smiled at my mother and had the pleasure of watching her blink and take an involuntary step back.

"When I was a child, my mother was a cruel, vindictive mistress. She never lay a hand on me. That was not her way. No." I shook my head. "Cliona deprived."

The banshees' eyes widened.

"My mother deprived me of love, touch, and kind words. Never food. Never shelter. I was dressed well and always had new clothes and new shoes. My hair was brushed to a dark sheen, decorated with pretty, shiny barrettes and braids. I was clean and well fed, sent to a good school, and educated about the human world. But she never held me when I skinned my knee or cried over a fellow student's cruelty. I learned how to console myself."

A silvery tear rolled down the banshee's cheek.

"I was allowed no friends and no family, no visitors other than those specific people my mother sought to show how good of a parent she was. And then, she gave me away right when I finished with the first school. I don't remember how old I was. Maybe three or four."

I met the banshee's eyes. "My mother saved my life by handing me over to humans. I would not have survived under her cold ministrations if she hadn't, but that is not my memory." I looked away from the banshee and met my mother's eyes. "Cliona came into my bedroom only one time, late at night when I was supposed to be sleeping. But you see, I rarely slept in that cold, loveless room."

Mom's eyes widened.

"She laid a flower on my dresser, one I'd never seen before, and whispered that if she knew how, she would love me. The next day, she dropped me off on the steps of a small house and left before they'd opened the door."

Silence filled the air. The five banshees stood like statues, each with tears in their eyes, before the first bowed her head.

"Accepted." As one, they shot into the air like a silver bullet and disappeared into the distance.

I took a step forward.

My mother floated from the top of her mound to the ground. She turned away from me and waved a hand, revealing a small entryway with a spiral staircase leading downward.

"Enter, daughter."

I sighed. "Can't we just talk out here? I have a date later."

I did not.

Mom's shoulders stiffened. "Can't you be serious for one single moment?"

She said nothing about the memory I'd given away, ignored the tension in the air between us, the possibility of something positive shimmering between us before it faded away like it had never been.

"For you?" I snorted. "Nope."

We started down the staircase, Mom's dress trailing behind her. Even in the dim light, she managed to still sparkle. "Why must you always be so antagonistic?"

I halted on the next step. "Me? I'm antagonistic?" A crack of laughter I couldn't hold back. "You've been trying to lure my banshee to you for weeks now, and you tried to kill me!"

A scoff. "Kill you?" Her dark hair shimmered against her back as she shook her head. "No, my darling. I was trying to save you."

Counting in my head wasn't working so well anymore. If I had a knife, I'd strongly consider raising it and stabbing her right in the space between her neck and shoulder. But I'd get bloody, and I liked this shirt.

"Save me," I said slowly, after a too-long pause. "Didn't you show up with Donovan to stab Caelan in the back and also work with Rhona to take me down?"

"Semantics," she said from over her shoulder. "Fae will work with anyone who furthers their goals."

"Good to know. I assume that's why I'm here."

We came to the bottom of the stairs, the area widening into a large room with bookshelves along the walls, soft cushioned chairs in blue and greens. Stunning carved wooden furniture surrounded a stunning gemstone table. Mom snapped her fingers, and a tea set appeared, complete with cream, sugar, and two delicate cups dotted with flowers and vines.

A bit on the nose for Mom.

"I made Earl Grey. I hope that's okay."

"That's Moira's favorite. I'm more of a coffee drinker."

Mom's lips thinned. "I can bring in coffee if you like."

"No. I know you prefer tea."

She waved a hand. "Please. Have a seat."

I sank into a chair and had to stifle my sigh. The chairs were amazing. And definitely not from a discount furniture store.

I would not ask her where she found these.

I would not ask her where—

"I'll have some delivered to your home, Evangeline," Mom said as she poured the tea.

Dammit. "Thank you."

"If you wish to walk among our people, you must learn to control your facial expressions. Every emotion shows in your eyes."

"Who said I want to spend any time with the fae?"

One of her eyebrows quirked up. "Your attendance at Cernunnos's dinner was a fluke?"

Fae spies sucked. "I was invited. Curiosity doesn't mean I want to move to the fae lands."

"Regardless, my point stands. Even if you do not entangle yourself in your kind, your relationship with the wolf will require your presence in delicate political situations. You must learn to position yourself as neutral, even if you burn inside."

My mother was making…sense. Why did it make me want to stick my tongue out at her and refuse to drink my tea?

"Why did you call me here?" I took a sip of my tea and wished it was coffee.

Mom rolled her eyes, wiggled her finger, and the scent of the brew changed into a dark, rich Colombian roast. Where was this mom when I didn't want to eat my vegetables?

"You swallowed the World Seed. Did you even once think about the consequences before you made such a foolish choice?"

"Bonding time is over, I guess?"

Mom set her teacup down and leaned forward, her vivid blue eyes burning. "You are a living gate, Evangeline. Your life will never be the same."

"My life hasn't been the same since a Chimera attacked me almost eight years ago. What's one more thing?"

"So flippant," Mom murmured. "Soon, when the worlds stop reeling from your decision, you will have the gods at your doorstep. You are their key home. But some won't be so magnanimous. Some will try to tear the power from your heart."

"And you?" I said, willing my heart not to thunder like a scared rabbit. "Will you tear it from me?"

"You think me terrible," she said. "A bogeyman in your life. Every decision I made was one that kept you strong, kept you alive."

"And my father? What about him?"

Her eyes flashed with fury. "I suspect you know who your father is. After all, he's taken quite an interest in you, hasn't he?"

Cliona wasn't stupid. Every time a god dropped by, they left a mark of power, an indelible stain denoting their presence that took weeks to fade. Cernunnos's touch was over much of my land. Cliona couldn't enter my property, but she would know he was in Joy Springs.

"And if he has?"

"The Fae King is bored. Such is the way with immortals. You are a new and shiny thing. Do not be surprised when he casts you aside for something else."

"Gee, Mom. You should go on the road with motivational speeches like that."

Mom reached down beside her chair and picked up a small suede pouch. "I have something for you."

"Beware gifts with teeth," I muttered to myself.

"This is your heritage," she said, ignoring me. "And your anchor to my lands. If you keep it in the pouch, you can use it to travel here at will. If you plant it..." Mom's voice trailed off. "Well, we will see what you choose. Either way, what is in the pouch and what comes of it belongs to you."

I did not take the pouch from her outstretched hand. "Is it a bomb?"

"Use your magic. It is nothing more than a seed made by my own hand."

I tested it before I took it, sending a questing tendril of magic toward the pouch. My magic seeped through the suede, touching the seed. I felt deep, earth-shattering power, a touch of Tess. No. Banshee magic and blood, soaked in greenery and earth magic.

Cliona wasn't lying. A seed, albeit a strange one, lay inside. I took the pouch from my mother's fingers and tucked it in my pocket, unsure if I'd ever use it. "Is this why you wanted to see me?"

"Do I need a reason to see my daughter?' Cliona asked primly.

I rolled my eyes. "Let's not do this." I waved my finger back and forth between us. "This mother daughter shtick where you pretend to care about me, and I pretend like anything you say is real."

A flicker of real hurt flashed over her face, there and gone in an instant. Mom straightened and rose. "Very well. Then I suppose this meeting is over."

I didn't rise right away,

"I assume you can see yourself out." Mom walked past,

pausing to brush a lock of hair from my eyes, her fingers soft and cool. It was the first time she'd ever voluntarily touched me.

And that made me immediately suspicious.

"Until we meet again, Evangeline." A wisp of power and she was gone, leaving me in this room with the amazing chairs and a pot of tea I didn't want.

"Dammit," I muttered. She was the bad guy.

So why did I feel so awful?

CHAPTER

Twelve

CAELAN

She smelled of another world. Evie turned the corner and startled when she saw me.

"You need to check your land before you walk it, flower girl."

Her eyes flashed with annoyance. "I never had any visitors until I started tangling with wolves."

I rose and waited for her to come up the steps. "Where've you been?"

She looked down. "Just a walk. My land needed tending."

"Is that why you smell like flowers and sky I've never scented anywhere on Earth?"

Evie sighed and came up the steps. "I don't have time for this right now."

Hurt stabbed me in the gut.

She stopped before me and reached out, pressing her palm against my chest. "I—I'm sorry. I've had a weird night. No reason to take it out on you."

I put my hand over hers, soaking up her warmth and vitality. Last night I'd dreamed of her wearing the crown, her presence in my life fading ever so slowly until she disappeared into the fae lands.

I refused to let that happen. She was mine, and I would fight for her.

I pulled Evie in closer, inhaling her scent, fresh and clean. My fist tangled in her hair, gently cupping her head. "I know you didn't go for a walk."

Evie tensed.

"But I won't ask you where you were. I suspect I already know."

"I'm sorry," she whispered.

"You don't trust me."

Her fingers tightened, wrinkling my shirt. "It's not—" She sighed. "You and I are from different worlds. I don't want any of this. Not the fae or my mother or being a Lady or being involved with a Lord."

"And what do you want?" I asked, oh so quietly. It didn't take a genius to figure out Evie didn't want what I was offering her. She might want me, but she didn't want the trappings of being my Lady. If I were younger and we had met sooner, I'd agree with Evie.

But I couldn't walk away from my people.

And I couldn't walk away from her.

Something had to give before it tore us apart.

My visit tonight wouldn't help things.

"Peace," Evie said. "Some down time would be nice." She smiled against my chest.

I wouldn't be bringing her peace tonight. "Come on. Let's go inside for a minute. I have something I need to give you."

She stiffened. "I hope that's a euphemism."

I waited while Evie turned and unlocked the door. "We'll see where the evening takes us."

Evie shrugged off her sweater and hooked it on the rack. "Coffee?"

"No thanks." I pulled the envelope out of my pocket.

Evie stared at it as if I were holding a snake. "Do I have to open that?"

"If you don't, the Council will show up on your doorstep."

Evie sighed and snatched the envelope from my hand, plopping down onto the couch. I sat opposite her. My "invitation" had come at the same time. Why they'd sent me hers, I couldn't fathom, but knowing the Council, it was meant to twist the knife into our relationship one more time.

When she opened it, her gaze skimmed over the contents, eyes narrowing the farther she read. A moment later, the parchment crumpled in her hand. "I take it you received one of these?"

I nodded.

"When are you scheduled to go?"

"Tomorrow. You?'

"Tomorrow. Two p.m."

"I'm at four."

"Do they think we're going to stab each other in the back?" Evie asked.

"They're only hoping."

Evie leaned forward, her shoes long since kicked off. "What's the story? Am I telling the whole truth and nothing but the truth, or are we being morally flexible?"

I grinned, loving how she didn't jump right to indignation and insistence on the truth. My Evie knew sometimes the truth only made things worse. Good in this case, but bad for our current relationship situation. "I plan to tell the truth. Ish."

Evie's eyes sparkled. "Ish? I'm pretty good at ish."

Oh, I know. "We stick as closely to the truth as possible. Donovan was working with other Chimeras to destabilize my region so he could make a power play."

"And my mother?"

"Up to you. We can leave her out if you wish and speak of only the Chimeras." I let the predator shine from my eyes. "The only Chimera witnesses are dead. Donovan is dead. I'm sure your mother would appreciate being left out of Council business."

Evie nodded. "Then we pretend we never saw her. But how do we explain how the Chimeras died?"

I thought about it. "Do we need to?"

Evie's mouth curved. "We can say they escaped. Give the Council something else to focus on."

"I like the way you think."

We talked for a little while longer to ensure our stories were straight. She yawned and stretched, her eyes growing heavy. I walked over and tipped her chin up, brushing a light kiss over her lips. "Get some rest. I'll send a car for you tomorrow."

"Not necessary."

No matter what I tried to do, she refused to let me take care of her. "The Council understands a show of strength. You and I are in this together. It's a small concession. A car. Nothing more."

She held my gaze for a moment before nodding. "I'll be ready at one."

"Good night, Evangeline." One more kiss, and I left her on the couch watching me leave.

I wanted to stay, but I was beginning to understand her, far more than she probably wanted me to. If giving her space, even though it went against every ingrained instinct, brought her to me in the end, I was willing to play the game.

In the meantime, I had a visitor at the Keep.

One I didn't want to keep waiting.

Seymour sat in the Fae King's lap, soaking up his attention. His pot tipped sideways as he reached up to rub his traps against Cernunnos's chest. Simone stood at the far back wall, her eyes wide as she stared at the king, then at me. The usually unflappable Omega could not have turned him away without offering a grievous insult, but the Keep had never hosted a fae visitor of his ilk before.

My Omega was out of her element and not pleased about it.

"Traitor," I muttered to the flytrap.

Seymour ignored me.

"My daughter's creation?" Cernunnos asked.

"Do you even need to ask?" I went straight to the bar and poured myself and the king a double of whiskey.

"No." His voice was amused. "Though I'm surprised by how sentient this creature is."

"Let me just say Evie was extremely pissed at me when she made him."

A delighted laugh. "Oh? Does he have any special abilities?"

"His bite is poisonous, and he stays angry at just about everyone."

Cernunnos brought the flytrap up to eye level. "You share similar traits with my daughter."

I hid my smile and added a large ice cube to each glass before carrying both over. I took the high-backed reclining chair opposite the king, who sprawled on the generous loveseat Simone added against my wishes.

Now I wouldn't part with the thing, much to Simone's amusement. It gave the sometimes-austere study a homey air. And now with Evie's botanical influence, I had Seymour and Hannah who were thick as thieves, and the loving turtle vine. She'd also given me a pothos vine with thorns, adding a cryptic warning not to forget to feed it, and that it would protect me if need be.

So far, the vine hadn't done anything except grow.

The king sipped the whiskey, nodding his approval. "You have good taste, wolf."

I barely restrained myself from baring my teeth. Demanding he call me Lord would begin a pissing contest I knew I wouldn't win.

"To what do I owe the pleasure of this visit?" I asked.

Simone had called me in a panic while I was waiting for Evie to arrive home, but I'd refused to return until I delivered the Council's missive.

"Trouble comes to your doorstep," Cernunnos said.

"Trouble never leaves my doorstep."

"Oh?" An amused smile. "Seems like much of your trouble started when you met my daughter."

"Some trouble is worth it."

"Let's hope it is."

"You're here to call in the debt." There was no need for it to come out as a question. Cernunnos didn't make house calls. He wasn't here because I was in love with his daughter.

He wanted something from me.

"You didn't think I'd give you a freebie, I hope." The king's smile was full of teeth.

"A freebie from a fae? Perish the thought," I said mildly.

"The favor is small and easily doable. Evie should not be aware or ever know."

I stilled. "Keeping secrets from her isn't part of the agreement."

Cernunnos's eyes swirled. "Consider the agreement changed. Evie cannot know."

I tipped the rest of my whiskey back. "Why?"

"It matters not. There is no harm to Evie now or in the future."

This creature might one day become my father-in-law, and I didn't trust him as far as I could throw him. "What's the favor?"

"I need shelter for someone in my kingdom. She will need a home or apartment or somewhere to stay and work that pays her enough to survive. Thalia is gifted and might be able to have a shop or contracted work she uses to make a living."

"What is her gift?"

The first flash of discomfort appeared in his eyes. "She's a seer. A powerful one. Thalia cannot drive or transport herself. Visions come upon her at any time, and they can become volatile."

Upon the surface, the favor didn't seem terrible, but fae were tricky. Cernunnos wasn't telling me everything. "Is she dangerous?"

"I would not unleash someone dangerous upon your town or my daughter."

"That isn't an answer. Yes or no."

His jaw tightened. "She can be dangerous to herself when she's in the midst of a vision, only because her magic paralyzes her. Thalia's visions are realistic to the point where she can no longer recognize herself when she's having one. If the wrong people were to get a hold of her, she could not protect herself."

"Then she needs a companion or guard."

He inclined his head. "If you provide her one, I will look upon such an action favorably."

Not admitting to a debt between us, but something I might be able to exploit later. "What else?"

Cernunnos hesitated, an odd reaction I'd never seen from him. "Thalia is simple," he said after a moment. "Sweet and easygoing. She's an innocent in an age that doesn't always appreciate such traits. Whoever you assign to her may need to treat her with kid gloves until she gets her bearings."

"If I do this, my debt is cleared."

The king's eyes narrowed. "You are a black and white kind of man."

I shook my head. "No. I do not like fae deals and want this one concluded. No strings, no gotchas. If I take Thalia on and keep her safe for a period of…" I thought about it, "six months, after one hundred and eighty days, our slate is clean. I will pay the rent for an extra six months to allow her time to save some money. After that, the girl is on her own."

"Twenty-four months," Cernunnos countered, just as I expected.

"Twelve." The Fae King could damn well afford to clothe and house the girl himself. But for some reason he either wouldn't or didn't want to. Interesting.

"Eighteen is my final offer. If you don't agree, I will walk away and finalize our debt in a much different way."

Fae speak for either take it or I'll fuck you over in a glorious way later.

"Fine. I'll set the girl up for eighteen months and give her the best chance to succeed. After that, our debt is cleared."

"Money. Food. Shelter. A job. And a protector or companion."

I waved a hand. "I'll do all of those. Though Thalia doesn't get to pick and choose who I pick to oversee her."

"Someone safe," Cernunnos growled.

I studied him. "You care about this girl. Why are you foisting her on me?"

"It doesn't matter," the king snapped.

His reaction told me it very much mattered.

"We have a deal." I stuck my hand out. "Deliver her to me in three days. I need some time to get everything set up."

I glanced at Simone who was furiously taking notes on her ever-handy iPad. She glanced up and nodded, her eyes a little feverish at the thought of such an interesting task. I'd talk to her away from Cernunnos' influence. After we checked the room for magical listening devices.

The king and I shook, and Cernunnos rose, his antlers almost brushing the ceiling fan. I'd seen him appear without those, so I knew he was here in an official capacity and wanted to try to intimidate me.

Granted, the thought of being mixed up with the Fae King made me a little ill, but he'd done me a big favor, and this Thalia thing was far less than what I expected him to ask.

Or it was on the surface at least.

"Three days," Cernunnos said.

"How will I get a message to you?" I asked.

"Leave it on the table in your secret library." With a wink at Simone, Cernunnos disappeared in a wisp of gold and green magic.

Simone slumped against the wall. "Do I even want to know why you made a deal with the Fae King?"

"Plausible deniability." I slumped against the back of the chair. "Do you know anyone named Thalia?"

"No one by that name. She's bound to be fae, and I only have a few such contacts, but I'll ask around." She tapped one more thing on the screen and tucked the stylus back into its slot. "Are you worried about not telling Evie about this?"

"Of course I am." I rubbed a hand over my face. "Feels like no matter which direction I turn, I can't win with her."

"The fae always complicate everything they're involved in." She tucked her tablet into her tote bag and picked it up. As she passed, she laid a hand on my shoulder. "Be careful. The king is leaving a lot of information out."

"I'm thinking of assigning Garrett to the woman."

Simone nodded. "Good idea. He won't tolerate any shenanigans." She laughed. "We just gotta keep him from killing her."

I groaned. "Don't even say that. If something happens to Thalia on our watch..." My voice trailed off.

"I hope this was worth it," Simone said quietly before she left the room.

If it got me Evie, anything would be worth it.

CHAPTER
Thirteen

I t was too damned cold for a dress, but jeans were a power move I wasn't ready for, so I settled for wool blend slacks, leather boots and a cashmere sweater. I put my hair up in a neat chignon and added minimal makeup.

I needed to look calm, collected, and professional. Not like the savage who'd killed two Chimeras in the woods a couple of months ago…and participated in other things with the Shifter Lord.

After making a coffee to go, I waited by the front door for Caelan's driver. My stomach twisted in anticipation. The Lords were all wildly different and the thought of standing before them getting grilled about something I didn't technically have a hand in pissed me off.

But that's politics, baby.

True to his word, a car pulled up at the edge of the driveway, inches away from my wards. I tugged a jacket on, grabbed my purse and keys, and hurried down the driveway.

The driver was a wolf I'd never met before.

"Ma'am. I'm Cain. Is the temperature okay?" The shifter wore a dark suit and mirrored sunglasses. He had a sharp jaw and full lips, but his expression was stone faced.

"Good with me. Thanks for the ride."

"Buckle up, ma'am. The Shifter Lord insists you arrive safe."

I obliged. "Ready when you are."

Seconds later we were on the road.

Cain pulled up to the entrance of a fancy hotel about forty-five minutes later. I reached for the door, but the door was opened and a tanned hand extended in.

Caelan's smell washed over me. I slid my hand into his calloused palm and let him help me out.

"We shouldn't be seen together," I whispered.

"I don't give a shit what they think this looks like. I'll never feel guilty for the way I feel about you."

My heart did a little skip. Something brushed against my ear, and I batted at it, thinking maybe it was a bug.

Caelan's eyes widened, a delighted smile tipping his lips up. "Blooming for me, Evie?" he murmured, his fingers brushing against my hair. The delectable scent of jasmine rose in the air.

My mouth fell open. I lifted my hand to feel soft petals entwined in my hair.

"Shit," I breathed.

"Don't pluck them," Caelan said quietly, tugging my hand down. "The Council needs to know who you are."

Yet another weird side effect of my magic. At least I hadn't blown anything up today. Yeesh.

My boot heels thumped against the stone ground, and I was glad I'd chosen sensible shoes. A fine mist of rain sent a chill across my skin. The sky was rapidly darkening, storm clouds rolling in from a distance, akin to the temper beginning to churn in my chest.

We hurried inside, seconds before lightning cracked in the sky and the heavens opened up. The hotel's interior was tastefully decorated in a mix of modern touches and old-world style. A wrought iron chandelier hung in the middle of the foyer casting a warm light on the tile inlay.

As we walked, my hair kept rustling, a multitude of floral and herbaceous scents wafting in the air as we moved. People gawked at me with wide eyes as Caelan kept a firm hold on my elbow, chuckling softly as my hair bloomed before their eyes.

"I'm going to look like a freak when I walk in there," I mumbled under my breath.

Caelan escorted me to the end of the hallway. "You're going to look like a goddess."

He tugged me down to the bench to sit beside him. We sat next to a room with large wooden doors and a do not disturb sign.

"The Council is meeting there?"

"They changed the location four times to make it difficult for anyone to get the drop on them."

"And they think hosting at a public hotel will be safe?"

"Everyone here belongs to one of the Lords," Caelan said. "The Council bought the place out for forty-eight hours."

I grimaced. "This isn't a day trip then? Bummer."

The doors opened. Simone poked her head out, saw me, and offered a grim smile. "Five minutes and you're up."

"Any tips?"

She tapped her ear.

They were listening.

"Just be yourself," Simone said, her eyes burning with anger. "That always seems to work."

With a nod at us both, she ducked back inside the door.

"I can't tell if she's telling me not to be myself or if she's saying be the Evie that grows twenty-foot flowering trees on someone else's lawn."

Caelan grinned. "The latter." He rose and touched my hair, sending another waft of floral scent up. "Stop being afraid of who you are. Use it. Show the Council you are not to be trifled with."

"Easy for you to say. You're a Lord. I'm a peon."

"You may live in my territory, but you are no peon. They called you here for information about Donovan, but don't be surprised if they try to dig into your background. Stay on topic and answer only the questions about the dead Lord. You owe them nothing except info on Donovan. And even then, you don't have to speak if you don't want to, but they will make your life hard if you don't."

"When does it end? When will they ever get off my back?"

Caelan's jaw tightened. "Follow Simone's advice. Show them you are not some mundane florist. Fear is power, Evangeline. When they know to fear you, they will back down."

I slumped. "This sucks."

Caelan snorted. "Eloquent as always."

The door opened again. Caelan gave me a meaningful look before walking away.

Simone stepped outside. "Evie. The Council will see you."

I squared my shoulders and followed her into the room. The hotel setting was a little odd for such a powerful gathering. A coffee set up rested by the back wall, white cups turned upside down on a silver tray next to large, hand labeled carafes.

The Shifter Lords sat side by side, behind a long table with a dark tablecloth. Rowan was on the end on my left side, a warning glimmering in his hazel eyes. Next to him sat Ethan, his gaze watchful and wary. Thorvin sat next to him, staring at me with friendly curiosity. Soren sat next to him, his face a carefully blank slate. But there was one sitting there who might have broken my heart if I had let him in.

Ben. He was as handsome as I remembered, but all pretense of friendliness in his eyes had fallen away. The Healer watched me, like a predator watches another worthy predator.

The way he looked at me hurt. I'd never done anything to him except keep my secrets. I'd never harmed anyone who hadn't brought harm to my doorstep, and I tried my best to stay in my lane.

And it had gotten me right here. Right now. In front of a bunch of Lords who wanted to own me. Anger sparked in my gut, fury at being put in this position when all I wanted to do was go home and play in the greenhouse.

I swallowed the fury down and put on a pleasant smile, while refusing to look at Ben.

Be myself, Simone said.

Here goes nothing.

"You boys look like you're up here for a celebrity panel. Am I early for the Q&A?" I turned in a slow circle, pretending to investigate the room. No windows to be found, but two doors on either side of the Lords' table. The double doors behind me were heavy and large, difficult to get out if I needed to exit in a hurry.

"You will speak when you are spoken to," one of the Lords snapped.

I turned to see Ethan glaring at me. He was the oldest of the Lords, silver edging his hair at the temples. His eyes were dark and flat, and he wore a cloak of restrained violence around his lean shoulders. Out of all the Lords, I knew him and Thorvin the least.

Ethan seemed to be the de facto leader, at least today. He sat in the middle of the table, hands crossed in a steeple. His navy suit was perfectly pressed, complete with a crisp white shirt worn underneath and a dark gray tie with a silver pin in the shape of a wolf's head.

I let a little Floromancy power shine through my eyes. "I am not your prisoner, Lord. Watch your tongue when you're speaking to me."

Soren's lips twitched. Rowan rubbed a hand over his face. Thorvin continued to watch me, seemingly memorizing everything about me. His attention was beginning to unnerve me. Ben's eyes narrowed.

Rage sparked in Ethan's eyes. He leaned forward a hair, hands pressed on either side of him. "Do not threaten me, witch."

Ethan had control issues. He liked walking in a room and being the most important thing inside. This man liked power and servitude. Too bad I had no intention of allowing him any over me. "I am no witch. The only one threatening here is you. Do not presume you can control me. Ask your questions and leave me be."

If Moira were here, I'd get a double high five for my haughtiness.

Rowan's slight nod told me I was doing well. Or that I was about to get my ass kicked off by pissed off shifters. Couldn't tell you. But no one had attacked me yet, so I planned to roll with it.

Ethan opened his mouth to speak, but Thorvin spoke before he could.

"Of course, Miss Quinn." His voice was deep with a slight European edge. "Please," he gestured with a large hand. "Have a seat. We won't take up too much of your time."

"A gentleman," I said. "Finally." Choosing a chair at the very back of the room, I sat and crossed my legs.

Ethan let out an annoyed sigh.

Thorvin's eyes sparkled. "Can you hear us all the way back there?"

"Of course I can. This seat is expedient. I have another appointment to go to after this."

"Your disrespect will be your downfall one day," Ethan growled.

"Maybe," I agreed. "But it won't happen today."

"Perhaps not," Ethan said, a vicious smile lighting his lips. "But I look forward to the future."

I pretended to yawn.

"Miss Quinn," Rowan said with an amused drawl, "thank you for agreeing to see us today."

"I didn't have much of a choice, did I?"

"We apologize if our missive sounded demanding." Rowan shuffled some papers in front of him. "All we're trying to do is get to the bottom of what happened to Donovan."

"Donovan was a traitor and an all-around asshat."

Ethan blinked in surprise. "A traitor? Explain."

"You're awfully demanding for someone who needs something from me."

The Lord's nostrils flared. A flash of gold streaked through his eyes. "Miss Quinn," he said through clenched teeth. "I'd appreciate it if you elaborated on your statement."

"Which one?" I asked sweetly.

Rowan choked and tried to cover it up with a cough.

Ethan rose, his face flame red with rage. I kept my seat, readying my magic for a strike if he came toward me. "I could kill you right now and no one would be the wiser."

We stared at each other, gold flaring in his slightly crazed eyes. "You could try. But I promise you won't find it as easy as you assume it might be." Vines crawled from my skin and slid across the floor, a new aspect of my power I'd been messing around with when I had time.

These vines were not normal. Poison dripped and hissed when it hit the ground, destroying the carpet as they slid ever closer to the Lords. Rowan was the only one who wasn't watching the vines. A curious expression had taken over his face, and I knew the man well enough to know he was wondering if he could do the same thing.

The soft shhhh of the vines was the only sound in the room. I stopped them an inch from his foot. "I am not yours to command, Lord. Treat me like an equal or I will walk out of here."

"We are in command of all the paranormals in this country!" Ethan shouted. "You have been nothing but a—" Thorvin reached over and put his hand on Ethan's arm, silencing him.

I stood. "A pain in the ass? A menace?" I shrugged. "Had you ever heard of me before this year? Had I ever done anything to stand out or gain power? I'd been in Caelan's territory for seven years before you started poking your nose into my business. This is your final warning. Leave me be or you will have me as an enemy."

Ethan's eyes flicked to the dripping vines. When he lifted his gaze, a chill walked down my spine. I'd always thought his eyes looked lifeless, but right now they held the chill of the grave. "You wish to make an enemy out of all of us?"

"You're the only one who's threatened my life."

Ben sighed loudly. "Evie, please withdraw your…"

"Super awesome vines?" Rowan supplied when Ben floundered.

"Poisonous weapons," Ben said.

"When Lord Ethan stops being a dick, I'll put my plants away."

I could almost hear Ben's teeth grinding.

"You are not helping," Ben whispered to Rowan.

"She's right." Rowan didn't bother to whisper back. "We've antagonized her for months now when we usually stay out of another Lord's business."

"She's here to answer questions about Donovan," Ben snapped.

"Then let's all shut the fuck up and let her do that," Rowan said, his eyes rolling with gold. I'd never seen Rowan truly pissed off before. His jaw turned to granite and claws had slid from his fingertips.

Thorvin rose and leaned over to murmur something low in Ethan's ear. The other Lord froze before nodding once. He retook his seat, but I remained standing.

"Miss Quinn," Thorvin said in a placating tone. "We apologize this meeting has turned so…acrimonious. If you'd please take your seat, we can resume."

"No. I don't think I will. You have two minutes to ask your questions. After that, you should think twice about summoning me like I'm a common peasant forced to live under your rule."

Thorvin's brow rose a hitch, and I waited for someone to leap over the table and go for my throat. Tension strummed tight like a drum before the Lord nodded once.

"Very well. Let's revisit your comments about Donovan being a traitor."

"He'd been working with Chimeras for months now."

Ethan reared back like I slapped him. "Lies," he hissed.

Thorvin, however, seemed more intrigued than shocked. "You've seen this?"

"He showed up to Caelan's Keep with the one who usurped and killed your other Lord and another Chimera named Rhona."

The Lords turned to confer quietly amongst themselves.

Rowan was the first to withdraw. "Did you have anything to do with his death?"

"Sadly, no."

Rowan let out a bark of laughter. "You disliked the Lord, then?"

"So far I dislike everyone here but you, Lord Rowan."

He grinned. "I'm apt to agree with you. Our behavior toward you today is appalling. Please accept my deepest apologies."

I inclined my head. "You can make it up to me by bringing me some more of those wonderful apples from your territory."

Rowan winked. "I'd be happy to as long as you give me one of those flytraps."

"Only for you, Lord Rowan."

"You are sleeping with two Lords?" Ethan snapped. "Typical."

A red haze obscured my vision. The floor rumbled under my feet. Regular, thick vines, green with new growth, snapped from the ground underneath Ethan, tossing him off his feet with a star-tled yelp. It took every ounce of willpower I had not to pop him with those poisonous vines. With a wiggle of my finger, they wrapped around his knees and ankles before he could react, and lifted him into the sky, dumping him upside down.

He hung from his ankles, swearing up a blue streak. The other Lords had dived from the table. Everyone except for Rowan who let out a heavy sigh.

"I'll give it to you, Evie. You do have style." He rubbed a hand over his face and let out a short laugh.

"Release me," Ethan snarled, struggling against the green vines. For every one he slashed with a wicked sharp claw, two more took its place.

"Sluts don't take instruction well," I said, my eyes wide with innocence. "We're too driven by the pulse of our overactive loins."

Soren, who'd been suspiciously quiet, strode over to me. I watched him warily. He wasn't an enemy, though I was worried about his fascination with Moira and how it might upset her life.

He held his hands up. "I just want to talk."

"We can talk without you getting any closer."

"Privately."

"If you try anything funny, I won't promise I won't poison you."

"Consider me duly warned."

Soren kept walking until he was less than a foot away. Like all the Lords, Soren was tall and built for violence. His eyes, a startling blue, held mine. "Ethan is not a good man to make an enemy of," he said in a voice meant for my ears only.

"And you think I am?"

"Caelan's fascination with you is well warranted," he said with an incline of his head. "He's never gone for weak women."

The words felt like a punch to my gut. Everyone had a past, but I likened myself to an ostrich. If I buried my head in the sand far enough, maybe I wouldn't have to hear about it. "What will it take for you fuckers to leave me alone?"

Soren snorted. "You need to ally yourself with one of the Lords."

"I already am." Ethan was still trying to escape, so I commanded the vines to shake him a few times, not enough to hurt him, just to rattle his skull a bit.

The Lord's snarling dialogue was a lullaby to my soul.

"No," Soren said softly. "It's not enough to sleep with him or occasionally allow Caelan to come into your life when you see fit."

I stared at him. "You think I should marry him." What was up with these misogynistic pricks trying to marry me off? "It's not the 1800s."

"Caelan has already told you why it's in your best interest to tie yourself to him. He's not a stupid man."

"And what about me?" I asked. "Where's my choice?"

"You are a threat."

Could I punch some sense into Soren or was I bound to repeat the same thing for eternity? "And I wouldn't be if you left me alone."

"You know it doesn't work like that."

"Well it should," I snapped. "I'm no one's plaything."

I took a deep breath and stepped forward, raising my voice to carry over Ethan's commotion. "Donovan died because he fucked around and found out. I had nothing to do with his death, but the Lord was justified in his use of force. It was either him or Donovan, and the world is a better place without that piece of shit in it. Do not summon me again."

I turned to walk out.

"Um. Evie?" Rowan called.

I stopped and turned.

"Do you mind?" He pointed at Ethan still struggling. "I think he's close to passing out."

My eyes narrowed. "I'll cut him down in a few minutes."

Soren snorted.

The doors slammed open, revealing Caelan. His golden gaze swept over the room, landed on me for a brief second before moving onto the Lords. When he spotted Ethan, his lips twitched. "I see you have things well under control."

I shrugged. "This is the last warning they'll receive from me."

One of Caelan's eyebrows tipped up. "Good to know."

I passed by. Caelan snagged me around the waist, his hand curving over my hip. "You look so fucking sexy when you're being violent."

Before I could respond, he pressed a hard, possessive kiss to my lips.

I blinked and brought his face down for one more, with the Lord happy to oblige.

"I've pissed them off," I whispered. "Ethan is a dickhead." I dragged my fingers through his dark hair, cherishing the feel of his silky tresses against my skin.

"What did he do?" His words were a rumble of fury.

Telling him might mean Ethan wouldn't walk out of here alive. "Don't worry about it. I took care of him."

The side of his lips tipped up. "I can see that. Anything else I need to know?"

"I told them Donovan deserved it."

Caelan's laugh made me smile.

"Rowan is supposed to bring me some apples."

"I'll ensure he keeps his promise." One more kiss and he let me go. "Can I come by tonight?"

I nodded. "Good luck."

Caelan eyed the table one more time. The Lords were reassembling in their seats, pointedly ignoring Ethan's plight. Not a single one of them tried to cut him down. "Do you think you should free him?"

"In a little while."

Caelan nodded. "As you wish. Cain is in the front waiting for you."

"Thanks."

He winked at me and strode forward. "Gentleman. I hope this won't take long."

I walked out, ready to get on with my day. If they came around again, I had no plans to waste my time trying to reason with any of them.

As far as I was concerned, any business I might have with the Council was concluded.

I strode through the hotel lobby, ignoring the people still staring at my flower strewn hair. Cain was already by the passenger door holding it open for me.

I slid in with a murmured thanks.

As we drove away, I cut the magic holding Ethan aloft and smiled.

I came home to a young man standing in my driveway.

"Do you know him?" I asked Cain.

The driver sighed. "Yes. The Council has sent you a …"

"Spy?" I offered helpfully.

Cain pulled into the driveway, carefully avoiding the shimmering wards. "He's a good kid, Miss Quinn. Take it easy on him, if you don't mind."

"Depends on how easy he takes it on me, but I have no plans to let him through the wards, so he may need a ride home."

Cain inclined his head. "Take care of yourself."

"You do the same. Thanks for the ride." I dug in my purse and tossed him a twenty.

The shifter rolled his eyes but tucked the bill into his shirt pocket.

I got out and walked up to the young man. "Whatever they've told you is probably a lie. You won't be allowed through the wards, and if you try to get through, I won't be held responsible for what happens. Do you understand?"

"Umm. Yes. I'm uh Marek."

"Evie." He was tall and lanky, somewhere in his late teens to early twenties, and still holding on to the scrawniness of youth.

One day, he'd be a handsome man, but right now, he looked like a kid who'd received an assignment he was totally unprepared for.

A pang of sympathy hit me. "Who do you belong to?"

"I'm one of Rowan's."

My eyes narrowed. Was this a favor or was there something else going on I wasn't privy to? "Who assigned you to me?"

"Lord Rowan volunteered me for this assignment."

"And when was this?"

Marek swallowed. "About five minutes ago. I was at that awesome cafe when I got the call."

"How long are you here for?"

Marek lifted a scrawny shoulder in a careless shrug. "Until Lord Rowan says I can go home."

"Great. And what are you supposed to do?"

Marek fidgeted. "Um. Not tell you what I'm supposed to do," he said sheepishly.

I'd thought about powering down the wards a touch until this answer. "Alright then, Marek. I like your Lord, but I don't take kindly to spies. The wards will fry your ass if you get frisky with them. Try, don't try. It's no skin off my back either way. Got it?"

"Er. Yes ma'am."

I held my index finger up. "And none of that. Call me Evie."

"Yes, Evie."

"Good. I'll see you around, Marek."

I stepped through the wards.

"Uh. Miss Evie?"

I turned.

"What if I have to go to the bathroom?"

Lord love a duck. "Then I suggest you find somewhere other than my driveway to go. If I smell wolf piss, I'll push my wards out all the way to the road. Got it?"

Marek swallowed hard and nodded, a tinge of fear rolling over his face before he dropped his gaze.

I turned away and headed up the driveway.

Several hours later, Caelan came into the house and kicked off his shoes. I'd felt his presence as soon as he entered, thanks to the souped-up wards. With Marek's still hovering around the driveway, I went ahead and juiced them up today, just as a precaution.

"The wards tingled this time," he said by way of greeting.

"You came in from the back?" I guessed.

Caelan stilled. "Why? Is there something out front?"

"The wards must be blocking his scent."

"Your favorite Lord sent a spy here?" he said in a deceptively calm voice.

"I assumed you knew about it. He was here when I arrived home from the inquisition."

Caelan closed his eyes for a moment. "Shit. I meant to tell you, but I got caught up. They insisted on sending someone for monitoring." He rolled his eyes. "Rowan jumped in and volunteered his person, and Ethan said something very interesting about your virtue."

I winced.

"Is he still alive?"

"For now." He let out a heavy sigh as he settled his bulk beside me and opened his arm.

I scooted under it and sighed. He was always so warm.

"You did quite the number on him." Caelan's chest rumbled with amusement. "He'll be healing for at least a week. The vines got a little…animated once you left the building."

Interesting. My power continued to grow in disturbing and sentient ways. "I deserve a little credit for not poisoning him."

"Maybe let them cool down a couple of weeks before you ask for it."

"My hope is I never see them again."

Caelan shifted. "Being with me will make that hope all but impossible."

I toyed with the buttons of his shirt. "They want me to ally with one of them. Same shit, different day."

The hand he held around my waist tightened. "And your response?"

"Do I even need to tell you?" I rolled my eyes. "Of course I told them to fuck off."

"What about me?" he asked quietly.

"As far as I'm concerned, we're already allied."

"But nothing more permanent?"

I was tired of talking about this. Tired of worrying and being pushed. So very tired of politics I never asked for. I popped my head up to stare at him, those stormy gray eyes already carved deep into my soul. "I care about you. More than I've cared about any man in my life. But I am not the kind of woman who can be pushed into something she doesn't want to do."

At his darkening gaze, I shook my head and barreled on. "I'm not saying no forever. I'm saying no for now. If you need a forever commitment right now, I am not the one."

What came next was a long and charged silence. I dropped my head onto Caelan's chest and soaked up his warmth for what might be the last time.

A Lord was not used to being denied.

"A courtship, then," he murmured.

I jerked my head up and stared.

"A proper one."

My eyes narrowed. "We aren't in the 1800s."

"I never said we were."

This felt like trickery of the highest order. "I'm not asking to be courted. Only respected."

"A courtship is the proper way to woo a woman a man wants to marry."

I scrubbed a hand over my face. This was going all wrong. "We rarely talk."

A feral grin. "We're usually preoccupied with other things."

"Caelan. I'm serious. I know very little about you, and you know even less about me."

His expression sobered. "You want me to know you before you say yes."

This still felt like trickery. "That's usually the way it works.

Boy meets girl. Girl meets boy. Girl and boy figure out one likes stone ground mustard, the other likes plain yellow."

"Dijon," the Shifter Lord said and shrugged.

"Same," I admitted.

"Mayo or no mayo?" His eyes glittered in the low light.

"Depends. Yes, on sandwiches. No on hot dogs."

Caelan's nose scrunched up. "People put mayo on hot dogs?"

"Twenty percent of the population."

"Sacrilege," he muttered.

"You forget how I was raised. I'm very much human when it comes to the tradition of love and marriage."

His strong fingers toyed with my hair. "Can you see yourself being married again? After..." His voice trailed off. "Is this why you're so hesitant?"

"I don't like being pushed into any decision I haven't made on my own, but my past makes me more reticent to tie myself to someone else in that way. Marriage is a sacred covenant, and I won't be bullied by anyone to enter into one."

He nodded. "Very well, Evangeline. I will only ask you when I have met your requirements."

I snorted. "There are no requirements other than to stop pushing me toward the altar."

"Mmm." The sound seemed like agreement, but I knew better.

"Do not mess with me, Lord."

Caelan chuckled. "Messing with you got me right here."

"Don't push your luck either."

He shifted and tilted my chin up, brushing a kiss over my lips. "I will abide by your rules."

I hadn't made any rules, but I felt like I'd somehow lost the rule book.

Little Shop of Florals was busy from the moment we opened the doors until closing time. When I finally locked the doors and sagged against the wall, Moira and I stared wide-eyed at each other.

"That was intense," I breathed.

Moira sank into a rolling chair. "When are Tess and Ash due back?"

Both called in sick today, though Ash admitted he was more heart sick than anything. Tess didn't elaborate, and I didn't press the issue. Even though none of us could catch mundane diseases, I allotted a few sick days to my employees because sometimes you just needed a free day to veg in your pajamas and ruminate about life.

"I expect Tess will be back sooner than Ash."

Moira spun in the chair. "This sucks."

"Yeah. Do you think I should ban employee relationships?"

The vampire laughed. "You only have three employees and both Tess and Ash are terrified of me. You and Ash won't be dating, and I can't see Tess dating anyone else for a long time. I don't think you need to worry about it."

Something in her first sentence made me pause. "Why are they terrified of you?"

Moira's jaw tightened. "Unimportant."

"Moira."

"Leave it be," she warned. "We've worked it out and everything is fine."

At my nod, she continued. "Needless to say, my dating life is drier than the Sahara. Tess and Ash will be fine, even if they decide they're better off apart for good." She smiled. "They're adults. Let them solve it their way."

"I was!"

Moira yawned and rolled the chair back. "You were getting all glinty eyed. I know that look. It's Evie speak for I'm about to get involved."

"Was not," I muttered, even though we both knew she was right.

Earlier in the day I'd told her about my visit with the Council, but we hadn't had much time to chat about it because of the stream of constant customers.

"Do you think this time the Lords will take the hint?" Moira asked.

"After what I did to Ethan?" I strode over to the coffee pot and made a fresh one. "Fifty-fifty."

She grinned. "I would have loved to see that prick get tossed around."

"It was awesome." The memory of Ethan hanging upside down, still fresh in my mind, made me grin.

"You probably made an enemy today."

"They've been enemies since the moment they stepped into my shop and threatened me."

Moira stood and slung her purse over her shoulder. "We have your back. Always. But tangling with the Lords is bad for business and our continued health. Be careful." To soften her words, she hip bumped me as she passed by on her way to the door. "Tangle with Caelan all you want," she said with a wink. "But the other ones smell blood in the water."

A gust of cool wind blew into the shop when Moira left. I shivered and locked the door behind her.

The Lords might smell blood in the water, but when the chips fell, it wouldn't be my blood they found.

CHAPTER

Fifteen

CAELAN

A shift in the wind and the scent of ancient pines and snow told me I was no longer alone. From behind the tree cover, a massive, glowing stag with moss hanging from its impressive antlers stepped out.

A snap of light and the Fae King stood before me, his eyes an unsettling multi-colored swirl of magic. "Your land still holds a taste of the ancient wilds," Cernunnos said before coming to sit beside me.

He was not my king, and I would rise for no authority other than my own, but Cernunnos took no issue. The king understood the way the modern world worked and knew the fae no longer held our world in a chokehold of fear. Their magic was still impressive, but using a spell on a human brought a death sentence if pressed, and shifters were more resistant to a fae's power.

Not Cernunnos's or another god's, but a lower fae would be hard pressed to unduly influence someone like me or any of my shifters.

But the Fae King had much larger problems than petty grievances.

"Did you bring her?" I asked. His favor had weighed on me

for the last few days. On the surface, the request seemed innocent, but a fae rarely told the full story. There was something about this Thalia woman Cernunnos wasn't disclosing. If she brought harm to my people, she would die, and if that brought war to my doorstep, so be it.

But Cernunnos wasn't known for breaking deals or dealing unfairly with people, though he was pure fae and had a great deal of mischief in his bones.

"She awaits my word. I wish to speak to you first."

"Everything is ready. Your Thalia will have shelter and a part-time job until she figures out another way to secure funds. Her protector is my Second, Garrett."

Cernunnos inclined his head. "Thank you. Thalia is…special."

My eyes narrowed, but I remained silent. Was this woman his lover? Something else?

"Her powers can be crippling, and my realm has made her visions worse. My hope is Joy Springs will bring her some peace. She is important to our future."

"Why are you being kind to this woman?"

Cernunnos' eyes flashed. "Do you know me as unkind to anyone? She is my subject, therefore, she is worthy of my attention."

I didn't believe him for one second. "What about Cliona?"

"Tread carefully, Lord," he warned.

"She has tormented Evie her entire life and has not warranted your kind attention."

"Cliona is a problem for another time. She is under the watchful eye of a few trusted associates."

I grunted. "My word stands. I'll ensure the care of your charge, but if she endangers my people, I will not hesitate to end her." Cernunnos might be Evie's father, but he was a conniving sonofabitch. Whoever this Thalia woman was, I planned to figure out her secrets and why she was so important to the king.

Cernunnos's lips pulled into a wry smile. "I think you will find

Thalia's influence an interesting addition to your current dynamic."

Whatever that meant. "Either way, she is a guest in Joy Springs and subject to our laws. A Lord's success relies on their ability to keep their people safe. If a guest breaks the rules of hospitality, a Lord is within his rights to enforce certain…stipulations." I let my teeth show. "Caution your Thalia to respect the Lord's authority, and she will have no issue here."

Cernunnos shook his head. "I care nothing for the other Lords' authority. The only reason I am sitting here with you now is because of Evie. She cares about you. As such, I will do my best to respect your territory." The Fae King rose. "But make no mistake, Lord Caelan, you exist by my grace. I will deal fairly with you as long as you do the same."

He swung a hand across his body. A shimmering portal appeared from thin air, revealing a land of emerald-green grass and brilliant blue skies.

"Thalia," Cernunnos boomed. "Step forward."

A small woman appeared on the other side. Her hair was dark and braided into a heavy plait. Eyes of hazel glinted as she watched us, set in a delicate, fine-boned face with high cheekbones and full lips. Thalia looked familiar, but I knew I'd never met her before.

The grass rustled from behind, Garrett's way of telling me he'd arrived. My Second could sneak up on anyone, but he tried to be courteous unless he was hunting.

When Thalia spotted Garrett, her eyes narrowed. With a slight squaring of her shoulders, the woman stepped through, the edges of her dress dragging through the portal and onto the damp grass. The portal disappeared plunging the night into silence.

Thalia stared at Cernunnos, anger glinting in her eyes. "Where are you dumping me this time?" She practically bristled with an ill temper.

A soft snort from behind. Garrett stepped forward. "Come with me, Thalia. I'll escort you to your quarters."

"Another prison," Thalia scoffed. She rolled her eyes. "Do I at least get three square meals a day this time?"

"Don't be difficult," Cernunnos said through gritted teeth. "You've never been abused in my care."

"It doesn't mean your care is up to necessary standards," Thalia said in an arch voice. She unslung a pack from her shoulders. "Is there a place where I can get some blue jeans? Ol' deer guy refuses to stock pants in his 14th century fortress."

My brows went up. Probably not a lover then.

"I'll take you," Garrett said, stepping up to offer his arm to Thalia.

The woman stared at him with suspicion. "And who are you?"

I lay a hand over my chest. "I am Caelan, Lord of this territory. This is my Second, Garrett."

"Second what?" Thalia asked, confusion flashing over her face.

Garrett watched her with the intensity of a predator discovering something interesting. A flash of worry shuddered through me, but I cast it aside. This was Garrett. Not some lovesick teenager. Even if he was attracted to this irate woman, and I couldn't imagine why he would be, he'd do his job.

"A Second is integral to the structure of the Pack," Garrett said. "We help the Lord maintain order, structure, and discipline."

"Garrett is also a trusted advisor and a protector for everyone in our Pack and those who've received our protection," I added.

Thalia looked at Cernunnos. "How long will I be here?"

"For the foreseeable future."

Thalia rolled his eyes. "Until you can decide what to do with me?"

The king's expression darkened. "I'm doing this to help you."

Thalia rolled her eyes and finally took Garrett's outstretched arm. "A cage with no bars is still a cage."

Lightning cracked in the sky, a physical representation of Cernunnos's fury. His eyes swirled with rage, and he stepped forward as if to grab her.

Thalia snorted. "You stopped scaring me a long time ago. Honestly, it'd be a relief if you killed me."

Garrett stiffened, a low snarl ripping from his throat.

"Know your place, wolf," Cernunnos said, his voice a rumble in the night.

I stepped forward. "Thalia is under our protection now. You have no say over her welfare until you decide our watch is over."

For a moment, I thought Cernunnos might call the entire thing off. His eyes swirled as he watched Thalia, her fingers wrapped around Garrett's forearm. His usually reliable second's posture was stiff, the rings of his watchful eyes flaring a bright gold. If I ever left, there was a good possibility Garrett would step into my position. A shifter's power only grew as they aged, and Garrett was almost as powerful as a Lord. It took incredible willpower for him to hold his position as my Second and not to get into dominance challenges with the other wolves.

Garrett was deadly enough to win most challenges that came his way, but intelligent and emotionally mature enough to defuse most before they resulted in a full out fight. Young shifters were full of testosterone and violence, and sometimes the only way to temper the urge to fight was for a more dominant wolf to put them on the ground.

"She is not your plaything," Cernunnos warned Garrett, seeing the potential of trouble as well as I did.

Garrett held the Fae King's gaze. "I'd never force a woman," he said, the wolf riding his voice.

Thalia dropped Garrett's arm. "I swear," she snapped. "If it's not one ridiculous thing, it's another. The last thing I want is some man bossing me around all the time. And a shifter to boot?" She rolled her eyes. "All the snarling and growling and possessiveness?" Thalia shuddered. "No thank you."

Garrett blinked owlishly at her. I ducked my head to hide my smile.

My Second cleared his throat. "My apologies. Please allow me to escort you to your apartment."

Thalia studied Garrett for a moment before nodding. "Fine."

"Do you have anything other than your backpack?" he asked.

"No. It's difficult packing ballgowns and corsets," she said with a dark glare at Cernunnos.

"My court is traditional," he gritted out.

I was beginning to see why he wanted Thalia out of his territory.

"I'm a young woman, and we don't live in medieval times."

"It's not like we have a department store in the fae lands," Cernunnos said. A heavy sigh bit through the air. "Never mind." He turned to me. "Lord, I'm entrusting her into your care."

"I can take care of myself," Thalia snapped.

"Obey the Lord's rules," Cernunnos warned before disappearing in a swirl of emerald and gold magic.

When he was gone, Thalia let out a breath of relief. "Did I really get an apartment or was Dad shitting me?"

Garrett and I both froze. "I'm sorry," I said slowly. "Did you call Cernunnos Dad?"

Thalia laughed. "I guess he didn't say a word?"

"Not at all. You being his child changes a few things." Many things. I wouldn't change her protection detail because Garrett was the best I had, but I'd have to add a few more wolves onto her security detail. She wouldn't be able to leave without an escort, adding an additional level to the pain of an ass favor repayment.

"It doesn't, actually," Thalia said. "You could let me leave right now, and I'd never say a word."

"Cernunnos would hunt you to the ends of the earth," Garrett said.

"I am not without tricks of my own," Thalia said hotly.

"Regardless, you are under our protection. If you try to escape, we will be forced to hunt you down as well," I advised her.

Garrett's eyes flashed gold. "I've got your scent, darling," he drawled. "You won't be able to run far enough to keep me from catching you."

Thalia's heart rate rose sharply.

Garrett's grin was full of teeth and menace.

Her fingers tightened on her backpack. "Take me to the apartment, please."

My second gestured for her to walk ahead. Thalia straightened and took a step, abruptly swaying.

A flash of speed and Garrett was behind her, ready to catch her if she fell.

"Roots," Thalia whispered, the irises of her eyes turning a blinding silver, "Twisting roots buried in skin. Too much power."

She sagged, her knees going out from under her, but Garrett swept her into his embrace. His eyes met mine. "Take her to the Keep?" His grip on Thalia was possessive, proprietary, and I knew it could become a problem. But Garrett had never been volatile or failed in his duties. In this, I had to trust him.

"No." Anger burned inside me at how I'd been bamboozled by Cernunnos. "Head to the apartment. I'll send Simone over."

"I'll contact you when she's settled in."

Without waiting for a response, Garrett turned and fled through the woods.

I was officially in charge of Cernunnos's daughter. Other daughter.

I'd be annoyed by the lie by omission regardless, but this one came with serious consequences.

He'd sworn me to secrecy concerning Thalia's identity. I couldn't tell Evie without violating the terms of our bargain.

My jaw clenched. I knew I was missing something.

Evie would be furious when she found out.

"Fuck," I snarled.

Neit, God of War and Mom's hot ex-boyfriend stepped into the shop. The bundle of dahlias I held slipped from my hand and onto the worktable, scattering petals from damaged blooms. It was still just me and Moira but today was less busy than the day before.

I wasn't surprised to see him. What stunned me was Neit's appearance. He'd foregone his typical dark, rune-riddled armor, and had chosen a pair of charcoal-grey jeans, black tennis shoes, and a forest green pullover sweater. His dark hair was brushed neatly away from his face, and he wore a knitted scarf tossed casually around his neck.

"You look like a clothing model," I blurted.

Neit's smile was darkly amused. "I tire of using glamour. Fitting in is the best way to enjoy my time here." He patted his stomach. "Plus the smell of that cafe finally won me over."

"Marnie's place is amazing," I admitted. "Try the Shepherd's pie next time it's on the menu. It's amazing."

Neit inclined his head. "I'll do that."

Silence fell between us, and I realized he had a reason to be here, one he seemed nervous to broach. "Coffee?" I offered.

"Please."

Moira held her hand up. "I'll get it. Why don't you two have a seat?"

She gave me a meaningful look and fanned herself when Neit turned away to find a seat. While Neit was smoking hot, all the gods were. I think it was part of their genetic blueprint or something. I always appreciated a little eye candy at breakfast time, but Neit was involved with my mom and that automatically put him into potential stepdaddy territory.

Neit was off limits and dangerous.

We settled in just as Moira brought two steaming cups of coffee over. Neit gave her a grateful smile.

"Thanks."

She touched my shoulder. "I'll be in the back. If the bell goes off, I'll come back."

Neit waited to speak until Moira was gone. "Evie, I find myself in a predicament."

"I'm not sure what kind of assistance I could offer a god." Nor did I feel particularly inclined to offer any assistance at all.

A small smile curved his lips. "I'm not here to ask for your assistance."

"Oh?" A tug of trepidation pulled inside me. "I know you aren't here for our store-bought coffee."

Neit leaned forward, his massive hands curved around his mug. "I need information."

"Depends on what it is." Information wasn't inherently harmful, but Neit had better ways of discovering info than I did, so I was skeptical of whether I could help him.

"Where is your mother?"

I blinked. "Err. Why?"

"She slipped away from me a few weeks ago, and there's something I must speak to her about."

What harm could it be for me to tell him where she was? I mulled the question over. Mom would have no issue with stabbing me in the back, but she'd kept me alive and safe.

Until she hadn't.

Hell with it. "She's in her domain."

His eyes narrowed. "Are you sure?"

"Unless she's moved over the last few days, she's there."

Neit nodded, a calculating look appearing on his face. "She must be blocking me."

"Can't imagine why," I said lightly. "Weren't you threatening to kill her not too long ago?"

His grin held a feral edge. "Don't you worry about that." He rose, carefully setting his mug down. "Thank you for the information. The game continues."

"Is there something I should know?"

"Not at all, Miss Quinn." Anticipation gleamed in his eyes. "I will see you soon."

In a flash of bright violet light, he was gone.

Moira walked out just then, probably sensing the lack of an extra heartbeat and knowing he was gone. "Everything okay?"

I stared at the place where he was standing a moment ago. "He's looking for Mom."

"Uh oh."

I shook my head. "I don't think he wants to kill her." A laugh bubbled from me. "If I had to guess, I'd say he still likes her."

Moira shuddered. "Your mother? But she's horrible."

"People lose their mind over beauty," I said more to myself than her. "That's why you rarely see terrible people who are beautiful walking around single."

Moira laughed. "I'll give you that one. Too bad Cliona's immortal. She'll keep stringing all the boys along with those looks for eternity."

But Neit was different. I felt it in my bones. Not good or bad, the god seemed to be giving my mother a real run for her money, in whatever game they were playing. I just hoped they kept me out of it.

An hour before closing, a woman I'd never seen before stepped into the shop followed by a shifter who didn't like me very much. They were arguing in hushed voices, his hand on her arm as he tried to stop her from going deeper inside.

Our eyes met. "Hello, Garrett."

Caelan's second was tall, blond, and full of muscle. His amber eyes glittered as I spoke. "Evie." No head nod, no smile. Nothing but an icy greeting.

The woman he was with was short and pretty, and even though I'd never met her before, there was something familiar about her that I couldn't put a finger on. She had dark hair woven in a neat braid and hazel eyes. Her face was delicate, though the stubborn tilt of her chin and the spark of anger in her eyes told me she was giving Garrett premature gray hair.

She yanked her arm away and straightened her shirt. "Evie. I'm Thalia."

"Hello, Thalia. Is there something you're looking for?"

"We were just leaving," Garrett gritted out.

"No, we are not," Thalia snapped. "Stop being an asshat and let me look at the flowers."

My lips twitched as Thalia and Garrett locked eyes in a glaring contest. "How do you two know each other?"

Thalia clicked her tongue. "He's my unwanted bodyguard."

A flash of hurt over Garrett's face. Impossible. The man had no feelings. "I've been assigned to your protection," he spat out. "As much as you hate it, you're stuck with me."

"Are you running from the law or something?" Why in the world did this innocent looking young woman need a protector like Garrett?

She snorted. "No. Just an overprotective father." Thalia rolled her eyes. "I have to drag this guy everywhere."

That would piss me off, too. Especially if I got stuck with Garrett. "She's fine here if you want to take a break," I said to the shifter. "You know as well as I do that I can protect her if something happens."

"I'm not leaving," Garrett growled.

Hope flared over Thalia's face. "Yes! You heard her! Give me twenty minutes." Her imploring look softened my heart. "For girl talk. And shopping without you snarling about how much everything costs. Please, Garrett."

But the shifter was a boulder, unable to be moved. "Sorry, peach. You're stuck with me."

The look of disappointment on Thalia's face broke something in me. Knowing I might regret this, I pulled my cell out.

Garrett saw the motion. "Don't you fucking dare."

I hit the speed dial button for Caelan. "Sorry. Us girls have to stick together."

The Shifter Lord answered on the first ring. Garrett's muscles tensed.

I held up a hand. "You know as well as I do if you come for me, I will flatten you." A crazy smile tipped my lips. "And we both know how much I would love to do it."

"Ooh," Thalia breathed. "You guys hate each other, don't you?"

"Let me guess," Caelan's voice rumbled over the connection. "Garrett's there, isn't he?"

"Yes. Has he kidnapped this girl? Do I need to stage a rescue while I wait for you to come gather your errant wolf?"

"I'm going to kill you one day," Garrett said softly. "Right when you least expect it."

"Tell my wolf to stand down," Caelan rumbled, fury tightening his voice.

"I don't need your assistance to deal with your guard dog," I said.

Thalia laughed out loud. "Did you guys used to date?"

"No!" We both barked at the same time.

"Any time you want to dance, darling," I drawled. "Let's dance."

"Evie..." Caelan said. "Please stop fighting with my Second."

"He started it."

His long-suffering sigh made me laugh. "I'm calling to see if you can relieve Garrett of duty for a little while and let this poor woman shop."

"You've met Thalia." There was an odd note in his voice.

"Yes. Why is she under Garrett's protection?"

"It's a long story," he said tightly.

"I'll have time tonight if you want to come over." Couldn't wait to hear how Caelan had gotten roped into babysitting. Or whatever this was.

Thalia's eyes widened. "Are you doing it with the Shifter Lord?"

Garrett pinched the space between his brows.

A long pause came over the line. My heart thudded in my chest. Something was wrong. "Caelan?"

A soft sigh. "I'm sorry, Evie. I can't tonight. Something came up."

I swallowed and tried to shake off the rejection. There was no reason for me to be weird about this. Caelan was a Lord. He couldn't always come over every time I asked him.

But he always had before, a negative voice whispered through my brain.

"Alright," I said, ignoring the knot in my stomach. "We'll catch up another time." I turned away. "And Thalia? Can you call off your dog for a little while? She wants to do some shopping."

"Yes, she does!" Thalia called. "And I still need some clothes!"

"How long?" Caelan asked.

I thought about it. "Two hours?"

"No," Garrett growled.

"An hour," Caelan bargained.

"An hour and a half. Final offer. If you say no, I'm growing a new vine and trussing up your Second and going anyway."

"I'd like to see you try," Garrett muttered.

"Take the girl shopping and do not let her out of your sight."

"You got it," I agreed.

"Bye, Evie."

My stomach lurched. He sounded odd. "Everything okay?"

Another too long pause. "Everything is fine."

I knew he was lying to me. "Alright then. Take care."

I turned to see Garrett watching me, an odd expression on his lean face. Ignoring the knowing look in his eyes, I smiled at Thalia. "We have an hour and a half."

The young woman clapped her hands together. "Awesome! Is there a discount store around here?"

Moira popped out from the back. "There's a shopping strip right outside town. You'll find plenty of stuff there."

Thalia gave me a hopeful look. I shrugged. "She's right. Ready to go?"

And that was how I ended up taking a perfect stranger on a shopping spree with a pissed off wolf pretending he wasn't following us.

An hour and a half to the dot we were back at the shop. Garrett leaned against the passenger door of his pickup truck, a blank expression on his face, but I could almost feel the burning fury beating from him when our gazes met.

"Uh oh," Thalia breathed from the passenger seat. "Why doesn't he like you?"

"Honestly? I have no idea. He's always been like this." I opened the door. "I'll help you carry your stuff over to his truck."

Thalia groaned. "Do I have to go back?"

"I can only push the Lord so far."

At Thalia's disgruntled look, I laughed. "Besides, Garrett is just doing his job." I didn't like the man, but I knew how hard he worked to keep Caelan and the Pack running efficiently.

"Yes, but he's being super annoying about it." Thalia rolled her eyes and grabbed a few bags. "Thanks for taking me. It was nice to hang out with someone who isn't worried about what I can do."

My hands stilled. "What can you do?"

Thalia blinked. "No one told you about me?" A bright grin creased her face. "This goes against everything I'd heard about small towns."

"Let's go," Garrett demanded, reaching over and plucking the bags from Thalia's hands. The shifter didn't bother to take any from mine.

I rolled my eyes and walked over to Garrett's truck to dump her bags in the backseat.

When I turned, Thalia stood there. She threw open her arms and brought me in for a tight hug. "Thank you, Evie. I'm so glad I met you."

Blinking in surprise, I pulled away and smiled at her. "Enjoy the new clothing. If you ever want to go shopping again, drop by the shop or give me a call."

"Only if I get to escape from Captain Grumpy Pants again."

Garrett shook his head and slid into the driver's seat. "Wrap it up, girl."

Thalia shot him a dark glare. "I'm not a girl."

He started the car, the engine rumbling loud enough to drown out the rest of her words.

I bit down my smile. "See you around!"

On my way back to the shop, I turned to give Garrett a mocking little wave.

He raised his middle finger and waved back.

I burst out laughing, even as I didn't envy him.

Thalia, as much as I liked her, seemed like she could be a real handful.

CHAPTER
Seventeen

CAELAN

I sat on the steps of the Keep waiting for the familiar rumble of my Second's truck. An hour ago, I sent two wolves to Thalia's to relieve him of duty.

The telltale purr of the engine sounded before I spotted Garrett's vehicle. My Second pulled up close and slid out of the vehicle.

"I knew you'd be out here," Garrett said, a sour note in his voice.

"You threatened to kill Evie." I'd stewed on it for hours, wanting to let it go. But a wild possessiveness toward her hummed in my veins, and I knew I couldn't let it stand.

Garrett's face turned wary. "So?"

"You haven't liked her from the moment you met her."

"Why would I? She's dangerous."

"We're both dangerous."

Violence bloomed in my blood, the urge to push Garrett into a fight almost overwhelming my good sense.

"Yes, but she's dangerous to every shifter in this territory." Garrett leaned against his vehicle and crossed his arms. "What's this about, Caelan?"

I ran a hand through my hair and sighed. "I'm in love with her."

No surprise on his face. My Second wasn't stupid. "Doesn't mean you have to take us down with you."

He and Simone were the only ones I'd allow to speak to me this way. We had years of history between us and rarely pulled our punches. "I've no intentions of doing any such thing."

Garrett snorted. "You damn well granted that woman liberties in our Pack, Caelan."

"Because she will be our Lady." A gold haze rolled over my vision. "Watch your tone when you speak about her."

Garrett's jaw tightened. "Every time you go to see her, every time she wakes up here, you lose a little bit of a grip on this territory. You need someone as invested in this as you are."

"A shifter, then."

He shrugged. "A shifter would love our Pack as much as we all do. As much as you do."

The thought of anyone else other than Evie warming my bed made fury heat my blood. "I don't want a shifter," I gritted out.

"Maybe not, but are you sure Evie wants you?"

I squashed the urge to punch Garrett, but his words left me uncomfortable, itching to shed my skin.

His question was right on the money. Evie might want me, but did she want me enough to fight for what we could one day have?

CHAPTER
Eighteen

Tess came in the next morning, looking no worse for the wear.

Ash was still nowhere to be found. I had an email from him telling me he planned to be off until Monday, and he'd call if he needed more time.

"Morning, Tess," Moira called, sipping from a cup of fragrant tea. "Nice to have you back."

Tess waved and set her purse down behind the register. "Thanks. I can close today if you want to take off early." She grimaced. "I could use the extra hours since I've been off."

"Are you doing okay?" I asked.

Tess nodded. "A breakup is weird, isn't it? It's a small death. An ending of something even if both parties are still alive."

Unsurprised she'd compared a breakup to death, I was none-theless impressed at her logic. "Did you know they call an orgasm *la petite mort?*"

The banshee blinked. "No. How interesting. Why do they call it that?"

Moira snorted, and I wondered if I'd made the wrong move with that fun fact. Apparently, she and Ash had not taken the final step in their physical relationship. "It means the little death and refers to the feeling that overtakes your body during an orgasm."

"You die?" Tess frowned. "That doesn't seem fun."

Moira hid her grin behind her mug and widened her eyes dramatically at me.

"You don't physically die, but the feeling is…indescribable." I shook my head. "Perhaps it was a poor way to explain. Many things in our lives are akin to death. There are many endings, but there are even more beginnings we experience. That's what makes life worth living."

A thoughtful expression crossed her face. "Maybe I should find someone to help me orgasm."

A bark of laughter from Moira's corner.

I winced and waved my hands. "No. Tess. No. That's not what I'm saying. Sex is important, especially your first time."

Moira rose and stretched her lean frame. "Tess."

The banshee turned.

Moira popped her head into her hands and leaned on the register desk. "Listen. Evie is right. Sex is important, but it's not the end all be all. Your first time should be special, but you don't have to do anything the traditional way. You don't need a boyfriend. You don't even need a first date. Hell, you could put an ad in the paper and—"

I gasped. "Moira! Don't you dare tell her to take a Craigslist ad out for her virginity."

Moira rolled her eyes. "I'm simply saying she could do it."

"You should definitely not do that," I urged Tess, who watched us like she was at a tennis match.

"I could auction it," Tess said thoughtfully.

Moira cackled.

I scrubbed a hand over my face.

"That way I wouldn't have to take out a student loan," she added, a brilliant smile lighting up her pale face.

This conversation was barreling out of control. "I, um. Tess, I

—" Sinking down onto my worktable, I stared at the banshee. "Shit," I muttered.

"No," Moira said, her voice thick with amusement, "please keep going."

"Shut up," I muttered.

Tess's eyes widened, pale eyes sparkling as she ran with the idea. "Maybe I could go national with it. See if I can do one of those clock video things—"

"TikTok," Moira supplied helpfully.

"Yes, and then I could go live and show them the goods."

I sucked in a breath, suddenly feeling lightheaded, when something occurred to me.

"You're messing with me!" I accused.

Tess grinned. "You're so easy sometimes, Evie. Like I would ever take off my clothes on the internet."

"Or auction your virginity."

When Tess didn't respond, I stared. "Or auction your virginity," I repeated. "Right?"

Tess's mysterious smile and failure to answer stuck with me the rest of the day.

I WAS the only one in the shop when pain ripped through my abdomen. A startled cry of agony tore from my throat as I went to my knees. No one was around, and my cell phone was up by the register. Trying to breathe through the sharp spikes of twisting misery took a slight edge off the pain, but it wasn't relief enough for me to rise and try to drive home.

Slowly I shifted to lay on my side, tears streaming down my face. My abdomen glowed a strange golden color and pulsed in time to my heartbeat.

I squeezed my eyes shut and moaned. A gush of liquid soaked my pants. Moving even an inch set agony tearing down my spine, but I couldn't stay here. I sent a trickle of magic into the earth, willing it deeper and deeper, sending tendrils out toward the one person I knew would come.

Blissful darkness came seconds later.

Shattering glass and a wrench of metal followed by a grunt of effort jerked me away some time later. A sob of pain tore from me, and I tried to raise my head but couldn't.

"Evie." Caelan's voice was barely human. Gentle, calloused hands touched my abdomen. "What happened?"

Shaking my head took too much effort. "Seed," I whispered, my dry throat clicking.

His face swam into view, stormy eyes glowing golden around the irises. "I'm taking you back to the Keep."

I was too tired to argue, but when his hands lowered and lifted me up, stars of agony bloomed behind my eyes.

Darkness swept in once more.

Voices flickered in and out of my senses. The sound of a door opening. Firm but gentle hands under my body.

Agony.

"Ground," I croaked.

"Evie—"

Caelan. The voice belonged to Caelan. I pushed weakly against his chest. "Ground. Please."

The sound of more voices raised in argument.

"Get the Keep healer," Caelan snapped. "And call Ben."

"No Ben." My argument was weak and thready. Ben couldn't stand me and there was nothing worse than a judgmental healer.

"I don't care if you two don't like each other. He's the best healer we have."

"Ground," I said again, seeing sparks at the edges of my eyes.

He gently laid me on the ground, his fingers brushing my hair from my face. "Tell me what I can do."

Tears streamed from my eyes, my nerves on fire. "Stay back," I whispered.

As I expected, Caelan didn't budge even when roots crawled from my skin, plunging into the earth, encasing me in the safety of Mother Earth's arms. My eyes squeezed shut, sobs of pain hissing from between my lips as I forced myself to think past the agony. Even wounded, I knew the earth would heal me if it could, but I'd never felt anything like this before.

I had a horrible suspicion about what was happening, and if I was right, this might be the end of me.

Or, a terrible thought whispered in the back of my brain, it might be only the beginning.

I grew and grew, my back pressing into the moist earth. The smell of loam and green and life flowed through me as I gave myself to the world, sending my power deep into its eternal heart.

CHAPTER
Nineteen

CAELAN

Ben stopped abruptly, his lips pulling back into a feral snarl.

"Do not," I snapped. "You know how I feel about her."

The new Lord stepped forward, his eyes on what might be Evie's living casket. "She's under there?"

"Yes."

His jaw clenched. "I'd rather you found someone else for this."

"Does our friendship mean nothing?" I asked quietly. "Does she mean nothing?"

"She's a liar."

I snorted. "And you aren't?"

Ben came to me scarred and haunted, and, against the advice of all the other Lords, I'd allowed him a place in my pack. We'd become the best of friends and stayed that way for years until his fascination with this Floromancer got in the way.

And she'd returned his fascination in the hesitant, sometimes ornery way she had. I was not a stupid man. If Ben had gotten his head out of his ass and questioned why she was so hesitant and allowed her to come to him, he very well might have earned her love. Even though I'd all but forced him out of my territory, she may have still gone to him.

And seeing him now, with glowing eyes and tight jaw, I think Ben knew it too.

"Dumbass," I said with a snort.

Ben sighed and crouched, placing his hand on top of the wooden construct her body had formed. I could see inside, Evie's form curled into a fetal position and dotted with crimson flowers. Blue magic flowed from Ben's fingertips, and the big man closed his eyes for a long moment.

When he rose, his expression was grim. "She's alive but in some kind of stasis."

"A coma?"

Ben shook his head. "Not quite." He jerked his head toward the small copse of trees.

I followed him over so we could speak in private.

"Tell me what happened."

I relayed as much as I could, telling him how all the flowers in my yard had bloomed at once and Seymour had jumped onto the table and bit me, fortunately not sending venom through his teeth. "All the signs were there, so I headed straight to Evie's to find her on the ground."

Only a select few knew what she'd done with the seed, and I left that part out. Yes, it was important, and if I had to speculate, the seed was probably behind what was happening to her now, but if Ben knew what she'd done, the info might not be safe from the other Lords.

Ben's moral compass was rigid and unyielding.

Thus why he'd fucked up so spectacularly with the woman currently trapped in a cage of her own making.

Evie and I both had strong morals, but whereas Ben was an oak, she and I were willows, pliable and able to bend when circumstances demanded so.

"What aren't you telling me?" Ben demanded.

"Nothing you need to know at this time. Will she be okay?"

Ben shook his head. "There's no way for me to determine. She's alive. All her vitals are stable, but she is out of it. I suspect she's put herself into a form of hibernation while her body repairs the damage." He eyed me. "The damage you won't tell me about so I can help her."

"Did you sense any damage?" I asked.

His eyes narrowed. "I didn't look closely enough. Mostly I wanted to make sure she was still alive. I'll look at her again in a minute." He crossed his arms over his massive chest.

Ben wasn't a wolf. Nor, like everyone guessed, was he a bear, though he had the barrel chest and tree trunk arms reminiscent of our bear brethren a few states over. He was something far worse —so deadly even my wolf hesitated to tangle with him.

"You aren't going to tell me." Flat words, annoyance flashing in his eyes.

"I will if she takes a turn for the worse."

Ben blew out an annoyed breath and turned toward Evie, going to his knees once more. His magic swept through the air, blowing through the trees and down into the ground, eyes turning the color of ice.

I knew the moment Ben found it. An explosive curse and the magic disappeared. He rose and stalked toward me. "What," he bit out, "is inside her?"

"Is she stable?"

"For now." Ben's nostrils flared. "What the hell have you brought onto your property?" He scrubbed a hand over his face. "And even worse, into your life?"

"Don't," I cautioned him, my voice a low growl in the quiet. A few trusted wolves kept watch on the area, ensuring curious eyes didn't get too close. I hadn't been subtle when I'd shattered the window to get to her, and carrying out a woman covered in blood was bound to get people talking.

One, Garrett, on break from his frustrating watch of Thalia, turned, his eyes glowing. I shook my head, and Garrett turned away.

"Thinking of siccing your wolves on me?" Ben said with a dangerous smile. "I'd hate for you to lose them."

"Can we at least try not to be dicks to each other?" I said in frustration. "I get it. You hate Evie. She feels the same way about you."

Ben flinched. "She does?"

I closed my eyes for a second. "Yes, you fucking prick. You haven't been exactly kind to her. She asked me not to call you."

Ben's eyes glowed with fury. "I'll cut the shit if you will. What did she do?"

I studied him for a long moment. "This can go no further than here. If you can't keep my confidence, tell me now. You're a Lord, Ben and no longer tied to my pack."

To his credit, he didn't answer right away. "How bad is it?"

I snorted. "She's unconscious in a cocoon of wood and flowers. I'd say pretty bad."

Ben rubbed the back of his neck. "Does it affect us all?"

"Only time will determine that answer, but if I had to guess, yes."

"Fuck," Ben snarled. "I hate you for making me a Lord, you ass."

My answering smile was not friendly. "I know."

The large shifter sighed. "I'll keep your confidence. Tell me what she did."

When I told the story, Ben's eyebrows rose in shock. "She did what?"

"Yep. She's in and out of consciousness, but I'd venture to guess the seed is what's causing this now."

Ben put his hands on his hips and bowed his head. "Why can't she ever do anything normal?"

The frustrated question made me laugh out loud. "Because it's Evie. Swallowing it was the only way to take the seed out of play. She took a wild gamble that her mother wouldn't kill her over the decision."

"The World Seed," Ben murmured. "Fucking wild." He blew out a breath and went back over. "Let me look at one more thing."

I came over and crouched beside him this time, watching his

power arrow straight into Evie's abdomen, a gentle probe. When he withdrew, his face was grim.

I stilled. "What is it?"

"I can't believe I'm about to say this, but the seed is… sprouting."

I blinked. "What? It's growing? Inside her?"

"Yep. Like the old wives' tale about not swallowing watermelon seeds, but way worse." Ben looked a little green.

"Is she in pain?"

"Not anymore. The stasis keeps her pain free, though she is oblivious to what's going on around her."

I thought about it. "Can you get it out?"

Ben shot me an incredulous look. "You want me to perform surgery on someone who's enclosed herself in a magical construct to extract a deadly, potentially world-ending seed?"

I shrugged. "Can it be done?"

"Christ, Caelan." Ben inhaled. "I might be a healer, but I'm not a mage. We need someone more versed in this type of power than we are."

"Like me?" A deep voice interrupted. Power punched through the air, ancient and wild.

Annoyance spun through me at his casual foray onto my property which was warded to the teeth against intrusion.

Ben swore, spinning to face the Fae King. His mouth fell open.

"Caelan," Cernunnos greeted.

I inclined my head. "This is Ben. We're debating surgery."

Ben punched me in the arm so hard I stumbled.

"No need," Cernunnos said as he walked over to Evie's construct. "She will be fine when the seed expels itself."

"Expels," Ben repeated faintly. "Define fine for me, please."

A flash of amusement in those ancient eyes. "The seed is doing what it's always meant to—grow."

"And what about Evie? She's hosting the thing in an odd, symbiotic way. Will she become the tree?"

Cernunnos reached out to touch the wood, a faint emerald and golden glow touching Evie's cage. "I'll ensure she does not, though she will always be linked." His gaze rose and locked with mine. "You will be responsible for a dangerous legacy, Lord. You've chosen this spot, and Evie was too weak to argue. If the World Tree grows here, you will have to allow divinity onto your property."

I swore, dark and heated. "Can we move her?"

Cernunnos chuckled under his breath. "Come over here and try, Lord."

I figured it wouldn't be easy. The good thing was I'd taken Evie to the very edge of the Keep's property, just in case whatever this was turned volatile. Giving access to even an inch of my property galled me, but Evie couldn't help what happened.

I was the one who'd brought her here.

"Fine. We'll figure it out." Evie was more important than the damned tree.

"She's stable, but the seed is…restless." He lifted his fathomless gaze. "I suggest you and your wolves move farther back in case any magic escapes."

He didn't mention Ben.

"Thunderbird, you're with me."

Ben snarled, his eyes flashing ice blue. I put a hand on his arm and gave a sharp shake of his head.

"Did your wolves hear?" he asked quietly.

"Your secret is safe," Cernunnos said. "Come kneel beside me. I need you to keep Evie still while I extract the seed."

"You're the Fae King," Ben said in a grouchy tone. "You can't do that yourself?"

Cernunnos went as still as the grave. When he spoke, the trees shook. "Tread carefully, Healer. The seed is like handling one of the human nuclear weapons. I need to focus everything I have on it rather than Evangeline."

Ben's brow furrowed at Cernunnos's familiar tone about Evie, and I knew he'd eventually put the pieces together. Shaking it off, Ben bent. "Tell me what to do."

I turned and jogged toward Garrett, planning to send them away but not going any farther than I had to.

Within seconds, my men were far away from any potential fallout, though Garrett appeared beside me.

"No need for you to be here," I said to the stalwart, sometimes homicidal shifter beside me.

Garrett grunted. "Simone will happily step up if your girlfriend turns us into crispy critters."

I slid him a look. Knowing how much it would piss him off, I asked, "How are things going with Thalia?"

Garrett swore under his breath. "She's a harridan. I thought Evie was bad, but Thalia makes me want to strangle the life out of her."

I grinned. "Do you like her?"

The look he shot me was pure menace. "I'd wash my hands of her in a split second."

We'd see about that. "Unfortunately, Thalia will be with us for a while, and you're the best I have. This isn't a normal deal. We can't afford to screw the Fae King over."

Especially knowing he was Evie's father and I one day hoped to be the bastard's son-in-law.

He and Ben were bent over Evie's shelter, their magic mingling. We were far enough away to get away in the event of a blast, maybe, but Ben wouldn't escape unless Cernunnos intervened.

I wasn't sure he would.

"Why is he so invested in her?" my Second asked.

I'd kept Evie's secrets, so far, but after tonight, we'd have a big issue with the gods, so I owed it to him and Simone to be truthful.

"He's her father."

Garrett sucked in a breath just as the world exploded.

Nonsensical whispers nudged me awake. I lay in a cocoon, encased in glowing magic. My abdomen no longer hurt, but gentle tugs against my skin were concerning.

"Stay still, Evangeline."

My father loomed above me, his brow furrowed as he concentrated. A soft beam of emerald and gold magic poured from his fingers into my abdomen.

"Oh. That's why it doesn't hurt."

"No," Cernunnos said. "I believe the magic inside the seed has numbed you in anticipation of tearing its way out of you."

I blinked. "Well. That's not very nice."

A soft snort above. I flicked my eyes to the left to see Ben close to my dad. "What are you doing here?"

"Saving your life," my father said.

I don't think I could move at all, thanks to Ben's gentle magic wrapped around me, but I heeded his warning and didn't even try. "This feels like the world's strangest C-section."

"Except the world might end if we tear this thing open before it's ready," Cernunnos said.

"You never told me I'd give birth to this thing."

"No one has ever swallowed the World Seed, so there was no way to know you'd be a mom," my father said dryly.

"Aww," I cooed, trying to quell the rising panic, "a bouncing baby tree."

"Evie," Ben said, his teeth gritting with effort, "stop talking, please."

"Sorry. I'm nervous."

"How do you think we feel?" Ben muttered. "I came because I thought you'd been hurt, not because you got pregnant by a magical tree. This one is out of my wheelhouse."

Cernunnos let out a bark of laughter. "I'm about to extract the seed. Can you take your structure down? Gently?"

"Um. I can try. It's usually automatic."

Cernunnos shut his eyes and let out a breath. "Alright. Try gently."

I closed my eyes and sent a thread of power out. Pain flared through my veins. A cry of pain tore from my throat. Tears squeezed from my eyes as I breathed in short, choppy gasps.

"How can I help her?" Ben asked.

"See if you can break it," Cernunnos advised. "Gently."

"Is it safe to drop my power?"

"Evie, Ben is going to release you. It's imperative you don't move a muscle."

"Okay. Got it. Maybe don't pull the seed out just yet?"

"Couldn't if I wanted to. I'm still working around your organs to extricate the roots."

"Dear gods," I whispered.

Ben shot him a dark look. "She could have gone without knowing that."

"Evie needs to know how delicate this is. There's a chance I won't be successful."

My heartbeat thumped against my ribs like a drum. "You're the Fae King. If you can't do it, who could?"

A faint smile. "This magic is older than I. It does not conform to our rules."

"Even better," I whispered. Swallowing hard, I looked at Ben. "Release me."

I felt the instant his soothing power fell away and locked my muscles tight.

Ben bent, placing his large hands on the wood. He grunted with effort as he pulled, but to no avail. His teeth pulled back, and his eyes glowed a strange, icy blue. Ben might be a Lord, but he was not a wolf. Whatever he was, he did not inherit the trademark golden eyes of the other Lords. He let go, adjusted his shoulders, and bent to try again, a glint in his eyes I didn't like.

"Don't," Cernunnos warned, sensing Ben saw the cage as a challenge. "Give me a moment."

A crack split the night, the wooden cage splitting in two. Ben grabbed both parts before they fell to the ground.

"I'm about to extract the World Seed. Once I give the signal, I need you to pull Evie away and run as fast as you can. It will attempt to reattach to her because her magic is familiar." His eyes swirled. "Its power hungers."

"Oh, goodie," I breathed.

His swirling gaze caught mine. "I'm sorry, Evangeline. This will be painful."

I figured it wouldn't be a cake walk. "What's the signal?"

His eyes met Ben's. Faster than I could track, I found myself ripped from the ground. Tearing agony ripped through my abdomen. I screamed, so long and hard my voice went out, and the new Lord ran like the wind, the cool night air slicing against my skin with his speed.

A percussive boom shook the world. Ben stumbled, righted himself, and kept running. He clenched me tight to his chest, the smell of wilderness clinging to him, as he ran for our lives. The agony had subsided once the seed was gone, and I reached up to wind my hands around his neck, burying my face against his chest. Warm liquid ran down my stomach and hips.

Blood. I wasn't out of the woods yet.

Another blast, this one so powerful Ben couldn't stay upright.

He cursed, stumbled, and fell, tucking me against his chest and rolling as he went down, careful to take the brunt of the fall.

We came to a stop, me sprawled and bleeding atop the healer. When I made to move off him, he held me in place by the hips.

"Don't." His eyes still glowed, his voice rough with effort. "You're still wounded. Let me move you."

He moved his hands up my back and carefully rolled before gently placing me on the ground.

His expression turned grim as he lifted my shirt up and examined the wound.

"How bad is it, doc?" I gave him a hopeful smile.

"Don't joke," Ben said quietly. "Stay still and let me attempt to heal you."

At his somber tone, I pressed my lips together. It must be bad if Ben wasn't sure he could fix me.

Cool blue light appeared in his palms. He tipped them over and pressed them gently to my abdomen.

A commotion in the woods came a moment later, revealing Caelan and Garrett.

"Evie!" Caelan came to his knees. He reached out for me

"Don't touch her," Ben snapped. "Not until I'm finished."

Caelan's upper lip curled into a snarl. "Watch it, Ben."

"You never interfered in a healing. Don't start now." Ben's hands moved over my stomach, the cooling touch of his power flooding my bloodstream.

"She's lost a lot of blood," Garrett helpfully observed.

"Giving birth to a tree is hard work," I quipped.

Ben's lips thinned.

"Sorry," I whispered.

"You aren't in pain?" Caelan asked.

I shook my head. "Not anymore."

"And that's why I'm concerned," Ben murmured.

"It's bad, isn't it?" I asked.

Caelan met my eyes. "Yes. And your natural healing ability isn't kicking in."

"Because she's drained," Ben said. "Whatever that thing did, it sucked every bit of power from you."

I sucked in a breath and reached deep within. There. A flicker of power.

"Temporary," Ben said. "You'll need a large meal and a couple of days' bed rest at least."

"You'll stay here." Caelan's jaw tightened in that mutinous expression I'd come to love.

But it also annoyed the hell out of me.

"No. I'll stay at home. All my things are there, and the land has always helped me heal."

Anger flashed in his eyes. "And who will take care of you?"

"I'll stay with her," Ben said.

My jaw dropped with shock.

"The hell you will," Caelan snarled.

Ben lifted his gaze. "You called me the best healer in the country. I'm not trying to steal your Lady. But this wound will require attention I can't give her if I'm not close." He lifted his palms and shook the residual magic off his fingers.

"Evie?" Caelan inquired.

I watched Ben. There was nothing in his expression that made me think this was anything other than what it was—a simple request from a Healer concerned about his patient. "You don't think I'll be fine on my own?"

I asked because Ben did not like me when we last parted. "There's really no reason for you to go to all the trouble. Caelan has Pack Healers he can send."

Cernunnos walked into the clearing stirring up the smell of pine and fresh air. "Take the big man with you. He has a profound gift."

My father bent and studied my wound. "I'm sorry, Evie. I can't heal you completely. The magic is ancient and will not respond to my call."

"Where's the seed?" I asked.

A faint smile. "Attracting attention."

Garrett let out a soft exhalation before turning and running in the same direction he came from.

"It grew?"

Ben's warm hands gently probed my stomach, his touch giving me goosebumps. My shirt and pants were soaked with blood, and I was freezing.

"She'll need a ride home—an easy one. I've done the best I can with the wound, but her magic is unstable right now. She's healing like a human, and I don't have the right tools to stitch her up." Ben sat back on his haunches, his face drawn.

I reached over and patted his knee. "Thanks for trying."

Ben sighed. "You are so fucking weird, Evie."

With that, he rose and stalked away.

I blinked at his back. "What did I do?"

Caelan lay his hand on my thigh. "You didn't yell or bite his head off for one."

"Do people do that a lot? Seems like a wild choice."

"Our kind as well as humans get angry about things we can't control. As a healer, Ben feels...*more* than most of us. It hurts him deeply when he can't help someone."

"Considering my intestines are still inside my body and I'm not bleeding to death, I'd call it a win."

"You aren't out of the woods yet," Caelan rasped, his gaze following Ben's back as he disappeared into the woods. "I don't like the idea of him staying at your house."

"You'd rather my wound open up, and I bleed out while I'm sleeping?" Jealous shifters and their insane tendencies made me want to punch them right in the kidney.

Cernunnos winced and took a few steps away, turning his back to us.

Caelan's eyes narrowed. A savage smile tilted his lips up. "I'd much rather be your doctor."

I rolled my eyes. "So you can yell at me every time I move? No thanks. Ben is a healer, and he's no slouch in the protective department either. And I'm no slouch at magic. It will be fine."

His jaw tightened. "I don't like how close you were to him."

"No shit," I said with a snort. "It's pretty obvious Ben does not like me any longer. I don't see why I can't attempt to be friends with him. Besides, that's not even what this is. Ben will be there to ensure I heal properly. There's nothing nefarious."

"You don't know how far a Lord would go to secure something he desires."

I stared at him. "Do you even hear yourself right now? Of course I know how far one would go. One of those Lords," I said, poking him in the arm, "is sitting on the ground with me after I almost bled to death bitching about a male healer staying with me for a day or two."

To his credit, Caelan's cheeks heated. Cernunnos interrupted.

"I think it's time to get you home."

I shook my head. "Show me the tree first?"

"I'll get her," Caelan said, gently scooping me into his arms. Careful not to jostle me, he headed through the woods, Cernunnos clearing a path with his magic. We stopped at the edge of the woods.

I sucked in a breath. "Holy shit. That's four times the size of the Jacaranda."

And it was. A massive, sprawling tree loomed above us, its trunk twisted into spirals. Long, sloping branches hung close to the ground, leaves of a brilliant greenish gold glowing in the night sky. I craned my neck up and couldn't see the top.

Caelan stood stone faced.

"Umm. Sorry?"

The Shifter Lord closed his eyes, and I could almost hear a phantom voice counting. When he opened them, he shook his head. "It's not your fault. It's mine."

"The bright side is this didn't happen in the middle of Evie's shop or the town square." Cernunnos laughed out loud when we turned identical thunderous expressions toward him.

Ben walked out from the woods gaping at the sight. He

stopped beside me, his hands in his pockets. "Is this thing permanent?"

Cernunnos shrugged, a human expression for him. "The World Tree is reborn with no set schedule. When it tires, it will cease to exist, and the seed will land in another worthy person's possession."

"Let's just hope they don't swallow it," I murmured under my breath.

"What happens now?" Caelan asked.

He still held me firm in the circle of his arms, his warmth seeping through my bloody clothing. I put my palm on his chest and lay my head against his shoulder. Guilt filled me.

Ben was right.

I am fucking weird.

Within twenty-four hours I was ready to commit murder. Ben and Caelan had all but moved into my house and had been involved in a never-ending pissing match. I wasn't strong enough to boot them both out yet, my power slowly trickling back to life. By tomorrow, I hoped to be at sixty percent normal. If things went well, I could toss them out on their asses if they didn't start behaving.

In the meantime, I'd texted Moira for help. She was on her way with donuts, coffee, and hopefully a healthy dose of sense to knock into the two shifters currently shoving each other in the kitchen.

"I swear to the gods, you jealous prick," Ben snapped when Caelan took the cream he was reaching for. "Can you cool it for five minutes?"

"I know you aren't here for the right reasons," Caelan said, pouring way too much cream in his mug.

"I'll be gone in two days. You asked me here, and now Evie is my patient. I'm not trying to sneak under her covers."

"Can you two please shut up?" I begged.

It was bad enough I had to have help to get to the bathroom. Listening to those two knuckleheads made me want to scream.

"Ben hasn't done anything untoward, and you know it."

"That's because I'm here," Caelan snapped, his eyes refusing to leave Ben's stiff form.

Ben sighed. "If I wanted to take Evie from you, I would."

"For fuck's sake," I muttered.

"Would you now?" Caelan said, a lethal glint appearing in his eyes.

The doorbell rang. I closed my eyes in relief. "Caelan, can you get that?"

"I'd much rather beat the shit out of Ben."

Ben rolled his eyes and went to answer the door, holding it open as Moira breezed in, her arms full of goodies.

She winked at me and headed straight to the couch. "Vanilla bean latte."

I snatched it out of her hands and took a long sip. "Mmm. You're a goddess."

"Yes, yes, I know." Moira waved her hand. "But that's not the best part." With a flourish, she opened the box of donuts revealing an astonishing array of wildly decorated pastries. "The new place downtown is owned by a pastry witch. You have to try the rocky road."

Caelan and Ben came over, both reaching for a treat.

Moira jerked the box back. "Uh uh. I've heard both of you've been misbehaving. Evie gets first dibs on anything she wants."

Ben had the grace to look sheepish. Caelan snorted and flopped onto the chair next to the couch. He exhaled. "Sorry."

I laughed. He sounded so disgruntled. "Good thing. I'm about to kick you both out."

Ben's brow furrowed. "You aren't well enough for me to leave."

"I can stay with her," Moira offered. "If you two hadn't brow beat her, I'd be the one taking care of her."

"I'm sorry," Ben said. "Her power levels are still low. She needs at least two more days of rest before I'm comfortable leaving her in someone else's hands."

"She is right here," I grumbled, choosing a rocky road and a coconut and pecan donut.

Moira lifted a questioning brow. "Do they deserve one?" she whispered.

"No."

Ben acted like he'd been shot, pulling a reluctant grin from me.

"Fine. But if anyone eats the blueberry one, there will be hell to pay."

Ben asked no questions, and neither did Caelan. Soon all conversation had died, and we were in a sugar coma.

Moira was the first to stir. She got up and made a new pot of coffee, then came back over and gently lifted my feet up before she sat down next to me. I wiggled my toes at her.

"Thanks for the coffee and donuts. How's the shop?"

"Just fine. Ash and Tess are back, and things are mostly back to normal."

"Ash is okay?"

Her eyes softened. "He will be. Tess is giving him space, and Ash is healing." She reached over and squeezed my hand. "Things are going to be okay."

"Good." My heart lightened. Ash had always been secretive about his relationships until the one with Tess. While I knew he wasn't a saint and had other relationships, I'd never seen him as happy as he was with the banshee. But sometimes, things weren't meant to work out. Maybe it wasn't their time, or maybe this really was the end. Either way, I wanted my friends to be okay.

I wanted us all to be okay.

Ben and Caelan went outside, and as soon as the door shut, Moira leaned in. "Are they driving you insane?"

I lay my head against the back of the couch and groaned. "It could have been the perfect scenario for a romance novel. Two hot shifters caring for me, making sure I had everything I needed, being a little over possessive. The tension between them and us rises in the air culminating in an explosive threesome where I have multiple orgasms and somehow wind up with a harem of sexy shifters who catered to my every need."

Moira cackled. "Since you're scowling on the couch, I assume it didn't go to plan."

"No. I'm getting ready to murder them both."

"Those are both glorious specimens of men. It'd be a shame for them to die."

I sighed. "Something good came out of this. Ben no longer wants to strangle me."

"Small favors." Moira yawned before a short laugh escaped her. "Before I forget, I thought you should know the entire town is talking about Caelan's new tree."

"He's not happy about it." Caelan hadn't said much about the World Tree in his backyard, but I could hear him discussing matters on the phone when he thought I wasn't listening.

"Who would be?" She rose, gently moving my feet off, and went into the kitchen. "Want another cup of coffee?"

"Not yet. I'm still nursing my latte."

She brought back a cup and sat down. "I'll stay if you want me to." Her eyes softened. "You look like shit."

I laughed, wincing as the still healing muscles in my stomach pulled. "Thanks."

"I'm serious. I've never seen you so laid up." She reached for her purse and dug around in her bag. "Have Ben or Grumpy make you some tea with this. It will help."

I took the small organza bag she handed me and held it up to my nose. Lavender, rose, cinnamon, and a few others I couldn't identify. Moira's lineage was a little mysterious. She was a vampire but not a full-blooded one. No fangs unless she decided to flash them at you, which was rare, and she preferred tea over blood. Her herbal concoctions were nothing to sneeze at, and I knew she had a brisk side hustle selling a cold and flu tea she'd come up with a few years back. Moira might be my best friend, but she held her secrets close.

I knew she had witch blood, but some of her talents made me think she might even have a little fae blood, both contributing to her leanly muscled, fine-boned appearance, not to mention her traffic-stopping beauty. She rarely talked about her past and didn't offer too many tidbits about herself, but she always had my back and that was the most important thing, especially given my own muddied heritage.

"What's in it?"

"A little of this, a little of that," she demurred. "It'll taste good and should help speed up your healing."

I tucked the bag into my cardigan pocket. "Not even Cernunnos could speed up my healing, but I'll give it a try."

She tutted. "Oh ye of little faith. I try not to let the boundaries cross between my apothecary and the flower shop, but in this case, I think this will do you good."

"I never said I didn't trust you. Cernunnos said the tree's magic was ancient, so old even he couldn't help with what it had done to me."

"Just give it a try." She had a weird look on her face.

"I'll have Caelan make me a cup of tea before bed. Just one dose?"

"One for the evening and one for the morning. Don't forget either dose."

"I won't." Chewing on the side of my lip, I debated whether to tell her something I'd discovered.

Moira knew my tells. "What is it?"

I picked up my cell and shot her a text.

Can you put up a silence barrier? My magic is too weak.

Her brows flicked up. *Done,* she texted back.

The bubble shimmered in an iridescent rainbow. Once we were encased, I looked over the couch to make sure Caelan and Ben were still outside.

"I found something."

"Like a weird rash?" Moira asked.

"Ass. No. I've been looking inside trying to figure out what the seed did to me, and with everything sort of moved around, I found this weird…lock."

That's the only word I could use. It was buried inside my usually full well of magic. Now that the seed had drained me until I was almost mortal, the lock wasn't difficult to spot. It looked like a glowing sigil, an odd symbol I couldn't identify, and alternated between gold and crimson.

"A lock," Moira repeated. "So you think if you could open it, you'd discover something inside?"

"Or underneath," I confirmed, explaining how drained I'd been and how that enabled me to see to the empty well of my power.

"Interesting," Moira murmured. "Have you poked at it?"

I shook my head. "Too scared. I'm already drained. What happens if it worsens things?"

She tapped long, elegant fingers on her knee. "Logical. But what if you can't find it once your magic refills?"

It was already getting difficult to see. "What could have done it?"

"Hard to say. Could it be self-imposed?"

"Why would I do something like that?"

Moira's delicate snort brought color to my cheeks. "Uh. Maybe because you're full of self-incrimination and guilt over the Chimera thing, and you weren't exactly all there during that period in your life." She sipped her coffee. "Have you asked Hazel?"

"Not yet." Hazel saved me after the Chimera attack when I'd lay dying on a Scottish field of wildflowers. She's the one who helped me contain the power while I figured out how to deal with (but mostly procrastinated about) it and gave me a tattoo that suppressed the power to prevent me from being identified as one. Chimeras were considered dangerous and often executed on sight.

It worked for many years. Then Caelan walked into my life and Finn, the now dead Chimera who'd attacked me, came right behind him. While the tattoo had been replaced, I could access the power any time I wanted, though I knew there were many, many things I could do if I only learned how. But the thought of working with the side of me I've always been terrified of kept any desire to master the power at bay.

"I'd call her first," Moira said. "She's well-versed in the Chimera power and saw you at one of the lowest points in your life. She'll know if you did it to yourself."

"What if I didn't?"

Moira exhaled, a grim expression on her face. "Then we figure out who tried to suppress your power and kick their ass."

I'd already been thinking about the culprit. While Moira's point about me was valid, I leaned more toward my mother doing this than anyone, especially if she didn't want me to know who'd sired me. The theory didn't fit exactly. Mom's magic wasn't crimson or gold.

Mine was, but the lock could very well be a spell and not a magical signature.

I wished I'd learned about this stuff as a child instead of having to stumble after it now that I was in my thirties.

"From the bubble we're under, I have to assume the Lords don't know?"

I shook my head. "Caelan has enough of my bullshit to deal with."

Moira's look was chiding. "That man could not be more in love with you if he tried." She tilted her head and studied me. "I know you well enough to know you love him, too, but you're holding yourself back. Big time."

"I literally just gave birth to a magical tree in his backyard. Hand over the world's worst girlfriend title. There's no competition."

Moira's lips thinned. "You only did so because he brought you to the Keep for safety. And, as bad as the location is, it's better than the middle of town where people would start asking questions. And once that happens..." She shook her head. "Once a small-town mob gets their curious claws inside of their target, it's game over for privacy. They're going to know what your favorite breakfast was when you were still shitting your pants."

"Blunt as always," I said with a laugh.

She shrugged. "Just saying. The small-town mob mentality is worse than the FBI."

"They're already going to be asking questions, but Caelan has made it his business to appear as a terrifying but fair overlord to everyone in Joy Springs. They might ask, but no one is going to answer. It's much different for the resident florist."

"True." I let out a sigh. "I do love him," I admitted. "But he holds himself back."

An arch rise of a dark eyebrow. "And I'm sure you're totally forthcoming with your past, too, aren't you?"

"Yeah. I suck, too."

Moira snickered. "And Ben?"

"He does seem to be here only in a doctor patient capacity." I shook my head. "He's kind and handsome, but honestly? He was also kind of a dick when I wouldn't share my secrets with him. Worse than Caelan and more judgmental. I don't think it would have worked out even if I had pursued it as much as I wanted to."

"I can overlook a lot for hotness," Moira admitted.

I'd seen it firsthand. "And Soren?" Those two had the hots for each other and made a striking couple when they were next to each other. Moira had kept mostly mum about the situation but said there was nothing going on. From everything I'd seen, she was telling the truth.

She scoffed. "Too busy looking at himself in the mirror to be interested in anything meaningful."

I winced. "If I were that pretty, I wouldn't stop looking in the mirror."

Moira grinned. "Shut up. You look like your mother, dummy. Cliona is the most beautiful goddess in fae history."

"Mom has the whole ethereal floaty goddess thing going on. I'm more down to earth and covered in dirt eighty percent of the time. Men are more into ballgowns than begonias."

"Except for a hot shifter Lord who looks like he's about to punch our dear healer Ben right in the throat." Moira pointed out the window.

Ben and Caelan stood almost nose to nose, baring their teeth at each other.

"Shit," I breathed.

Moira turned her palm up and moved her fingers in a gimme gesture. "Give me that bag. I'll make the brew now. Maybe by tonight you can kick those teakettles of testosterone out of your house."

I fished it out and handed it back. Moira untangled her length and rose. "I'll calm the idiots down and brew this."

She dropped the silence bubble and went outside. After some raised voices, Ben and Caelan came back inside, Moira following behind them red-faced.

Caelan threw an elbow at Ben, shoving the larger man against the wall. A massive hole cracked in the drywall.

Everyone froze. Rage filled me, and my blood pressure skyrocketed. No matter what I felt for Caelan, right now, he was annoying the shit out of me.

"Get. Out," I said through clenched teeth.

Ben snorted. When Caelan made no move, the healer teased. "Did you hear her? Get out."

I turned my furious gaze on Ben. "Both of you. Get out of my house."

Ben's eyes widened. "Evie. That's unnecessary. You need—"

"If I have to get up, I'm never speaking to either one of you again. What I need is some peace in my own damn house. Get your shit and get out."

Caelan's eyes flared gold, but after being with me for a while, the man had learned. He went straight to my bedroom and packed up the small duffel he'd brought. Before he left, he came over and crouched beside me. "Call me if you need something." His eyes softened. "Though I doubt you will." He let out a heavy breath. "Sorry I'm an asshole."

I snorted. "Give me a few days."

He nodded. "There are some things we need to discuss." Brushing a kiss over my cheek, he rose and headed out the door with a nod at Moira.

Ben, not as smart as Caelan, had not moved. "Evie, that wasn't my fault. You need someone to stay with you—"

"I'm here," Moira said. "I'd listen to Evie if I were you."

His teeth flashed. "This doesn't concern you."

"Ben," I said, feeling my frayed patience about to snap. "Moira is here. She's more than competent enough to help me to the bathroom. I won't ask again. Leave."

His eyes flashed that frightening, icy blue. With a tight jaw, he started to speak again, but Moira held up her hand. Her eyes flashed a vivid emerald. "As much as we appreciate you staying here to help Evie, please consider your services rendered and your time here at an end."

For a moment, I thought the situation might devolve into a fight, but after a long, tense moment, Ben stalked into the guest room and grabbed his bag. Without a word, he let himself out, slamming the door behind him.

"Fuuuuuuuck," I said in a loud groan. "Why do women ever get married?"

Moira laughed. "Normally, there's only one asshole to deal with."

I sank deeper into the couch and adjusted the blanket around my hips. "I can feel the testosterone draining from the air."

"Like a deflated balloon," she said as she set a kettle on the stove to boil. "I'll stay tonight and see how you're doing tomorrow."

"Are you sure? I'm fine to stay by myself."

She rolled her eyes. "You haven't moved from the couch since I've gotten here. I bet you can't." Her eyebrows flicked up when I didn't respond. "Exactly," she said quietly. "Do you need to pee?"

"No." Yes.

"You will after you drink the tea. I'll help you then." She came back over and plopped down. "Now let's discuss this lock and how you're going to open it."

CHAPTER
Twenty~Two

After a quick call to Hazel, Moira and I were stumped. The older witch was adamant I did nothing of the sort to myself while I was there. When I described what it looked like, Hazel had consulted some texts but came up empty.

Her advice was to "poke it with a mental stick and see what happened."

"Should we wait?" I said.

"Up to you." Moira shoved a French fry into her mouth and chewed.

She'd gone to pick up dinner, and I wanted to kiss her right on her pretty mouth, because all Caelan and Ben had let me eat was soup and bread. I was immortal, not an eight-year-old child. Moira had picked me up a double cheeseburger from one of our favorite mom and pop restaurants and some of their to-die-for curly fries.

I voted for now. "What the hell was in that brew you made me?"

About twenty minutes ago, I was able to get off the couch and take myself to the bathroom. On top of that, I poured myself a cup of coffee and went back to the couch, all without getting out of breath.

Moira's smile was secretive. "Witchy secrets. But I'm glad you're feeling better. Your color is improving, too."

"Ben will bug you to death for that recipe if we tell him about this."

"Which we won't," Moira said, an intense look in her eyes. "He has his way, I have mine." She sniffed. "Plus, it's a private family recipe. And we don't like Ben right now."

"True. But why do I feel like you aren't giving me the whole story?"

"Don't look a vampire horse in the mouth."

"Idiot," I said affectionately.

"And yet, you adore me."

Someone knocked on the door. My power levels still weren't high enough for me to tell who it was, though my senses tingled when someone passed through. Maybe two someones.

Moira hopped up and wiggled her finger at me. "Stay there."

As soon as the door opened, I knew who it was.

"Ash!"

The dryad kissed Moira on the cheek and breezed over. Tess followed behind him, and I breathed easier because riding together was serious progress.

Ash reached over the back of the couch to ruffle my hair. "Hey. Glad we finally got to visit. Your harem was not receptive to outside visitors."

Tess came around the couch and reached in for a lavender scented hug. "I'm glad you didn't die."

Ash snorted softly.

"Me too," I said solemnly. "What a bummer that would have been."

I eyed Ash. "As far as my non-existent harem, both of them have been shuffled out the door. They won't be back."

The dryad winced. "Everything okay?"

"It hasn't been okay since we met, but it's not worse. Not really. He's just annoying me, that's all."

"Caelan is possessive, and it's making Evie itchy under the collar," Moira said.

Another knock on the door. Moira's attention sharpened. "Expecting any other company?"

"No."

When Moira answered the door again, Simone stood there.

"Evie?" Moira called, asking for permission to let her in.

"I come in peace, I swear." Caelan's Omega held a covered dish. "And I brought goodies."

"What kind of goodies?" I asked before I answered.

"Salted caramel cookies and shortbread."

"I'll allow it," I said.

Ash rose and took the container from Simone, knowing us well enough to get some plates and napkins out. As he dished everything up, Simone kicked off her shoes and settled into an oversized chair.

"It took you long enough," she said.

"What were the betting pool odds?" I asked.

She grinned and didn't deny it. "Twenty-four hours. You held out far longer than anyone thought you would."

There was something she wasn't saying. "How much did you walk away with?"

Simone laughed and dug through her purse to pull out a massive wad of cash. "Almost two grand!"

"Holy shit." I shook my head. "Next time, I want in on those odds."

"Only if it's to do with Caelan. Can't have any collusion going on in the betting pool."

We grinned at each other. Ash came back in with his hands full of plates and handed them out.

"It's good to see you looking well."

Moira gave a sharp shake of her head outside of Simone's peripheral. Interesting, she did not want anyone to know about her brew. I'd grill her later and make her spill her secrets. She knew most of mine. It was about time she trusted me enough to tell me hers.

"It helped getting the bullies out of here," I said instead. "My air conditioner couldn't keep up with all the hot air those two were putting out."

"Tell me about it," Simone groaned. "Ben almost never gets angry until Caelan gets involved."

I bit into the cookie, the crisp salt crunching under my tongue and the caramel rich and creamy in my mouth. "This is amazing," I said after a moment. "I didn't know you liked to bake."

"Stress baker," Simone confessed. "Things get weird around the Keep when Caelan's not there."

"He wasn't gone that long," Moira said.

"The length of time never seems to matter. Imagine a house full of hyped-up toddlers without parental supervision, and that would be the Keep." She rolled her eyes and bit into her cookie. "It's a madhouse."

"You need more women," Ash observed.

"I wish it were that easy," she said. "Unfortunately, female wolf shifters aren't all that common."

"Is that why Gianna was chosen?" The woman had been a swan shifter.

"Partially. Her family background clinched the win." Simone's brow furrowed. "Speaking of her, Caelan had a guest while he was gone."

My stomach clenched. I had a terrible feeling I knew who'd shown up. "Oh?"

"Her cousin dropped by to see if Caelan had any further updates on Gianna's disappearance." She rubbed her hand over her face. "The entire thing is so strange. She just disappeared off the face of the earth. Odd behavior for someone so in love with the spotlight."

A fine tension hummed in the room, and Simone wasn't stupid. Someone had to say something before she got suspicious. "Caelan hasn't contacted her since the last time he spoke to her?"

I'd been there for the conversation, but Caelan hadn't known then where Gianna was or that the swan shifter was dust in the wind after I found her buried on my property.

He knew now, and shifters had a keen nose for sniffing out lies.

Simone shook her head. "He's been caught up in other things, but it's also unlike him not to follow up on something that serious."

"Is she still at the Keep?" Moira asked. "Caelan's on his way back."

Simone snorted. "He didn't tell me what happened here, but he was more subdued than usual when he called. Nadia left yesterday, but I know she'll be back if Caelan doesn't get into contact with her."

"He will," I assured her, mostly in an effort to turn the conversation to other things.

"We'll see." Simone bit into her second cookie and eyed me. "Something's on your mind."

"At any given moment of the day, I have approximately four hundred and twenty-six things on my mind."

Simone blinked. "Weirdo. What's going on?"

"We can't tell you all the cool stuff because you'll tattle to Caelan," Moira said.

Simone's lips thinned. "Mean."

"But true," I added. "Sorry. As long as you're linked to him, we can't be true blue besties."

"I don't tell him everything," she said.

"But if he compelled you to, you would have to spill, wouldn't you?"

Simone glared at me. "Fine. I get it. Are you okay, at least?"

"She's fine," Ash interjected.

I almost laughed. Shifters couldn't tell when a dryad lied to them, something we'd discovered a long time ago. Whether it was because his genetic makeup was mostly earth or what, Ash could claim pink bunny rabbits had come in on spaceships and no one would be able to sniff out a lie.

Simone's eyes narrowed. "Are you lying?"

"Not at all," he said. "I looked at the wound when I got here. She's healing well. By tomorrow, I think she'll be on light duty."

She slowly shook her head. "Caelan made it sound like you wouldn't be up and about for days. He's usually not wrong."

"There's no way he knows what's going on inside me unless he has x-ray vision." I smiled and hoped she didn't push it.

"I'll let Caelen know you're doing better." She rose and took her plate to the sink to rinse off. "I'll get out of your hair. I'm sure you're tired."

Moira's eyes widened a little as she got up behind Simone. "I can walk you out."

When they disappeared out the door, I closed my eyes and sank into the couch.

Tess let out a warbly sigh. "She'll figure out what happened to Gianna. Simone's too smart not to."

"Let me just dream for a little while," I said dramatically.

Moira came back in and sagged against the door. "Too close," she said with a groan. "Caelan needs to head Nadia off at the pass."

"I'll call him later," I promised. We needed to talk anyway.

Ash and Tess sat across the room from each other. Tension still sang in the air between them, but it wasn't as much as before. "And you two?" I asked. "Is everything okay?"

Moira grinned. "That's our Evie. Not much subtlety with her, is there?"

Ash snorted. "Tess and I talked. Time will help."

Tess nodded. "I know I have a lot of things to work on to be... normal."

Ash paled. "Tess. No. That's not what I meant at all."

I shot him a disapproving look. What had they talked about? "None of us are normal. The best we can do is pretend."

"Ash said I talk about death too much and it makes people uncomfortable."

"Ash," Moira said, a disapproving note in her voice. Her lips thinned. "Tess, you're a banshee. Death is the family business. None of us expect you to be anything other than what you are." Her eyes lingered on Ash. "Right, bark boy?"

Ash's stricken expression tugged at my heart. "Of course. Tess." He cleared his throat. "I'm sorry. I never meant to imply you were less or abnormal."

Tess tilted her head and studied him with her pale, curious eyes. "It's okay, Ash. You don't have to lie."

Ash opened his mouth, frowned, then snapped it shut.

Moira jerked her head at Ash. She walked into the guest room, and Ash followed behind. The door slammed and hushed voices murmured so low I couldn't make anything out.

"Is Ash mad?" Tess asked.

I swung my legs over the couch and patted the seat beside me. "Come over here."

"But you're sick." Pale, guileless eyes blinked at me.

My heart softened. "I'm not sick. Only wounded, and I'm already on the mend."

Tess rose and came over, curling her feet underneath her. I put an arm around her shoulders and hugged her close. "Are you okay?"

She nodded. "Why wouldn't I be?"

Tess was young and unusual even among her peers. She had one foot in the world and the other in the land of the dead. As much as it pained me to think about, Tess might always have a difficult time in the world. Banshees weren't common in Joy Springs, and Tess was unusual even for one of her kind.

"Sometimes people can say something that hurts us, even when they don't mean to. It's okay to be upset by those words, Tess. We don't always have to be strong."

Tess swallowed and looked down at her lap. "Ash is hurting. Because of me."

"I know he is, honey. But he's going to be okay. I promise."

She sniffed. "I can't help but be what I am. I tried really hard to be what he wanted, but I couldn't."

Oh, to be young again. I blinked away the tears forming in my eyes. "You don't have to be anything other than Tess. Someday, someone will come along and love you in all the ways you need them to. Maybe that person will be Ash. Maybe it won't. But I promise you, it will happen."

Tess's gaze lingered on the still-closed door Ash and Moira lingered behind. "I want us to be okay. But when he looks at me, I see pain. And it hurts me here." She laid a hand over her heart. "I don't know how to fix it."

"Again, Tess, it will take time. Everything is new and like any wound, it needs time to heal."

Tess nodded. "I'll try to do better."

I shook my head. "No." I pulled her closer and kissed her temple. "You don't need to do anything." Whether she would listen only time would tell. "Keep being you. That's all we can do."

The door opened. Moira came out, her eyes flashing a bright emerald. Ash walked out with his head lowered and his hands in his pockets.

"You ready to go?" he asked Tess.

She slid out of my arms and walked to the door. "Ready when you are."

Moira went to the kitchen and put the kettle on. Her shoulders were tight, and her mouth was pressed into a white line.

"Evie," Ash said. "I'm glad to see you're doing okay."

"I'll be at work before the end of the week. Hopefully in the next couple of days."

"Don't rush on our account. Everything is fine." He bent to brush a kiss over my cheek. "Get some rest."

I waved at Tess who smiled shyly.

A moment later they were gone.

Moira didn't speak for several minutes until she set a steaming cup before me. "Drink one more of these. I want you to go to bed early."

"Aw Mom. But I wanna watch tv!"

A reluctant smile tugged at her lips. "Brat." She flopped onto the chair. "Ash is an idiot."

"Did he really say she wasn't normal?"

She sighed and nodded. "He put his foot in it. I don't think he'll do it again."

"Not after that tongue lashing I suspect you gave him."

Moira groaned and curled her feet underneath her. "Men can be so dumb when it comes to the opposite sex."

"True story." I tilted my mug in a salute. "Bottoms up."

When I finished, Moira took the mug. "We'll look at your weird lock tomorrow. I can see in your eyes you're exhausted." She motioned for me to get up. "I'll tuck you in."

I laughed and shoved her shoulder. "Jerk."

She looped her arm within mine and lay her head on my shoulder, though it was awkward because she was a little taller than me. When I went into the closet to get my pajamas on, she turned down the covers and waited.

My stomach still pulled a little, but I was worlds better than I was this morning. I took my shirt off and examined the still healing skin, the angry pink scar already lighter than earlier. Once I was ready and had brushed my teeth and washed my face, I slid under the covers next to Moira.

"Want me to stay here or sleep in the guest room?"

"I'm fine to sleep alone. Whatever the hell was in that brew was miraculous. You could sell that stuff and be a millionaire."

She wiggled her fingers. "It's magic!"

"Uh huh. Keep your secrets for now, but one day I hope you trust me enough to share them."

Moira rolled onto her side and watched me, her dark eyes serious. She reached a pale hand out, and I entwined our fingers. "I trust you more than anyone in my entire life," she said quietly.

"Then why don't you share things about your life with me?"

A small smile touched her lips. "Because I don't want to look back. Looking forward is the only way I can survive." She reached out and touched my cheek before pulling away. "One day, maybe," she promised. "But not today."

Moira reached over and adjusted the blankets, making me laugh when she tucked my feet in like a little kid.

"If you're good, I'll make waffles tomorrow," she said.

"As long as you use real maple syrup." A yawn escaped me.

"We'll see." She flipped the lamp light off. "Night, Evie."

"Night. Don't eat all my cookies."

Her soft chuckle made me grin.

A few days later, I stood on Caelan's property staring up at the world's largest magical tree.

Caelan loomed behind me, arms crossed over his powerful chest. Things hadn't quite been the same since I'd thrown him out of my house. I was giving him the necessary time to get over it and realize I was not the one in the wrong.

"Has Dad been back?" I asked, looking over my shoulder to see Caelan staring at me.

"No, but we've had some magical disturbances around the wards. Everyone is curious."

I grimaced. "I'll ask him if there's a way we can conceal it."

"There can't be. This tree is the path for the gods. They need access to it."

I turned around to face the Shifter Lord. "I'm sorry about this. Maybe it won't last long here."

One dark eyebrow rose. "What are the odds of that happening?"

"Admittedly low."

"How are you feeling?" He hadn't moved toward me, but his eyes possessed me, everywhere they lingered. Storm clouds brewed in his eyes, and I steeled myself for an argument.

"I'm much better. My power levels are fully recovered and I'm back at work."

"That's good."

It didn't sound good the way he said it. "You can be angry," I said softly, "but not at me."

His nostrils flared. "I don't require your permission to be furious."

"No, but I'm not apologizing for telling you to get out."

"You shouldn't," he agreed.

I blinked. "Then why are you pissed off?"

His powerful chest rose in a long breath. "I screwed things up, didn't I? Things are weird, and I'm not sure how to fix them."

"Things have always been weird between us."

He tilted his head in acknowledgment. "Because you have doubts."

"And if I do?"

"Doubts are normal, but you're keeping secrets, too."

"And you aren't?"

A faint smile. He took a step forward. "I'm a Lord. Secrets are my business."

"I'm not ready to share everything with you."

The smile widened. "No one said I wanted everything. But I need more."

He came closer and rubbed his hands over my arms, his heat soaking through my sweater. Unable to resist, I moved into the circle of his arms. He smelled like the woods, the cold scent of pine in winter. Caelan's hand curled around my nape, fingers sliding up through my hair.

Sensation tingled against my skin. Every time he touched me, I had the urge to burrow into his skin and never let go.

"Why do you resist?" he murmured, lip against my hair. "You know we're good together."

"I'm not good for you." I tilted my head to look at him, tracing my fingers over his jaw. "And I'm not convinced you're good for me."

Caelan stilled. "Oh?" His fingers dug into a knot at the base of my neck.

I whimpered and sagged against him while he used those clever fingers to work it out. My hand slid up his back, tracing the lean muscles close to his spine. "You're jealous."

A huff of laughter against my hair. "Guilty. You're a little crazy."

I smiled against his chest. "Guilty. You ask too many questions."

"Mmm. You don't ask enough."

"True. You're bossy."

"So are you."

I snorted. "You're responsible for thousands of other people. How could you ever be a full partner to me?"

Caelan stiffened.

I winced. The words had fallen from my mouth before I realized what I was saying. "I don't mean it like that. You are a Lord. I'm…" I let my voice trail off.

"You're the heir to the Fae King," Caelan said quietly. "I could ask the same of you."

I froze. "How'd you know?"

"I may not be a genius," Caelan said quietly, "but I'm not an idiot. You're a princess and it's not hard to connect the dots. With his constant attention, it's no secret he's grooming you for other things." He bent and scooped me into his arms, ignoring my stunned yelp. "You're pushing me away. Again."

"Caelan."

"Don't argue with me, woman. Not now." His voice was a low growl, an assault on my senses.

I shivered. "See. Bossy." My fingers slid up his neck and curled in his unruly hair, the satin strands sliding against my skin.

Caelan's eyes flashed gold. "Do you want me to stop?"

I chuckled. "Nope."

A flash of teeth turned into a full-fledged wild grin. Caelan gathered me closer and took off at a swift run as a delighted laugh tore from my throat.

Hours later, I untangled myself from the Shifter Lord who promptly objected and pulled me back against him with a snarl.

"I have to get home."

"Stay," he murmured against my bare shoulder.

"I've neglected my land and the greenhouse. If I don't get it taken care of tonight, I might have to replace some windows."

"I'm rich. I'll pay for them."

I laughed and smacked a kiss on his forearm. "Let go."

"Don't make me get bossy again."

Wiggling my way out of his firm grasp, I bent to grab my bra and shirt, dressing quickly as he rolled over. The gleam in his eyes made me go even faster. His eyes flashed.

"You could stay here, you know."

"I know. But I just told you why I had to go."

"That's not what I mean."

I stilled, fingers pausing over the button to my pants. He could not be asking what I thought he was asking. A couple of hours ago, we were fighting.

"From the deer in the headlights expression," Caelan said, amusement in his voice, "I can see you suspect where I'm going with this."

"Moving in?" I squeaked.

Caelan slid down the edge of the bed, movements lethally graceful. "Don't you think moving in would be the natural progression?"

"Um. If we were a normal couple, yes," I allowed. "But we haven't dated for that long and, if you haven't noticed, your counterparts hate me."

He studied me like prey. "I don't give a shit what the other Lords think. And, evidenced by you tossing one of them around like a baby rattle, neither do you."

My heart pounded against my ribs. I was a little out of breath and a little sweaty and I had no idea what to say. Sensing my distress, Caelan went in for the kill. "There's more room here and much more land. Bonded to me, you'd be untouchable."

"I have several acres, and I'm bonded to my land." Sighing, I walked over and sat at the edge of the bed. Caelan lay his head in my lap and closed his eyes. I sent my fingers through his hair, dragging my nails gently against his scalp.

He hummed and smiled. "And you could do that every day."

"I'm not ready," I whispered.

His eyes opened. "Okay."

I blinked. "Okay?"

He nodded. "Okay. We'll wait."

My eyes narrowed. "Why are you suddenly agreeable?"

He laughed. "I was kicked out of my woman's house the other day because I was…and I quote, 'being an insufferable jackass.'"

I'd put that one in a text for him later because I was still mad at him. "Maybe I should call you a jackass more often," I mused.

"Or you could just move in with me."

"There you are."

Caelan's eyes glinted. "Fine. I can wait."

"How long? Because I won't be ready in five minutes. Not even ten."

He let out a dramatic sigh. "You're breaking my heart."

I bent to kiss him just as a loud explosion rocked the Keep, sending me sprawling to the floor.

Strong hands gripped me, helping me to a standing position. "Stay here."

A moment later, he was gone.

CHAPTER
Twenty~Four

My mother stood at the edge of Caelan's property, a ball of light floating in her hand. She wore a gown of pale gossamer silk, her dark hair streaming away from her face.

"I told you to stay inside," Caelan snarled.

"Do I need to remind you how bossy you are?" I murmured as I stepped up to stand by his side.

"Evangeline," my mother said. "Still lying down with the dogs, I see."

Oh. So this was how my evening was going to go. Awesome. "And you're still a massive bitch, I see."

Caelan's lips twitched.

Mom's nostrils flared. "Congratulations, Caelan. You've finally landed a worthy mongrel."

"Ooh. Ouch, Mom." I clasped my hand to my chest like she'd shot me.

"I'd argue," Caelan interjected coolly, "that no one has successfully landed Evie yet."

"It's true. I play hard to get."

"So hard it's like trying to drill through an adamantine wall."

"Funny boy," I murmured to Caelan.

We both smiled at my mother who stared at us like we were a strange-looking bug.

"What do you want?" Caelan asked when Mom stayed silent.

"I need access to the tree."

A fine tension racked the Lord's frame. I stepped closer and looped our arms together. "I'm sorry," I whispered.

I hadn't seen Mom since I'd traveled to her lands, and we'd left things weird between us. So weird I'd been thinking about it almost every day. For once she'd seemed almost human—or at least like a woman who'd made terrible parenting choices and regretted them.

Glad to know I was wrong. Cliona seemed just as frosty and impenetrable as she always was.

"You are on the edge of my property trying to break my wards," Caelan finally said. "Why should I grant you access when you haven't stepped foot on my land and have already proven yourself a terrible guest?"

Mom's gaze turned cold. "The tree is fae property. You are not authorized to keep us from it."

I shook my head. "I know you can access your lands without the tree. Why are you being weird about it now?"

"Who said I was going to my lands?" Mom responded. "The tree allows fae to travel to multiple lands. It is the only way we can access some of those places." She returned her attention to Caelan. "I have already given you the courtesy of not tearing down your wards. If you do not open access, you will feel the might of the fae."

"Big words," Caelan mused. "Would you risk starting a war with our kind? You might have magic, but we have teeth and claws and vast numbers."

My fingers tightened around Caelan's arm. We could not get involved in a war, especially not since this situation was my fault. I wouldn't bring that down on the shifters.

Mom's eyes flicked to me. "You still carry remnants of the seed's power."

Was she just going to ignore Caelan's tense threat? "Maybe it will wear off now that I don't have the seed anymore."

Mom's faint smile said fat chance.

"You could probably still act as an anchor." Mom's eyes narrowed as she focused on my healed abdomen. Something flickered over her face before she schooled herself into stillness once more. "If you don't wish me to enter your property, allow my daughter to come to me. She can help me cross."

Caelan liked that idea even less than letting my mother onto Keep property.

"I'll go to her," I whispered.

"But Lord," my mother said, "I suggest you figure out a way to allow fae to cross here. For most, Evie won't be an option."

Say one thing about Cliona, she'd never sold me out when it really mattered. Try to kill me? Yep. Although she denies it. But she'd never sold my secrets to the highest bidder.

"Noted," Caelan said, a snarl in his words.

I stepped away. "Once I help Mom, I'm heading home."

His jaw tightened. "I'll come with you."

Mom bristled. "Evangeline is my daughter. She is perfectly safe with me."

Caelan laughed. "Just like she was a few months ago when you tried to kill her?"

"How little you know, wolf," she snapped. "Come." Mom crooked her hand. "It will only take a moment. I will escort you home beforehand and you can send me on from your property."

Caelan opened his mouth to argue, but I shook my head once. "I'll let you know when I'm home."

"I don't like this," he said, the words brimming with anger.

"She's not lying. Mom had multiple opportunities to take me out."

"And she tried last time."

"Did I, Lord? Or did you see what you wanted?"

"I can't believe she might be my mother-in-law," he muttered, making me laugh.

"And I can't believe my daughter would settle for someone who'd leave fur all over the furniture," Mom retorted.

"Please stop," I said to them both. Reaching up, I kissed him on the jaw and headed toward Cliona, lifting my hand in a wave right before I passed through the wards.

Mom stared at Caelan for a long moment before she turned and took me by the elbow.

One second of dizzying disorientation, and I was back at my property, just on the edge, inches from the wards.

"One day," Mom said, "you will realize I've always had your best interests at heart."

"Mmm. I'm not dropping the wards for you."

Mom snorted. "Honestly, Evangeline. This is ridiculous."

I never met someone who could play the victim as well as my mother could. "You keep ignoring whenever someone brings up the fact that you betrayed me just a few months ago."

"Because it wasn't like that."

"Even if it wasn't, you haven't explained anything."

Mom's eyes tightened. "You wouldn't believe me anyway."

I studied her, the pale, proud, staggering beauty who shared genetic material with me. "You're probably right." Shaking my head, I brushed my annoyance away. "Tell me why you think I can act as a gate."

"You won't even offer me a cup of tea?"

I crossed my arms over my chest and stared, suspicion bubbling in my gut. Mom was trying too hard to get past my wards. She might be able to rip Caelan's apart, but she couldn't tear mine down. "You can have one when you get to where you're going."

Mom clicked her tongue. "Fine. Magic doesn't leave our bodies when we're exposed to something as powerful as the World Tree Seed. Not exactly. What you fail to understand is most fae magic holds at least a small amount of sentience. All our magic is based on the world's power in some way, shape, or form." Something like sympathy flashed over her face. "The seed left you with a…gift, if you choose to look at it that way."

Horror roiled in my gut. Beware the fae who leaves a gift behind. "What kind of gift?"

Mom tilted her head and watched me. "I recognize enough to know you can act as a gate."

"Will everyone else?"

She shook her head. "I'm your mother. We're bonded in a different way than every other. Other fae will sense something not quite right, but they shouldn't piece it together unless you tell them."

"Or you do."

"When have I ever spilled your secrets?" she asked, a flicker of hurt in her eyes, there and gone.

"There's a first time for everything." When Mom stayed silent, I waved my hand. "Anything else I should be aware of?"

"You're the only one who knows your magic inside and out. You'll know when you sense something different."

"And there's no way to get rid of it?"

Mom's amused chuckle sent a chill down my spine. "Have you ever heard of a fae gift that disappeared voluntarily?"

That's what I was afraid of. "Tell me how to send you on."

"Quite simple." She held out her hand. "Touch me, think of the tree, and open yourself to the magic. You don't need to know where the other person is going. You only need to act as the conduit."

A thought occurred to me as I took her hand. "Can I go wherever I want?"

Mom's grip tightened. "Yes, but I urge you to think long and hard before ever venturing into any of the other worlds unless you have to. Far more dangerous things prowl outside of the realms of your world, Evie."

That might be the first true warning she'd ever given me. "Noted."

"Ready?" Her grip was cool and tight. Magic pressed against me, the feel of it familiar and as staggering as it ever was.

I glanced up at her. "Mom?"

"Yes?"

I chewed on my lip for a moment. "You should come to lunch with me next week."

Mom's lips parted in surprise. "Err. Yes. I—I will. If you're sure."

I wasn't sure of anything these days. "I am," I lied. "Meet me in town at Marnie's restaurant. How about Wednesday at one?"

Mom nodded. "I will be there."

Our identical gazes met. "Good," I said and spiraled down into my magic. Like she said, it was easy enough to find now that my power had refilled. The seed's magic had mixed within my own power easily...too easily. I thought of the world tree, standing at the edge of Caelan's property, the massive low-hanging branches and the strange ethereal glow.

A slight tug and a pop, and Mom was gone, disappeared into thin air.

I blinked in surprise. "Cool trick," I murmured to myself as I wondered how it might benefit me in the future.

A rustle in the brush had me stepping quickly through my wards.

Cernunnos stood there in stag form. One quick flash of light and my father appeared, dressed in his preferred casual wear—joggers and a t-shirt. "Evangeline."

"Want some coffee?"

He inclined his head. "I would."

"Come on in."

As he passed through the wards, it occurred to me that maybe I shouldn't blindly trust him. My mother didn't have access, and she'd been in my life forever. I'd only known Cernunnos for a few months.

"You're thinking so hard, I can almost see your thoughts," he said as he held the screen door open for me.

When we were inside, I started up the coffee pot. "How do you trust anyone?" I asked.

My father blinked and settled into his favorite chair, my oversized reading lounger. Every time I sat in the thing, it felt like a warm hug.

"A loaded question," he murmured. "What would you say if I told you I don't?"

My hands stilled. "Not even me?"

"You are different," he acceded.

"There's no need for flattery. If you don't trust me, it's okay. We haven't known each other that long."

Cernunnos' eyes swirled. He curled his massive bulk into the oversized chair and smiled. "I've known you since before you were in the womb, daughter. There is no other I would trust more."

My breath caught. No one had ever said something so kind to me. Tears swam in my eyes and caught in my throat. I swallowed hard and still couldn't say anything.

Cernunnos rose in a liquid movement and stood next to me in a heartbeat. He gathered me in his arms, holding me close. I dragged in a ragged breath, my face pressed to his chest.

It was the first time he'd openly embraced me. My hands gripped his shirt tightly.

"I didn't mean to upset you."

I shook my head. "That's not it."

"You are touch starved, Evangeline. Such is anathema to one born of the soil of the world."

I thought about Caelan and almost laughed.

"Not in that way," he said dryly, rightly sensing where my thoughts had gone. "People like us need the constant contact of our family, friends, and lovers. Casual brushes, touches, hugs, those are almost required for us to retain our sanity."

I was able to drag in a normal breath and tilted my head up to study him. "What about you?"

"I am…different."

"But not much different."

"I am able to survive without such touches, though I do crave them."

I hugged him tighter, and we stood like that for quite a while, our arms wrapped around each other. My father always smelled like ancient forests and magic, and this time, even aware of what he could do, I was no longer afraid.

When we let go, the coffee pot beeped. My father went to the cabinet and pulled two mugs down. "I will bring you another coffee contraption," he said as he poured us both a cup.

"This one works fine." Did he know something I didn't?

"Your machine is plastic on the outside, but the inside has plastic components. The water temperature causes the plastic to weaken every time, sending thousands of tiny microplastics into your bloodstream."

I gaped at my father. "How—" I started. "How do you know about microplastics? Is that a topic of conversation among the fae?"

"Anything that pollutes this world is a topic among us."

"Interesting. You don't need to bring me one. I can find one without plastics, though I didn't think the fae needed to worry about those."

"We should all worry because those tiny plastics are destroying the world. You will find it difficult to source such a machine without resorting to manual means." He smiled when he saw my wince. "Allow me to provide this for you."

"Soon?" I asked hopefully.

"Soon," he agreed. "Now. Come sit with me and tell me how you've been since we extracted the seed."

My father left a few hours later, and I felt more centered than I had in years, his words about being touch-starved resonating deep inside me. I wasn't as touchy with my friends as they were with me. I wondered if they knew something I didn't and were trying to help in their own quiet ways.

Sighing, I shook my head and went back inside, planning to ask them first thing in the morning.

Yet another lesson, I, Evie Quinn, had managed to learn the hard way. At least this one hadn't tried to kill me.

Small favors.

Twenty~Five

An angry pounding on the door came before dawn the next morning. I'd been up for half an hour and was on my second cup of coffee, but no one wants to be disturbed at such an ungodly hour. I sent a trickle of magic out only to freeze.

Shit. I'd forgotten about Marek.

I scrambled off my chair and hurried to the door, tugging my robe around me. When I opened it, Rowan's furious face greeted me. Sheepishly, I held the door open and allowed him to stalk in. Power ebbed and flowed around him, his face set in an angry mask.

"You almost died and didn't think to send me a text?" He headed straight for the coffee pot and poured himself a massive mug.

"I'm so sorry. I forgot about Marek and how he might report back—"

"Screw Marek!" Rowan shut his eyes and took a deep breath. "I am your friend. Or at least I thought I was. When a friend has a near-death experience, it's a good rule of thumb to tell them about it so they can help you!"

I winced. "I didn't think. I'm so sorry. Caelan and Ben were here, and that was a whole thing—"

His brows flew up. "Both of them were here?" He hooted with laughter, his anger erased like a rushing river. "How'd that go?"

I put my hands on my hips. "You know damn well how it went."

He grinned. "That doesn't forgive what you did, but it helps."

Rowan gestured for my mug. I reached down and handed it to him. As the Lord refreshed my mug, he kept talking. "Marek was really worried about you, but he felt like he would betray you if he called me." He rolled his eyes. "He's a terrible spy."

I grinned. "Which is exactly why you volunteered him."

"Yes, though I regret it now that I had to find out what happened to you two days later!"

He touched our mugs together.

"Is Marek here?"

"I sent him to a hotel."

"Wait. Where was he staying before you arrived?"

Rowan's dark brows went up.

"Rowan! You did not make that young man sleep in my driveway!"

"The Council wants what the Council wants." He grinned at my outraged look. "Besides, it's good for Marek. He's gotten way too spoiled back home."

"When does he get to stop?"

"When you give him something they can use against you, I suppose." He sat on the couch and gestured for me to come over.

To his surprise, I sat beside him, only a few inches away. Rowan's brow furrowed. "Everything okay?"

"Do you know anything about touch starvation?"

Rowan huffed a laugh. "I was wondering about that. When I first met you, you were the most standoffish natural mage I'd ever seen. Our genetic makeup is different, but earth mages and humans with earth magic, and I, require more grounding. For me, touch helps. I assumed your background was so varied you didn't require it."

"Nope. I'm just dumb."

His look was chiding. "We both know that's not true. Ignorance is far different than stupidity. Who told you?"

"Cernunnos."

His hand jerked. "The Fae King?"

"Yeah." And since it was Rowan, I told him the truth. "He's my father."

Rowan stared at me for a long moment, his expression unreadable. "That...explains a lot, actually."

A snort escaped me. "Yeah. I'll say. But the touch thing never occurred to me. Isn't it weird to bring up to people?"

He kicked off his shoes and moved to the edge of the couch, turning so his legs were stretched out. "C'mere."

I didn't move for a moment. "You're not going to make this weird, are you?"

He grinned, a sly, sexy thing that made me laugh. "Only if you want me to."

Deciding to hell with it, I scooted closer and turned, settling in between Rowan's legs, my back resting against his chest.

I felt an immediate sense of relief. "Shit," I muttered.

"Yeah," Rowan agreed.

"Why don't I feel like this with Caelan?"

"Probably because you two are constantly having sex."

I swatted his arm.

Rowan chuckled. "I'm serious. You two haven't settled into anything yet. You aren't quite friends, and even though you're intimate, you don't consider him a bonded lover."

"And you?"

"I'm a friend, and I care about you, and you care about me. We have no complications. You and Caelan are a tangle of complications."

"Is it really that easy?" I muttered.

"And that hard," Rowan said.

"Would it have been easier if you and I had gotten together?"

I liked Rowan. He never made me want to kill him like Caelan did.

He toyed with my hair. "Maybe? I'm different from Caelan. All the Lords are different. But we all have a mega possessive streak when it comes to things or people we see as ours. Why? Would you want that?"

"I don't know what I want. None of this is Caelan's fault."

Rowan snorted.

"Not completely," I amended. "I'm a hot mess all on my own. I didn't need his help."

"You're keeping a lot of secrets, Evie. It makes Caelan crazy."

"He knows most of them," I muttered.

"And you didn't want him to. That also makes him crazy, FYI."

"I don't think we would have worked. You're far too logical."

Rowan tugged a lock of hair. "Hush. I'm lying with a beautiful woman giving her advice when I should be ravishing her."

"Are you a big ravisher?"

He sighed. "Not really. I like plants. It doesn't attract the ladies."

"Then you're looking for the wrong ladies. A lot of women love a guy who gets his hands dirty." I thought of Gianna, my heart tugging at her loss. "It's all the power you Lords collect. That attracts a certain kind of woman."

"Women not like you."

I grunted. "I almost ran, you know."

"From Caelan?"

He didn't sound surprised.

"Yup. Once I realized how enmeshed he was becoming in my life, I was so tempted to move the shop somewhere else."

"He'd chase you to the ends of the earth."

"I'm well aware."

Rowan shifted and scooted me higher, wrapping an arm around my waist. I was warm and comfortable, and...content.

Which made me realize I had a fundamental problem with Caelan. There were too many secrets between us. Good—okay, mind-blowing sex—would not solve our issues.

"Do you want him, Evie?" There was a note in his voice I was unsure of. Rowan was rarely serious, so when he was, I listened.

"I want him."

He filled in my unspoken words. "But not what he comes with."

"Right. And he doesn't want what I come with."

"The Fae father?" He stilled. "Oh. Shit. You're full fae." Rowan laughed in amazement. "I forgot about your mother."

"Yay for me."

"Wait till I tell all my friends I snuggled with a fae princess. They're going to lose their shit."

"Shuddup, Rowan."

His laugh made me smile.

"But that isn't all."

"Oh?"

"And I can't tell you what it is, but Caelan knows."

Rowan went still, his hand splaying across my abdomen. "Is it harmful?"

I'd gotten control over the beast. As much as I could. And my murderous tendencies had gone way down with Caelan allowing me to siphon magic on his lands. My shifting was mostly under control, and things had been especially calm since the seed had exited my body.

"It has the potential to be."

"Hmm. How does Caelan feel about it?"

"I'm not sure much rattles that guy."

Rowan fell silent for a couple of minutes. When he spoke, his tone was grave. "Your Lord feels deeply, Evie. Deeper than the majority of the other Lords. He is not typical in his relationships. The man has never been a saint, but he never used and cast women aside. He never fell in love, either. Until you."

Tears sprang to my eyes, but Rowan wasn't finished.

"If you can bear to lose him, maybe you should let him go. But if you love him, truly love him, you have to realize he's a package deal. Few Lords want to be in their position."

"Donovan?"

Rowan scoffed. "I said few. There are some, like our recently deceased Donovan, who feel like it's their birthright to gain power. People like Caelan, Thorvin, and I hope myself, we have the position thrust upon us and muddle through the best we can."

"You don't want to be a Lord?"

"Evie, if I had the choice, I'd be a hermit in the woods, surrounded by dirt, plants, and adorable forest creatures that fly into my cabin when I sing."

I grinned at the imagery. "You're the best person for the job, then."

"Yes, I suppose I am. No good politician wants the job. But Caelan is better at the long game than the rest of us. He sees in you a genuine partner, someone who will love him and help him rule. If your distaste for power is stronger than your love for him, then you know what you have to do."

"What's your opinion?"

"I think you're being weak on purpose."

"Rowan!"

"I'm serious."

"I don't think I want you to snuggle with me anymore."

"Liar. This is the best snuggle session of your life."

I made a disgusted noise but made no move to get up because he was right. This was the best non-sexual snuggle session I'd ever had. "I do love him," I said softly.

"I know." He stroked a powerful hand through my hair. "It sucks that our parents and events in our lives can fuck us up so bad. He's shown you how he feels. Maybe it's time for you to do the same. If you don't come to him eventually—if Caelan can't see a light at the end—it may kill him, but he will walk away."

"Dammit," I muttered. "I'm not any good at this."

"You don't have to be. It's Caelan. I've known the man most of my life. Show up at the Keep in a trench coat, drop it when you see him, and tell him you love him. Bing bam boom, you're pregnant."

"You're such an ass," I said with a laugh.

"You know you love me. Set your coffee down and take a nap with me."

"It's six a.m.!"

"Yes," Rowan agreed. "It's the perfect time for a morning nap."

CHAPTER
Twenty-Six

I sank my fingers into the ground, seeking the heart of Mother Earth. My magic responded faster than ever, a heat-seeking missile headed straight for the core of the world. Her presence surrounded me, and I sank down into my meditation, allowing the earth's power to ease my aches and pains, and wipe my mind of worry.

It'd been far too long since I communed with nature of my own free will. The last time I'd been close to death and was forced to. This time, I wanted to pay homage to her, thank her for my power, and check over my land.

Once I finished here, I needed to shift. My Chimera power had been suppressed for too long, and I was getting itchy under the collar. After the last shift where I'd gone into what was apparently the legendary Chimera form—whatever the hell that meant—I could feel the urge scratching at me to shift almost every day. But there were other things I was neglecting with this power, and I knew I had to master them if I had any hope of protecting myself against my mother or other threats that might arise when people realized who I was and exactly how I was related to Cernunnos.

Once that happened, I'd be a target for every fae gunning for the position, no matter that I was a blood relation.

I released a breath and wiped my mind of everything but the feeling of the earth's gentleness brushing across my skin.

Two hours later, I opened my eyes. Winter had come to town, or as much as we ever received winter. Joy Springs was its own little place, and when things got too hot or too cold, there were a number of folks who could fix that right up for us. They didn't do it all the time, but I couldn't remember a day when it stayed over a hundred during the summer. Winter was a little more flexible because it was rarely dangerous. This evening was chilly, the temps having dropped into the low forties. But even with winter's kiss upon our brows, it couldn't stop my Floromancy power.

The ground bloomed with wildflowers, a vivid and startling array of color surrounding me as far as the eye could see.

It had happened before, but never during the colder months. Yet another thing to chalk up to my genetic weirdness, but since wildflowers were harmless and no one but me would see them, I didn't worry too much.

I rose and stretched, sending a tendril of power out to double check I'd touched every piece of my land. A brush of contentment curled over my senses, the land sleepy and sated.

Good. With a bare thought, I shifted into a falcon, rising high into the air. The avian form was my favorite so far. My fae form was a wren, and I loved it, but the falcon could fly far longer. I could feel the power stretching my wings wide, the cool wind sliding underneath my wings. I opened my beak and let out a harsh cry, banking left and sailing through the air.

A dark form came at me from the right, quick and agile. I rose into the air and slowed down, allowing Poe to catch up with me.

I couldn't speak in this form, but Poe was happy to explore with me for a while.

When I landed on my porch and shifted, I shook out my robe before tugging it on. Poe hopped onto my shoulder.

"Let's go inside and get warm."

The raven dipped his head in acknowledgment.

"I've missed you. How's Fee?"

Fee was a phoenix I technically stole from my mother. Well, I stole the egg, not the bird, not dreaming for a second the shell contained a mythical bird of untold power. She stayed with Poe inside the basement of my home for quite a while until I struck a bargain with Caelan for Fee to stay with him so she could remain hidden but still take to the skies and experience some form of freedom.

It had worked out far better than expected, but, to my surprise, Poe had elected to stay with her. Now the two were inseparable, and Fee had grown into a stunning multi-colored mythical beast.

"Happy Fee."

"Good. I was at the property not too long ago." Poe and Fee stayed away from the main area of the Keep because of all the guests and business going on. It wasn't safe for anyone to catch a glimpse of Fee, so she stayed on the ground during the day as much as she could and kept to the back of Caelan's property. At night, she and Poe flew to their heart's content, her natural magic matured enough to where she could mute her orange and purple glow.

I'd visited a few times over the months, but I was careful not to draw attention to either one of them. Poe could take care of himself, but Fee was young and vulnerable.

She also belonged to my mother, or at least Cliona would claim her if she saw her, so I wouldn't do anything to jeopardize her safety.

I scratched the back of Poe's neck. "Hungry?"

He dipped his head, and I got busy chopping up some fruits and cheese, tossing some into a bowl with some nuts for Poe and adding some to a small tray for me. Shifting burned a ton of energy, and I always ate like a horse for the first several hours afterward.

Poe hopped onto the coffee table and dug into his food while I curled up on the couch and munched. When he finished, he lifted his head.

"Gods unhappy."

"When are they not?" I muttered.

"Angry. Tree."

I stilled. "They're angry about the tree on Caelan's property?"

Another dip of the head. "Technically, that's not my fault."

"Court of Gods. Danger. Danger. Danger."

The summons I'd received was only a few days away. I'd almost forgotten. If Poe was here to warn me, the circumstances I was walking into had to be dire.

"Any tips?"

"Survive. Survive."

"That's not exactly helpful, Poe."

"Betrayal."

"Who?"

"Gods. Trickery."

"Alright. I was already somewhat prepared for getting stabbed in the back, but that was before the tree incident. It's worse?"

He bobbed his head. "Mother. Father. Worry. Betrayal."

I reached over and stroked his head. "Thanks for the warning. So Mom and Dad will both be there and someone is going to try to stab me in the back?"

He made a frustrated quarking sound. "Tricks. Betrayal. Tricks."

"Maybe not a complete betrayal, but they're going to try to trick me?"

He bobbed his head. "Be careful." Poe flapped over to land on my shoulder. He rubbed his head against my cheek. "Love Evie. Love Fee."

"I love you too."

"Open door."

I snorted. "Done with me already?"

"Home. Fee."

"Alright. Don't be a stranger, Poe."

He flew off into the night in a flash of purple blue. I was just about to head back inside when I felt a disturbance at the edge of my wards.

Garrett stood there, holding Thalia's limp form in his arms, the woman's eyes glowing an unearthly silver. She mumbled something under her breath I couldn't hear.

"Let us in!" Garrett shouted. "Thalia needs help."

I rushed downstairs. "Then why aren't you helping her?"

His jaw tightened. "Because, you quarrelsome woman, she insisted on coming here."

"I'm not a medic!" With a word, the wards opened. Garrett stalked inside.

"Follow me."

For once, Garrett didn't argue. When we were inside, he carefully laid the young woman on the couch. Thalia's face was etched in lines of misery, her eyes wide open and unseeing.

"Evie. Evie. Are you there?"

I took her hand, concerned by Thalia's frigid touch. I reached for the wool blanket and covered her up. "I'm here."

"A decision. A crown. A tree. Death or Dominion. Blood. Family." A sob bubbled from Thalia's lips.

I stroked her hair. "It's okay." I glanced at Garrett. "Can you sit with her for a minute? I'll make her some tea."

"No!" Her hoarse bark made me freeze. "Understand. Heed me. You must choose, Evie. Choose what you want to be. Or you will die."

Her eyes fluttered shut, fingers going limp in my hands. Garrett went to his knees, eyes wide with concern. I slowly backed away, wondering at the force of his reaction to her. The usually unruffled Garrett was very much ruffled for this girl.

"She's unconscious," I said quietly. "That's all. Seers expend a lot of energy during their visions, and this seemed like a powerful one."

Garrett brushed Thalia's hair from her face and didn't respond.

I touched him on the shoulder on my way to the kitchen. "I'll make some coffee too."

While both were brewing, I texted Caelan.

Is she okay? he responded.

Unconscious but breathing. She should be fine in a little while.

And Garrett?

Unusually kind to Thalia. Something going on?

Wolves have a protective streak, was all he said.

Caelan speak for yes, Garrett has the hots for her.

Keep me posted. I'll come if Thalia takes a turn for the worse. Garrett can handle this.

I made sure the kettle stayed on to keep the water hot for when Thalia woke up, put my phone in my pocket, and brought Garrett a cup of coffee.

He grunted a thank you and curled his hands around the mug.

Garrett didn't like me. Considering how he treated me, the feeling had proven mutual. But seeing him here now, his eyes tight with worry as he fussed over Thalia made me see him in a new light. He lifted her head up and sat on the couch, gently adjusting her so her head rested on his lap. His fingers stroked through her hair absentmindedly.

Wolves might have a protective streak, but Garrett's was totally focused on the woman next to him. A monster from legend could smash through the house and swallow me whole and Garrett probably wouldn't look up from Thalia.

This made me like him a smidge more. Not much, but a little.

"What did she mean?" he asked, his voice sandpaper rough.

"No way to tell," I admitted. "I've been summoned to the Council of the Gods convening in a few days. That's the only thing I can think of."

He frowned. "Why would Thalia have visions about you when you don't know each other?"

"I'm not well-versed in seers, but I don't think Thalia gets to choose. We went shopping not too long ago, so maybe our trip triggered the vision. Or maybe the gods' council has the potential to change a lot of lives, and it was important enough for Thalia to warn me."

"Why are the gods so interested in you?"

"I'm not sure how much Caelan has told you, but the short answer is it's complicated."

He shook his head, ragged blonde hair flopping into his eyes. "Not much. I'm Caelan's enforcer, not his gossip buddy."

"Are you always so pissy?" I rubbed my face and sighed. "Can we not have one normal conversation between us?"

He lifted amber eyes and met my gaze. "Thank you for opening your wards."

I blinked, waiting for him to follow it up with something shitty, but he didn't. "Of course. You're one of Caelan's most trusted people. Why wouldn't I?"

He grunted and turned his attention back to Thalia.

She stirred a few seconds later, her eyes blinking open. Her brow furrowed when she spotted Garrett.

"Where—"

"You're at my house," I said.

Thalia turned and frowned. "When did I get here?"

"You had a powerful vision and insisted you come here."

She sat up abruptly and scooted away from Garrett. I pretended not to notice the flicker of hurt on his face. Thalia groaned and winced, pressing her thumb to the space between her eyes. "I have a horrific headache."

I hurried to the kitchen to make her some tea and carried the cup back with a small saucer. "Peppermint and some other herbs. It should help."

"Thanks."

Silence fell as we sipped our drinks. When Thalia spoke, her voice was shaky. "I don't remember much. There's some event or something coming up, and I remember it being dangerous."

"Yes," I agreed. "In a few days I'll be called before the gods."

Thalia sucked in a breath. "What did you do?"

"Planted a tree."

Garrett snorted.

Thalia's brow wrinkled. "That doesn't seem important enough. Did something else happen?"

"Lots of somethings. You were trying to warn me, but…" My voice trailed off.

"I know. My predictions are shaky at best." Her fists clenched. "Which is so annoying because how can I help people if I keep spouting off weird shit like *water fiiiilllltteeer*." She wiggled her fingers. "Or *darkness faaaallllls*."

She seemed so disgusted with herself, my heart hurt. "It's not your fault. I haven't met a lot of Seers, but all their predictions came with a heaping side of confusion." I slapped on what I hoped was a comforting smile. "But I've always been good at puzzles, so I'm sure I'll figure it out."

"Are you ready to go?" Garrett interjected.

Thalia sent him a hot glare. "Can I finish my tea first?"

His jaw tightened. "Fine."

Thalia rolled her eyes. "How did I get here?"

I decided to throw Garrett a bone. "Um. Actually, Garrett drove you here and carried you in."

Thalia blinked. Her eyes narrowed. "Did he smack my head against the door a few times beforehand?"

"No," Garrett growled, "but it was tempting."

These two were so going to do it. I bit down the grin threatening. "Want some more coffee?" I asked the prickly wolf.

"Please." He held his mug out. "Half, please. We'll get out of your hair as soon as the princess finishes her tea."

"Maybe the princess will throw it in your face and ask for a fresh cup," Thalia said sweetly.

"Try it and see what happens." Garrett snapped his teeth.

Thalia blushed and sipped her tea.

Garrett mumbled a thank you and took the mug I handed him. We sat in awkward silence for a few more minutes until Thalia rose. "Thank you, Evie."

"I should be the one thanking you."

When we got to the door, she reached over and gave me a tight hug before sliding past Garrett outside.

"Thanks for bringing her to me," I said.

"She asked to go."

I couldn't help my smile this time. "Be careful, Garrett. She seems like a feisty one."

Garrett pinned me with his amber gaze. "How about you mind your business, and I mind mine?"

"You're the one who carried her over the threshold like Prince Charming."

Garrett made a disgusted noise and walked outside, leaving me standing in the doorway laughing.

CHAPTER
Twenty-Seven

CAELAN

Rowan walked into the study, hazel eyes brimming with anger.

Seymour hopped off the desk and launched himself at the other Lord who caught him in one hand and tucked him into the crook of his arm.

"What's crawled up your ass?" I asked, pen paused in the middle of the hundredth damn form I had to sign. Simone was amazing, but the paperwork made me want to scream.

"You need to get your shit together, man. You're going to lose her if you don't."

I froze. "Excuse me?"

He came close enough for me to catch a familiar scent in the air. The pen dropped. Fury boiled in my blood. I came to my feet and leaned on the desk, claws making gouges in the wood. "Why do you smell like Evangeline?"

"Because I was at her house earlier since you didn't tell me she almost died." He shoved a hand through his hair and plopped into one of the leather chairs. "Fucking prick."

Rowan would have been acting guiltier if he'd done something unforgivable, but her scent...

Evie was all over him.

"Tell me," I demanded.

Rowan scoffed. "I didn't sleep with her. Nothing of the sort. Do you have zero faith in either of us? We're just friends."

"Then why do you smell like you're involved with her?"

"Because I am. I care about her, and I'm starting to wonder if I care more than you do."

The cracking sound of wood was the only noise in the room for a long moment. "Take care with your words right now."

He snorted and watched me with his strange hazel eyes. "How about you rein your shit in and talk to me?"

Rowan's levelheadedness had always appealed to me both as a friend and as a Lord, and the other man had been my friend long enough to speak to me even when I was being unreasonable.

Even though I had every reason to be unreasonable.

It took me a while to stifle the urge to rip his head off, but eventually my claws retracted and I retook my seat. "Talk." My voice sounded like I'd been gargling gravel.

"Evie's magic is bound to nature. She is a creature of the earth, and now that I know her full biological heritage, things make a lot more sense."

"She told you about Cernunnos?"

Rowan nodded, and I studied the man a little closer. Evie trusted almost no one. How had Rowan gotten underneath her prickly tight shields so quickly?

"I'm aware of her magic."

"But not of the requirements. She is full fae, and while the fae's magic is tied into the natural world, they are not like her. Evie needs constant touch to thrive."

My claws came out again, this time poking holes in the thighs of my jeans where my hands rested. "And you met this need for her?"

Seymour's traps moved to and fro as we spoke, his body shivering inside his pot. The poor thing looked like he wanted to bite someone, but he wasn't quite sure who was in the right yet.

Rowan stroked a finger over Seymour and said, "Shut up for a moment and listen to me, please."

Every muscle in my body was tight and poised to leap over the desk. "Hurry up," I growled.

"You scare Evie."

The wolf inside me recoiled, horrified at the accusation. "Rowan, I swear to the gods—"

The other Lord leaned forward. "Put away your fucking ego and listen to me."

The seriousness in his tone and the ferocity of his words made me blink. My anger drained away. "Fine," I said quietly. "I won't interrupt again."

"Wolves and shifters are tactile creatures. We feel better when we're surrounded by people we care about. They ground and settle us. It's no big thing for one of our Pack to reach out and provide a comforting touch."

I bit my tongue. All obvious observations from Rowan, but he was going somewhere with this, and I promised to listen.

"Pack is family. But what about those who have no family? Those people who've gone through traumatic circumstances and have since become hypervigilant and independent? Some fae are tactile, some are not. What if that person had no idea who she really was and had inadvertently starved herself from an act that could help center her magic and help bring stability?"

Rowan paused. I added in a hesitant comment because I didn't like where he was going with this. "I would touch Evie as much as she wants."

"If she asked you to."

I gritted my teeth. "Evie is prickly on a good day."

Rowan snorted. "With you, yes."

"Goddammit, Rowan."

The bastard had the nerve to laugh. "You might be having sex with her, but she needs more without any strings attached." A pause. "And you, my friend, are a fucking ball of tangled yarn. You are all the strings, all of the time."

I sat back in my chair. Seymour took pity on me and hopped from Rowan's arms into mine. I stroked his trap and mulled Rowan's words.

"Any advice?" I asked after a long moment.

"Besides get your head out of your ass?" Rowan said with an unrepentant grin.

"Don't make me kick your ass."

He laughed and stretched, bringing his arms behind his head. "Stop trying to push the poor girl into marriage."

"And the Council?"

"Fuck the Council," Rowan snapped. "Evie picked Ethan up with a whisper of power and tossed him around like a rag doll. The Lords should be afraid of her, and frankly, so should you. The woman can take care of herself, but you bastards have been coming at her from all sides. Evie has been fighting since you came into her life months ago, and her system is in overdrive with stress. While sex might be a decent stress reliever, you're more apt to win her if you just love her. No strings. No bargains. Nothing but you and her. Caelan and Evie. Do that, you idiot, and I'm all but certain you can make her yours. And for the love of the gods, touch the woman. Show her she matters because of her, not what she can do for you or your power base."

"I thought I'd been doing that."

"If you had, the woman wouldn't have snuggled up with me and taken a nap."

My fists clenched. "You lay with her?"

The asshole laughed again. "Yes. Because unlike you, I have no designs on her body or her soul. She can be herself with me. If you were smart, you'd let her be the same."

Rowan's words were a difficult pill to swallow, but as I sat there mulling over the decisions that had brought us to where we were, I realized he was right. And that enraged me.

Rowan held up a hand. "Don't misplace your anger. I'm here as your friend. I am no competition for Evie." His eyes glittered.

"Unless you continue to fuck this up. And if you do, I can promise you, I will go for her, and you will lose."

"I should put you in the ground for that," I said, the wolf in my voice.

"Again, you can try." Rowan stood, Evie's scent beating from his skin and clothing.

Claws pushed from my skin and power came to the forefront of my brain, scrambling for escape to show Rowan whose dominion he was in.

Rowan smirked. "I'll be out of your property within the hour so you can calm down." He turned his back to me, a brave move when faced with another Lord more powerful, and left the office. I didn't move a muscle until I was sure he was out of the Keep.

And when he was, I stood and carefully set Seymour down on the credenza behind me, tucking him into an unexposed crevice.

Then I picked up my desk with one hand and threw it against the side of the wall, reveling in the splinters of wood slicing my face and exposed skin. My breathing came fast and heavy, blood pooling in the wounds, and I sank to the ground, tipping my head up as a mournful howl tore loose.

How had I managed to fuck this up so badly?

I hadn't seen or heard from Caelan for two days. Unusual, but I received no response when I texted him this morning.

Concerned, I texted Simone to check on him. She gave me no information other than telling me he was okay.

Moira, Tess, and Ash were all back in the shop, and things were slowly beginning to normalize once more. We had a massive pile of baskets and flowers on the table, each of us putting together a rustic centerpiece for an upcoming ladies' luncheon. We'd chosen a mix of pretty winter flowers—ranunculus, anemones, roses, and a variety of seed pods and branches.

The event was a fundraiser, so as each basket was finished, I added a simple charm to help nudge generosity toward the cause. Simple, fulfilling work, and something I needed after the last few weeks.

Mom and Cernunnos were quiet. Thalia had visited yesterday with her ever-present grumpy shadow. No more disturbing visions, though she'd come mostly to check up on me to ensure things were going okay. Funny, because I was more worried about her than she was.

Garrett watched her like a hawk the entire time, and I

wondered how long it would take Thalia to realize his interest in her was not completely protective.

"What's going on with Caelan?" Moira asked as she picked up a stunning maroon ranunculus. "He's been quiet these days."

"No idea." In the back of my mind, I wondered if he'd found out about Rowan coming over. Looking back, I should have declined his offer, but Rowan had been right. Ever since I'd seen him, I'd felt sharp and steady. "I'm assuming he's busy."

A thought occurred to me. "Shit. I forgot to tell him about Gianna's cousin." I reached for my phone one more time and typed out a simple message.

Ash winced. "I'm surprised they haven't squashed the search or come up with some excuse to fend her off yet."

"He's been a little busy, I think, but I agree. Simone usually gets involved in all his goings on, but this one is delicate."

My phone beeped.

Working on it, was his response.

Short and sweet, no flirty undertone. Huh. Had he broken up with me?

The thought made something twist inside me. I guess I had no right to be surprised by such an outcome. I was a hot mess and every time I was around, I seemed to make things worse for him.

"Evie?" Ash asked. "You okay?"

"Have you ever heard of being touch starved?" I blurted.

Ash and Moira's eyes met, some silent communication happening.

"Shit," I whispered. "You already knew."

"No," Ash said quickly. "Only suspected until we found out about your relationship with Cernunnos."

Moira reached out and touched my hand. "This isn't uncommon, but you…" She paused. "You've had a lot of good reasons to push someone away."

"Is that why you guys have always been a little touchy feely with me?"

"I'm a dryad," Ash said. "While not as hungry for touch as others, I do require it more than many."

"Who does that for you?"

Moira chuckled. "His harem."

Tess's shoulders stiffened. Moira noticed immediately, her face falling. "Oh, no. I'm just kidding. We all know Ash doesn't have a harem. If any of us had one, it would probably be me."

"Evie could have a harem if she wanted," Ash added.

I shuddered. "I can barely handle the testosterone of one shifter. Having four or five? Absolutely not."

"Valid," Moira said. "But could you imagine all the di—"

"Moira!" Ash snapped.

Tess snorted. "I know what a dick is, Ash."

Ash looked like he wanted a hole to open up and swallow him.

"Let's reel this back a little and talk about the touch starvation. How do you know when you're suffering?'

Moira's look of pity almost made me get up and walk away. "You feel like you're going out of your skin. Your magic builds up until you have to—"

"Siphon." I sighed. "Shit."

"You would have needed to siphon regardless," Ash added. "You have much more magic than we do. But this could have contributed to the buildup."

"Why didn't any of you say something?" I wasn't angry but knowing this might have helped.

Moira saw my look. "Sex might take the edge off a little, but it's intimacy that matters. The feeling of safety you get in a lover's arms, and you know they would burn the world down for you. Simple sex is a biological urge. There's touching and release, but it's not the same."

Ash sighed. "You and Caelan haven't bonded on the true intimate level, have you?"

"I don't even know what that means," I muttered.

"Then the answer is no," Moira said.

"I don't think I get the intense need for touch," Tess interrupted. "Sometimes I think I could float away and dissipate in a mist of vapor, and I'd be totally fine."

"And we would miss you terribly and gather up all that vapor and make you into a rain cloud so we could keep you with us always."

Moira smiled at Tess who furrowed her brow and said, "That's not how banshee vapor would work."

"I'll make it work. I'll find a cute mason jar with a little metal lid and trap your vapor inside and decorate it with a pretty little black ribbon for all your moods and set it in the window so I can watch it rain all the time."

Tess shook her head, but she couldn't hide her tiny smile.

Moira grinned. "We can all be touch starved in our own ways." She returned her attention to me. "How'd you find this out?"

I hesitated for a moment. "Rowan."

Moira hooted. "Did you and that fine Lord have a snuggle session?"

My cheeks burned.

"Oh shit," Ash said with a laugh. "Is that why Caelan hasn't gotten back with you?"

"Probably," I muttered. Shaking my head, I pushed away from the table and stood. "Nothing happened, truly. I like Rowan, but I care about Caelan."

I rubbed my hands over my arms and went over to the window. "He's just so intense sometimes. It freaks me out."

"Maybe you should tell him," Moira said.

"If he ever talks to me again." Sighing, I rubbed my temples. "The gods council meeting is tonight."

Ash straightened. "Do you have an escort?"

"No. I expect they'll either send instructions or an escort. Any tips?"

Ash frowned. "I've never been called before one. Dress nice and be respectful."

Moira cackled. "The first one is fine. The second might be too big of a request."

"Shuddup, Moira."

Ash sent her an admonishing look. "Do you know why they want you there?"

I shrugged. "The summons came before the tree incident, so I'm not sure."

"The tree will definitely come up," Ash said.

"I have no defense other than what goes in must come out."

Ash gave me a withering look. "You truly have no respect for any form of authority, do you?"

"Where would the fun be in that?" I grinned and poked a cream colored rose into floral foam, gently pushing aside an anemone.

"These are not Lords," Ash said gently. "Their power can crush you."

"True," I agreed. "But why would they bother with me? I'm low on the totem pole and they have much bigger things to worry about."

Ash's hands stilled. "I think you constantly forget who and what you are. Being of the Fae King's blood doesn't put you low on the totem pole, more like close to the top. Chimeras are an unknown. They can do amazing things but they're so secretive, it's difficult to rank them." He gave me a probing glance. "You haven't spoken much about that side of you. Everything under control?"

"As much as it can be. I shift when I need to but still have a lot to learn. Finn could do some cool tricks, and all I know how to do is turn into another animal."

"Still a cool trick," Moira acknowledged. She picked up a rose and hissed when a thorn pricked her finger. "We didn't get the de-thorned ones this time?"

I shook my head. "New supplier. Our regular one had a rose slug outbreak, and it decimated their crop." A disgusted scoff came from me. "They charged an obscene amount to de-thorn them, so I figured we could do it."

"And then you forgot?" Moira accused, waving a bloody digit at me.

"Yup. I was busy giving birth."

Tess let out a chortle. "Seed jokes will never get old."

We worked a few more hours on the arrangements before I called it quits. On my way out, Ash stopped me by the door and pulled me in for a hug.

"Be careful," he said quietly. "If you can't be respectful, be quiet."

I snorted. Like that would ever happen.

His heavy sigh made me grin. "If you don't take my advice, at least keep your mouth shut. Admit to no wrongdoing. The fae are tricky and will use all kinds of deceit to bend you to their whims."

I patted him on the back. "Remember who my mother is. I'll be fine, Ash. I promise."

His grim expression when he pulled back said he didn't believe me at all, but he didn't argue. "Text me as soon as you're home, no matter what time it is."

"Will do."

He held open the door for me and waved as I drove away.

The first hint of dread sang through my bones. Four hours from now and I would be standing in front of more power than my mind could comprehend.

I'd been dancing right on the line of danger with the gods for months now. The summons wasn't out of left field, but I'd hoped I could delay being called to the carpet until I got a firm handle on my magic and learn my limits. Now I had to walk in and hope my Floromancy and shifting ability would get me out of any serious trouble I might find.

Mom and Cernunnos would be there, but I wasn't confident

enough to tell if their presence was a good thing or would serve to make things worse.

Ash's doubt about me being okay only heightened my own. I was walking into the unknown, and I did *not* like surprises.

Unfortunately, the fae and the gods have proven to be nothing but a surprise.

A disturbance at the wards had me making my way outside, wobbling as I adjusted to the kitten heels I wore. I shoved a pair of slippers in my bag in case I changed my mind, or in the event of needing to run.

Either scenario was highly likely when it came to my luck.

Marek, Rowan's wolf, waved at me. He'd come back yesterday with little fanfare, though the relief on his face when he spotted me hale and hearty had thawed my heart a little.

Next to him stood a man of my similar height with pale skin and swirling green eyes.

Birch, the strange tree man I'd met at my father's introduction party.

I reached back inside and grabbed my shawl, then headed toward him.

Birch gave me a little bow once I was outside the wards. "Well met, Evie. You look lovely this evening."

"And you look quite handsome, Birch." He wore a shiny suit of forest green with a black shirt and green tie. His nut-brown hair was swept away from his face, showing off his strange eyes.

"Thank you, my dear." He held out his arm. "I am your escort this evening."

I wrapped my fingers around his elbow and turned to Marek. "I'll be home around—"

Birch's eyebrows lifted. "The fae have no concept of time, but if I had to guess, I'd say a few hours."

"Around eleven, I hope, though there's no reason to be concerned if I'm a little later."

Marek nodded, his gaze drifting away from me to rest on Birch. He was young enough to have never met a fae.

"This is Birch, a friend of the Fae King."

Birch offered Marek a tiny bow of his head. "Well met, wolf."

"Marek," I said. "He's one of Lord Rowan's."

"Ah," Birch said. "I do not personally know your Lord, but he seems like a fair ruler."

Marek nodded eagerly. "He is, sir."

Birch smiled with a little too many teeth making Marek blink in surprise. "Keep an eye on our dear Evie's house." He reached into his pocket and handed Marek a small round device. "If anything happens, you can reach me by speaking my name into this device. It will only work once, so make sure to use it only for an emergency."

"Th—thank you," Marek said, tucking the device into his pocket.

"I'm assuming I'll have no cell service?"

Birch gave me an amused look. "Hold on, dear Evie, and I'll have you there in a jiffy."

I tightened my fingers. Seconds later came a disorienting jolt and a sense of strange otherness.

Seconds after that, I stood in a hall of gleaming marble and gold.

"Welcome to The Hall of Fae," Birch said.

I gawked. "There's no sports memorabilia," I murmured.

Birch gave me a strange look. "Sports?"

"Hall of Fame?"

His brow furrowed.

"Never mind," I said with a sigh. "It's a human thing."

"Of course it is," Birch said.

We were alone, our voices echoing in the massive chamber. A glowing fountain stood in the middle, sparkling, iridescent water flowing up and over, the sound settling my nerves. Fae art was displayed on lined pedestals—everything from carved musical instruments, strange stones I'd never seen before, vases and pottery, and other strange and fantastical things.

Portraits lined all three walls, a mix of male and female fae, only two I recognized—Mom and Cernunnos. "What's the purpose of this place?"

Birch grinned. "Vanity."

Sounded about right. "Fair enough. Anything I need to know about this council?"

Birch stared at me for a long moment. "Your father didn't tell you anything?"

"Not much," I admitted. "He seems to have a laissez-faire attitude about a lot of things."

"Hmm." He stepped forward and headed toward the large silver doors at the back of the room. "I'm not of your father's rank and will not be allowed in the room. Do you know what this is about?"

"A half dozen things come to mind."

Birch laughed with delighted surprise. "I see your father in you and yet, you are your own unique and mischievous person. Cernunnos got up to his fair share of shenanigans in his youth, but I think you'd give him more than a run for his money."

"It's hard to imagine him as a child."

Birch nodded. "He is an ancient and has long since forgotten many things. It's difficult for any of us to remember so long ago when fun was the most important thing in our lives." We stopped at the door a few minutes later, after I'd gawked suitably at some of the more interesting treasures set up on the pedestals.

He lowered his voice. "Have you done anything illegal?"

I blinked. "Erm. According to whose laws?"

Birch shook his head. "I should have been more specific, but I wasn't aware I was in the presence of a criminal mastermind," he said dryly. "The fae have many laws, but only a few bring consequences if they are broken. The rest are flexible."

"If I did break one, I wouldn't know. I haven't killed any fae or anything like that."

"A good start. Killing one of our kind can bring a death sentence, though some get extremely creative with murder."

"Good to know." I think?

"If you've committed no crime, then I can only assume you have nothing to worry about. Perhaps they only wish to meet Cernunnos's whispered-about daughter."

I grimaced. "I would have preferred to have a barbecue or something rather than travel into the faelands in uncomfortable shoes."

"Wouldn't we all." Birch dropped my arm and stepped back, bowing low with a dramatic flourish. "Best of luck, Evie. The doors will open in just a moment. When you are finished, they will send you home."

"Wait. You're leaving already?"

The doors boomed open.

Birch disappeared.

An ancient voice beckoned me inside.

I smelled flowers first, a mix of rose and jasmine, combined with the heady scent of a floral bloom I'd never smelled before. Making a mental note to ask about it before I left, I straightened my shoulders and walked inside.

Flora surrounded me, fat green glossy leaves hanging from the ceiling and climbing up the walls. A riot of blooms entangled in vines wrapped around large marble supports. The floor was made of grey stone, the sound of my heels loud in the silence.

Before me rested five ornate chairs. One made of antler horns, one made of greenery and thorns, another of pure gold, one of silver, and the last pure gleaming crystal.

I was the only one in the room.

"Come closer, child," the ancient voice said.

I did as they bade, my gaze everywhere all at once as I looked for threats. My magic was calm and lazy inside me, feeling at home in this strange place. I stopped a few feet away from the thrones and waited, my senses seeking out the flower with the irresistible scent.

There. I itched to step closer but didn't want to seem overly curious.

"You may explore, daughter of Cernunnos," the voice said.

Had I detected a note of amusement? The voice was deep but female.

I didn't wait to be told twice. Moving from my spot, I made a beeline toward the crystal chair. A strange double-bloomed flower waved in a phantom air. The color was mixed with vivid purple and burgundy, its glowing filaments bright, electric blue.

Taught at a young age to be wary around unfamiliar plants, I came close enough to examine it but stayed far enough away to avoid any airborne pathogens or pollen.

A shimmer in the air revealed five fae.

I turned. My mother sat in the crystal chair. Cernunnos took the antler horn seat. A massive red-haired man with two axes strapped to his back took the silver one. A stunning woman with flowers woven in her pale hair took the greenery chair, and an older woman with long silver hair and proud features took the gold.

I moved away from the flower to retake my original place. Knowing I should do something, but also conscious of my position, I dipped my head and offered them a short bow before rising.

"Welcome, Evangeline," the silver-haired woman said. "Thank you for attending our summons."

The invitation literally said attendance was not optional, but I chose not to point that fact out.

Look at me. Maturing already.

I dipped my head again and stayed silent.

Mom's azure gaze rested on me, but Cernunnos looked past me, at a point over my shoulder.

When no one spoke, I cleared my throat. "May I ask about the unique flower I was looking at before you entered?"

The pale-haired woman smiled. "We simply call it a fae flower. It blooms only when and where it wants to, but seeing such a bloom is a good omen."

Evie - 1, I guess. "Is there a way to grow it in the human world?"

"I'm afraid not," she said. "Earth's atmosphere isn't quite right for the bloom to flourish, even on fae owned land."

"Too bad. It's stunning. Is it poisonous or in any way harmful?"

"No. It's merely what it appears to be—a rare, stunning bloom."

"Thank you for the knowledge."

A small dimple peeked from the woman's cheek. "I am always happy to share knowledge of flora and fauna. Please call me Aine."

A goddess. One of summer, I think. "It is a pleasure to meet you, Aine."

"Likewise."

"Do you know why you are here?" the huge red-haired man asked.

"No idea," I said honestly.

"You are Cernunnos's chosen heir. We wished to see you for ourselves," the giant boomed.

Again, this could have been a casual barbecue. "Alright," I acknowledged. "I'm here."

"We know," he said. "We can see you."

"Right." Maybe the red-haired man had been hit in the head too many times.

Silence fell again and went on for so long, I jerked a thumb over my shoulder and said, "Is that all? Am I free to go?"

"Patience, child," the silver-haired one said. "We are examining your aura."

"Oh." Internally, I was screaming. What could they see inside me and were they secrets I wanted them to know? Suppressing my almost overwhelming urge to squirm, I did my best to wait patiently for their perusal to end.

No one had mentioned the tree, so maybe they hadn't noticed? If that were the case, and I skated out of here without having to answer for that debacle, I was going straight to the gas station and buying lottery tickets.

My mother's brow furrowed, just a slight mar on her perfect face. I stilled and tore my eyes away. Was it me or something else?

"Enough," Cernunnos snapped. "You've ogled my daughter enough. There is nothing alarming in her aura or her magic."

"That is for us to decide," the silver-haired woman said tartly.

Cernunnos turned those strange ancient eyes to her. "Enough," he said again. "Evie is not used to our ways. She was not raised in our world."

The furrow in Mom's brow grew deeper.

I chanced sending a message to her, something I hadn't done in so long, I wasn't sure I remembered how.

Mom?

Evangeline. Something is wrong.

With you?

Faint exasperation came down our bond.

No. But something.

I almost sighed aloud. *Entirely unhelpful, but okay.*

Cernunnos rose.

A shift of air, three gasps of surprise, and a tug at my arm revealed a flustered Tess. Her hair was in tangles, and her skin was chalk white. Tears streamed down her cheeks.

My mouth dropped open. "Tess," I breathed. "What in the hell are you—"

"*Death,*" Tess moaned. "Marked for death."

I froze. "Me?"
"Evangeline," my mother snapped. "You must—"
Tess opened her mouth and screamed.

CHAPTER
Thirty

I'd never heard a banshee wail. One star. Would not recommend.

The sound was indescribable. It echoed through my bones, vibrating my very cells with a shockwave of power.

Everyone except for my mother went down. In a graceful leap straight out of some kick ass spy novel, my mom vaulted over the table straight for me. Her eyes were wide with terror.

I slammed my hands over my ears and fell. My heart hammered against my chest, and I couldn't think or do anything. All I wanted was for Tess to stop screaming.

Three masked fae appeared behind my father's prone body, armed with glittering swords. To my horror, all three raised those swords high above their heads, aiming straight for the Fae King.

Before I could shout a warning, Mom's arms wrapped around me, and all I could think was that she smelled like flowers.

She yanked Tess close and a moment later we stood outside the wards of my home.

Except ... there were no wards. Someone had torn them down.

Mom was saying something, but I couldn't hear her, Tess's scream still infused into my veins.

Evangeline came the whisper of Mom's voice inside my mind. *Why are your wards down?*

I—I don't know.

The sound of snarling and an explosion of blue light came from the front of the house. I took off running.

Three Lords stood on one side, three on the other.

Ben, Rowan, and Caelan stood closest to me. Ethan, Thorvin, and Soren stood on the other side, but behind them stood a tall, pale woman with hair so light it could be mistaken for white.

Mom touched my shoulder. My ears popped and I could hear again.

"Thanks," I whispered.

She didn't respond, her attention fixed on the woman. "Titania."

I went still. Titania was a figure of lore that I didn't think existed, but if there was a true fae queen, this woman looked like she could be it. Pale hair, bright green eyes, fine features and a gossamer gown of pink and green, Titania was just as tall as the Lords, but she vibrated with magic.

Her lips curved when she spotted my mother. "Cliona. How wonderful for you to come. I see you've brought me a pet."

Tess was silently weeping behind us, her small frame shivering with exhaustion.

"Why are you on my daughter's property?" Mom snapped.

"No one owns property," Titania said with a laugh. "Not on this plane. It belongs to us. Your daughter lives on our land."

What an entitled 'pick me' girl. "The hell I do."

Titania's eyes narrowed as they focused on me. "You must be the sniveling brat I've heard so much about."

Ethan held a hand up. Mom's eyebrows hitched when the fae fell silent. "On a Lord's leash, Titania? Oh, how the mighty have fallen."

"You know nothing," Titania hissed.

"We're here for Evie, Caelan. If she comes with us, there will be no bloodshed."

Caelan's gaze flicked to Soren. "All of you? Or just you? Soren, have you chosen a side?"

Soren's lips thinned. "I don't like any of this."

I moved to stand next to Caelan. A proprietary hand snagged me around the waist and hauled me close. Ethan's lips curled in disgust. "You continue to choose the mongrel over your own kind."

Fury bristled from Caelan, but he calmed when I smiled.

"Aww, Ethan. Are you still butt hurt over getting smacked around by a girl?" I clicked my tongue. "We can go for another round if you'd like."

Caelan's hand tightened around my waist in approval.

Ethan's eyes flashed the gold of the Lord's. "If you'd like to go again, little girl, I'd be happy to oblige."

"No need," Titania said. "We aren't here to kill you, Evie."

"Evie," Tess said quietly.

What did Titania mean by that? I did a quick scan of my land. Nothing seemed amiss except for the wards, and the reason for that was standing in front of me looking like a fae cosplayer. Did fae really wear glitter or was Titania just a poser?

"Then why are you here?"

"Evie," Tess said, a note of urgency in her voice.

I turned.

"We're here to crown you," Titania said.

Mom sucked in a shocked gasp.

Caelan froze. "What?"

"Don't look so surprised," Titania said. "Cernunnos made quite the statement with his little introduction party. You're his heir. All the fae know it. I've been sent here to speed up the process."

"Mom?" I whispered.

One sharp shake of her head, and I believed her. Mom knew nothing about this. "Evie was just at the Hall of Fae. No one said anything about it."

My father had said nothing either. He'd agreed to me waiting to give him a firm answer, and he had never backed out of a deal with me before. What, if anything, had changed?

Titania rolled her eyes. "Because we needed the land open to recognize the crowning, and we all know how…reluctant Evie is to trust anyone on the property."

This smelled rotten. My land should have nothing to do with wearing the fae crown. "If what you say is true, there's no need to do this right now. I still haven't said I'd take the crown."

Mom stepped closer. She had never given me comfort during our relationship. Everything regarding her felt like a test, but in this moment, we felt united.

Titania's eyes gleamed. "Normally you'd be right." She studied her nails, a satisfied smile curving her lips. "But with the odd appearance of the World Tree and your continuing connection to it, your safety is at risk if we don't move the schedule up."

"Cernunnos has said nothing about this," Mom snapped. "Perhaps we should bring him here to settle things."

"You can if you'd like, but he will be overruled."

"Cernunnos is the Fae King," Mom said. "He is the final authority."

Titania snapped her fingers. Caelan's hand was ripped from my waist. He, Ben, and Rowan were tossed away like bowling pins, Caelan's snarl ripping through the air.

"Evie!" Tess grabbed my arm. "Don't—"

Titania knocked Tess away, the banshee hurtling through the air, her scream short and shocked.

Standing my ground, I reached for my power. Boosted by being on my property, my magic rose, tingling against my palms. "I refuse."

"Titania, there's nothing more for you here," Mom insisted. "Do not make me come for you. There's no need for this to be a fight."

Titania smirked as the other Lords closed in on me. Soren was the first to reach me, his calloused hands closing around my arms. He leaned close and whispered something for my ears only.

"It's a trap."

Titania's eyes flashed. Soren's hands were ripped from me, his snarl as he struggled to maintain his footing helpless under Titania's power. I sent magic tearing from the ground, vines dripping with thorns and poison wrapping around the fae's legs.

Titania laughed and shook them off.

Mom held her hand up. "Titania! Enough!"

But Ethan's hands wrapped around me next, his grip punishing. Vines tore from the ground, but Titania pushed them away with little effort. Thorvin approached carrying something glittering and covered in bone.

His steps were jerky and halting, his eyes glowing burnished gold. "I'm sorry," he whispered, hands rising to place the crown atop my head.

I didn't understand what the fuck was happening, and why she was so insistent I take the crown. It didn't matter if I did today or tomorrow or two years from now, did it?

A flash of silver blew past us and slammed into Titania. *Tess.* The fae's mouth opened wide, her eyes glowing a familiar icy pale shade. She swayed on her feet, Titania's golden beauty in stark contrast to the death that had invaded her bones. Her cheeks hollowed and sank into her skull. Pale skin turned the gray of death, and her mouth opened, Tess's banshee scream shaking the world.

"Oh," Mom breathed, eyes wide as she watched a fae queen die right before her eyes.

Tess's flickering form appeared from the ruins of Titania's body, relief spearing through me, but when she lifted her head and opened her mouth, her form went transparent before disappearing in a pop of sound. The rest of Titania's skin flaked off, blowing away like ash in the wind, and just as her bones sank to the ground, I realized it was too late.

Thorvin slammed the crown atop my head.

Betrayal. I remembered Thalia's prophetic words as the crown's magic snaked into my soul.

The World Tree sang through my mind, its staggering power colliding with my blood stream. I sank to my knees, trying to push the magic into the ground, but it was too intense, too much. Magic poured from every orifice in my body, bubbling up through my skin.

It took me a moment to realize what was happening.

Titania exploded into ash, releasing Thorvin from her strange hold. His eyes went wide with horror, and he reached for me, trying to remove the crown. Mom grabbed him by the arm and pulled him away. Once he was safe, Mom hurried over and sank to her knees before me.

She placed her hands on either side of my face. "You have to conquer the magic."

"Can't," I said through clenched teeth. "Too much."

Caelan, Soren, Rowan, and Ben had come back and gathered around, as close as they could while the magic roared through me. This crown and the tree were inexorably linked, but we couldn't rule side by side. This was not the path my father had chosen for me. This was something else. Something corrupt.

The World Tree planned to absorb me, the magic it had left me with no gift at all. It'd been a path back to claim me. Cernunnos might have expelled the seed, but he'd failed to wipe all the traces from my body, and maybe couldn't have even if he'd wanted to.

The tree wanted all of me, every bit of its power back and every bit of my magic. I might have made the snap decision to swallow it to keep it from those who wanted to misuse it, but looking back maybe that's not what my mother had been trying to do at all. Maybe, in her own way, she'd been trying to save me from myself. But once the seed had spent time inside me, it liked what I had to offer. With me, it could expand its power, could claim all the realms and control who entered them at will.

The fae had never truly had control over this astonishing power, but they'd leashed it to their will. Until I made the choice to expose it to my very essence.

Hindsight, as the humans would say, was always twenty-twenty.

"Help her," Caelan begged.

"Tess," I whimpered, even as fae magic tore me apart.

"She's fine," Mom said, cool fingers pressed against my brow. "Banshees do not die. They…" She pressed her lips together. "She will be back, I swear to you."

Tears slipped down my face. I held my hands against my abdomen, the weak spot there caused by the initial rupture flaring with pain. Taking the crown off, even if I could remove it, was futile. The spell had already triggered and buried its way through my psyche.

"Who?"

Mom knew what I wanted to know immediately. "I do not know, but I plan to find out."

Caelan crouched beside me, his warm hand splayed on my back. "Why didn't you do anything?" he asked Cliona.

Mom's skin pulled tight against her bones. "We cannot harm one of our own. It is one of our oldest laws."

"Even if she's killing your daughter?" Caelan snarled.

Mom closed her eyes for a brief moment. "It is our oldest law," she whispered, but I saw the grief swimming in her eyes.

A flash of emerald and gold magic revealed my father, bare chested and savage. As I watched him walk toward me, the wounds on his body, given to him by those warriors in the hall sealed. He crouched next to Cliona and touched my brow, closing his eyes. A tendril of his magic soared through my mind and swept through my body.

When he opened his eyes and I saw an endless well of grief, I knew it was too late for me.

"What will happen?" I croaked.

"Your body and essence will be absorbed into the tree," Cernunnos said, his eyes a swirling vortex of power.

Mom shook her head. "No."

Cernunnos lay a hand on her arm, but she jerked away. "No. Cernunnos. We did not work this hard for this to happen."

I could feel my body slipping away cell by cell, but this moment…I'd waited my entire life for answers, and Mom had finally given me one.

"You worked together?" I whispered.

Mom bowed her head. "I would have done anything to keep you safe, even if it made you hate me."

Her eyes, a carbon copy of mine, shimmered with tears. "I have failed you."

Caelan's grip tightened. "No. Evie. You must fight this. You have to fight this. Rowan finally talked some sense into me, and I planned—" He cut himself off.

I looked up at him and saw all the possibilities between us slipping away as my life force flowed through the ground and into the roots of the World Tree miles away. Lifting a trembling hand to his face, I cupped his jaw. "I wish we had more time."

Caelan's face went white. "Evie." He bowed his head and let out a choked curse.

Rowan put a hand on his shoulder and crouched beside him. "If anyone can fight this, you can." He shook his head. "After all of this, I refuse to believe this is what fate has in store for you."

Mom looked at my father. "There's nothing you can do?"

"The magic predates me. It does not recognize nor respond to my power."

My attention focused on those words. "Moira," I whispered. "Call Moira."

"A vampire cannot help you," Mom said. "But she can say goodbye."

I shook my head. "She helped me heal. Last time."

Ben had stayed silent the entire time, but at that, he jerked. "How?" he demanded. "Maybe I can do the same while we wait."

"I have no idea," I said on a half sob. "She made me a tea that counteracted the magic."

Cernunnos stared. "A tea?" he said disbelievingly.

Soren, thank the gods, already had his phone out.

He spoke into the phone a second later. "I know you don't want to speak to me but get to Evie's property as soon as possible. She needs you."

Moira would not dismiss a summons like that. I only hoped she was close. Her being able to help was a serious long shot, but one I was willing to take.

And if she couldn't, at least she'd be here while I faded.

"Want me to call Ash?" Caelan asked.

I nodded.

It took twenty minutes, and I was hanging onto life by my fingernails. The tree demanded everything from me and had taken some of the most important parts, my legs sank half into the ground, roots climbing up the sides of my thighs and dug into my hips. But this was no communion of a Floromancer with Mother Earth.

This was a brutal claiming by a power I couldn't hope to beat.

Moira dropped her bag and slammed to her knees before me, Ash not far behind her. Her dark eyes swept over my face and body until a choked cry came from her throat. She reached out to touch the roots and jerked back her hand in horror when she felt what had claimed me.

Ash was more circumspect in his reaction. He sat beside

Moira, his eyes roving over every inch of my body, lips pressed tight when he realized what had happened.

"You can't break free?" he asked quietly.

I shook my head.

Moira dug through her bag, holding and discarding several items before letting out a frustrated cry. "I can't—I can't help," she choked, eyes wide with horror. "I can't help you."

Soren came to his knees beside her and brought her into the circle of his arms. Claws slid from her fingers as she gripped the front of his shirt and buried her face in his chest, her mouth twisted into a rictus of grief, bloody tears sliding down her face.

"I'm so sorry, Moira."

She reached out a hand and put it on my knee as she tried to collect herself. But when she did, she turned to my father and launched herself at him, lethal claws sliding out to gouge his face.

"Moira. No!" I tried to lunge for her, but I was trapped tight.

Cernunnos made no move to attack her. He let her claws slide against his cheek, flaying open his skin. He let her fists pummel his chest and her screams rend the air, and when she'd exhausted herself, my father gathered her into his powerful arms and held her, allowing her to grieve against him even as he knew Moira blamed him for everything.

Ash bowed his head. Magic spooled into his palms, and he touched my heart, his hand splayed over my breastbone. Tiny leaves spouted from his skin as he worked inside me, his power encasing my heart in a cage not even the seed could touch. "Just in case," he said, his breath coming in gasps when he finished. "Fight, Evie. Like you've never fought before." He lifted his head, eyes sparkling with an emerald glow. "Use everything you have. It's going to take you, regardless, you might as well go down fighting if you can."

"I can't do anything," I confessed. "Every bit of my power is being funneled away." Tears spilled down my face. "How can I fight something the Fae King cannot? Something the most powerful fae bow to?"

A sad smile and endless grief etched lines in his face. "You have something none of those people do, Evie." He leaned forward and murmured in my ear, the words so low only he and I could hear.

"Use everything. *Everything.*"

I didn't know what he meant, but I knew I didn't want them to see me...end. Not like this. Not this horrific, slow purge of my very being. "Take her," I whispered. "I want you to remember me how I was. Not like this."

When he pulled back, he withdrew his magic and touched my cheek. A moment later he rose and gathered Moira from my father's arms.

The vampire screamed my name and fought against him. Ash whispered something in her ear. Moira's eyes widened, and she turned her attention to Ash. He held a finger to his lips and carried her away.

A drop of pure silvery magic appeared in Mom's palm. She pressed her hand to my collarbone. "A piece of me," she whispered and leaned to kiss my brow. "Fight, Evangeline."

She rose and took her place beside my father who held his hand out. A piece of gold and emerald magic sank into my forehead. Seconds later they were gone.

Soren touched my hair and walked away. Rowan cupped my jaw and gently pressed a kiss to my lips that made me laugh.

Rowan grinned even as I watched his heart break. "This is the one and only time I could get away with that, so why the hell not."

Caelan's grief-stricken eyes didn't waver from me. Soren touched my shoulder and walked away with Rowan. Ben was the last to go.

"For what it's worth," he said in a soft voice. "I'm sorry."

By now my hands were trapped inside the earth, forcing my body into an awkward angle. "Me too," I whispered.

He bent and brushed his fingers over my cheek, then turned and walked away.

Caelan and I were the only ones left. He sat before me, gold ringing his stormy eyes.

"What can I do?" he whispered.

"Stay with me." I gave him a wobbly smile. "It won't be much longer."

Caelan's jaw tightened.

"I wish I would have said yes," I whispered. "I'm sorry I fought you for so long. I'm sorry…for all of it."

He shook his head. "No. You have nothing to be sorry about. I'm the one who's sorry. For being brash and impatient and insisting you do things my way." He blew out a breath. "I'm an idiot and I promise you if we can get you out, I will never take you for granted. Never again."

"We still have a lot of things to work out."

He sighed. "I know, and I don't care. We'll work through them. All I want is you by my side. In whatever way I can have you."

I only had a few minutes before I stopped breathing, the roots inside me moving slowly toward my lungs. Everything below my belly button was blissfully numb.

"I love you," I whispered. "I don't know when it happened. I was too busy alternating between craving you and wanting to kill you, but one day I opened my eyes, and I knew that I loved you more than breathing."

A soft smile. "Who knew you were capable of such pretty words?"

I snorted. "Dying will do that to a girl."

One sharp shake of his head. "No. I refuse to believe you're dying. We'll figure a way out of this. We always do."

My breath was coming in short gasps, the roots pulling me all the way to the ground. "If we do, I reserve the right to kick Ethan's ass."

"Garrett has him." A savage grin crossed his lips. "We plan on holding him for a while."

"Your Lords are falling like flies."

"Good," Caelan snarled. "Let them fall. Who has need of a Council if they play games like this?"

"Where's Thorvin?" He'd disappeared just as Titania was dying.

"No idea, but I don't care right now."

"It wasn't his fault. Titania had him under some form of mind control. He couldn't help himself." Thorvin appeared as horrified as I was.

"I'll deal with Thorvin later."

I turned my cheek as my face touched the ground, barely able to get a tiny bit of air. "I love you," I whispered one more time.

"Stay with me," Caelan begged. "Evie, please."

But I could fight no longer. The ground opened under my body, sucking me under and straight into the burning, beating heart of the World Tree.

CHAPTER
Thirty~Two

CAELAN

I had no idea how long I sat on the ground staring at the place where Evie sank into the earth and disappeared. The sun had peeked above the clouds some time ago, casting a cheerful pink light across the sky. And still I sat, hoping against all hope she'd appear and tell me this was all some horrible joke.

She was unhinged enough to pull something like that off, and it only made me love her more.

But when the sun finally rose, and the temperatures warmed slightly, and the only sign Evie had ever been there was the depression of where her body had been absorbed into the ground, I knew this nightmare was real.

I bowed my head and buried my face in my hands, a mournful howl tearing from my throat to shatter the quiet morning.

It wasn't long before a heavy hand dropped onto my shoulder, and Rowan sat down beside me.

"I can't go back," I rasped. "Evie—she's—"

"I know," Rowan said. "The tree has…changed."

I turned a hopeful look his way, but the other Lord shook his head. "There's no sign of her, but I feel her magic soaking the area."

"How did this happen?" I turned my eyes to the heavens and

fought for a semblance of understanding, a moment of clarity in this madness. And even though no answers came from above, I found one in my heart.

Power. Wasn't that what it all came down to? Humans fought and climbed over each other to reach the pinnacle of their careers. I'd done the same thing, scrambling over others who might have wanted this position, killing them to take the title of Lord. And what had it gotten me?

A depression in the earth and a bright light extinguished like she'd never existed.

Except this horrible hollow feeling in my heart knew her, loved her, grieved her.

"Fuck," I said, my voice breaking. "You were right. As much as I hate to admit it, I should have done a million things differently. Why was I so—"

"Wolfish?" Rowan said with a chuckle. "Possessiveness is in your nature, but Evie is not something to be owned."

"I've fucked it all up, and it's too late to fix it."

Rowan didn't say anything for a long time. He inhaled and exhaled a heavy breath and finally shook his head. "If there's anyone who can get out of this, it's her. Don't count her out yet."

"Do you know something I don't?"

He shook his head. "No. But we both know her well. The only thing we can do right now is believe she will find her way back."

He clapped a hand on my back and rose, holding his hand out for me to rise.

As much as I wanted to curl into a ball and let the earth take me so I could be next to her, Rowan was right. Evie was a fighter. I could *not* believe she was gone. If I believed that, I would have no purpose.

"Let's go back to the Keep," Rowan said. "I posted a guard of our most trusted people around the tree. Some of the fae have shown up asking for access, but I denied them and will continue to do so."

"Moira and Ash?"

Rowan's jaw tightened. "Devastated. Tess hasn't been seen since…"

"Yeah," I said with a heavy sigh.

"Her shop will be closed for a while."

"Understandably so."

The ride to the Keep felt like it took no time at all while simultaneously taking forever. When Rowan pulled up to the front, I didn't wait for the vehicle to stop all the way before I was out and running to the back.

The tree stood, a glowing beacon of power, but all I could feel was hatred toward it and what it had taken from me.

But where the leaves had once been a vivid green, a red and gold thread ran through the bark and the leaves now, giving the tree a slightly sinister look. My lips twitched.

It was just like Evie to give the thing one final fuck you as she died.

Tears filled my eyes, and I had to turn away lest I tear the goddamned thing down with my two bare hands.

She would come back to me.

It was the only thing keeping me going.

CHAPTER
Thirty-Three
FOUR WEEKS LATER
MOIRA

Nothing mattered when the thing you loved most went away.

I sat at the table piled high with petals and wanted to set the entire thing on fire. Flowers were a symbol of hope, and all my hope had died the moment I watched my best friend get absorbed into the ground like fae fertilizer.

Claws slid from my fingers, and I had to take a deep breath before I went into a killing rage. A warm hand reached over and squeezed my shoulder.

"Moira," Ash said as he set a steaming mug of Earl Grey before me. "Have faith."

I scoffed. "Four weeks, Ash. She's been gone for four weeks. When does our faith die and we come to terms with her death?"

"Evie is a powerful being." Ash's nostrils flared. "So much power I can barely stand next to her without feeling like I'm going to burst into flames. And not only that, she has the Mother's blessing. The world loves her and that matters."

"Not even Cernunnos could save her," I muttered. "If the Fae King could do nothing to save his daughter from such a terrible fate, do you think the Mother could?"

Ash's measured look made me feel awful. He was right. Faith

could bring you through the direst of circumstances, but we hadn't just lost Evie.

Despite Cliona's promise to the contrary, Tess had not returned.

The shop had lost its spirit. Both literal and metaphorical. With Evie gone, Little Shop of Florals had lost its heart. With Tess gone, we'd lost curious innocence and hope.

I swallowed hard and clenched a handful of petals in my fist, crushing them in my grip. The scent of rose and jasmine filled the air. It should have been pleasant, but all I could think about was our loss.

I was a thing of teeth and claws and burning rage, and Evie's love and care was the only thing keeping me tethered to this world. Without her…

"I miss her," I whispered.

"Evie is well-loved." His lips twisted. "I wish she were here for us to tell her so."

"I miss both of them. What happened? What brought this on? One minute she was there and the next, she was just…gone. What kind of world could let something like that happen? She mattered so much. And now she's not here. Just gone. Like a fucking soap bubble or something." I laid a fist against my heart. "She lives here, and I know she will always be there, but I want to hear her voice. I want—" My nostrils flared. I shoved the basket off the table, the air filling with a riot of pink and burgundy petals.

Ash's face softened. "I know it's difficult to have faith when circumstances seem so dire, but I choose to believe she's still in there fighting to come back to us. Eventually, even I will lose that faith, and when that time comes, then we can discuss what happens next. But remember, Moira, Evie is not only fae. She's kept one secret from almost everyone."

My head snapped up. "You think the Chimera part of her might save her?"

"There's no way to tell, but it's unaccounted for. If the fae trapped her, maybe the Chimera will be the thing that frees her."

I didn't see how. She always felt the thing inside her was a monster, a ravaging beast raging to claim power, but I'd never seen that. I mean, yes, she ate way too much red meat since she'd accepted its claim on her, and I knew she hoped we didn't notice, but there'd been no real change in personality other than her physical hunger and the occasional mood swing when she hadn't siphoned off enough power.

Neither one of those two things was enough to make me believe she'd changed from the Evie we all knew and loved. It was only one more thing to deal with—a terrible thing in how it happened, but one that had saved her when all hope seemed lost.

Maybe it would do that for her again.

"She doesn't know how to use the power," I said, thinking through some things aloud.

"Evie has always been good with intuitive magic," Ash said as he bent to scoop the scattered petals back into the basket.

I got down on my hands and knees to help. "She overthinks," I mused.

"Absolutely. And what does she have plenty of time to do now that she's been absorbed into a tree?"

I sat back on my haunches. "Think about how she's going to get out. If she can think at all."

Ash nodded. "Trust me when I say, she can. I've touched that tree. Evie's essence burns inside the thing. She's still there. I can feel her."

Ash's magic worked much differently than mine. I had little domain over the earth like he or Evie did, though I used its bounty in some of my work. If he said he could feel her, then I believed him.

"How can we help her?" I asked.

He scooped up the last of the petals. "She said you helped her heal after she was wounded when Cernunnos and Ben's magic couldn't. Is that true?"

I hesitated, unwilling to divulge everything, but still nodded.

This was Ash, one of my closest friends. If my power could help Evie, I'd carve my secrets into my skin to assist.

"Hazel will be back in a few days. She's been working on a few things to help us see how much of Evie is left. We'll need to clear the visit through Caelan—"

I snorted. The Shifter Lord was even more obsessed with Evie than we were. "He'll grant us access anytime we wish."

Caelan had come by once every few days every week since Evie had left us. He kept a twenty-four-hour guard on the tree, and any fae who managed to get inside the Lord's wards had met a gruesome end by the teeth and claws of angry shifters. It'd gotten so bad, the fae and shifters were close to being in a full out war.

The fae couldn't travel to the other realms because Caelan flat out refused anyone access. Cernunnos had stood by him in that regard, though more of a silent partner because of his position in the fae kingdom. He'd strengthened Caelan's wards and rebuilt the ones on Evie's property to keep curious gossip hounds away.

For our part, we'd told our customers and all the nosy Nellies coming in that Evie had taken an extended vacation to Scotland, and she had no return date as of yet. When someone pushed, I was happy to show them my teeth and claws.

Evie was only unhinged when someone pushed her too far.

I was unhinged all the time, while keeping a false and shiny veneer of civility around me, and I was spoiling for a fight. *Come at me bro, and I'll fuck you up and call your mother to gloat about it.*

Business had dropped by about thirty percent. Again, Evie was sweeter than me and had a way with people I did not. I much preferred to be out of the spotlight and in the shadows. Ash was too introverted to deal with customers for too long before he retreated into the walk-in refrigerator.

Tess…well, Tess was gone, but she'd be even worse than the both of us combined.

If Evie didn't come back, we were fucked.

And so was the shop she'd lovingly built with hands and

sweat equity, because we were shit business owners. We were here because of her love and mercy. Ash had come to her damaged and broken.

I'd come to her angry at everything and everyone.

Tess had come to her a lost wanderer who needed love and care.

And Evie being Evie had given it to all of us while keeping none for herself.

I hurried to the walk-in freezer, buried my face in my shirt, and let out a bloodcurdling scream, one after the other until my throat was raw and my tears had dried.

She had to come back. She had to.

If she didn't, there was nothing left for me.

The accursed tree taking up so much of my property hadn't changed since the moment I'd returned home after Evie's…fuck. I refused to believe she was dead.

Evie's absence. That felt better to say. Her forced sabbatical.

Temporary, explainable, fleeting things. Never the permanence of death.

"Gods," I swore to myself. "I'm an idiot."

Seymour bumped his main trap against my hip. We'd taken to sitting out here each night, watching for any sign of change. Seymour, as intuitive as he was, knew something was wrong. He'd gone right up to the tree, tipped his traps up as if he could see all the way to the top, and let out a strange, warbling keen, as if he, too, knew his mistress was inside.

I'd found him out here every day, his pot leaning against its rough bark.

Simone's familiar figure exited the back door, too far away for me to make out her face, but every one of my shifters moved a certain way. I could tell each one of them by their gait, but Simone's hair gave her away every time.

I didn't get up. She made her way through the yard and came to sit beside me, straightening her legs out before her.

"Anything?"

I shook my head.

Simone sighed. "I feel like I can sense her in there." She shook her head. "Sounds insane, I know, but Evie just has such a brilliant presence. Every time we stood beside each other, I felt like I was standing next to a supernova."

I understood. "She's there. I feel her too."

Simone nodded, even if she didn't understand. "Her turtle vine has faded, as if it knows Evie is gone from this world."

My jaw clenched to hold the angry words back. Evie was not gone.

Only absent.

"Seymour misses her. I often find him out here."

Simone scooted a little closer, a wolf seeking comfort from Pack. But I didn't have any comfort to give her. Not since I'd lost Evie. I was an animated shell of the Lord I'd been before, and my people were beginning to notice. If things didn't change, I'd find myself on the receiving end of challenges designed to take my position.

I couldn't muster up enough feeling to give a shit.

"Nadia returned," Simone said after a few minutes. "She's growing impatient."

I didn't care about her, either. "Tell her Gianna is dead. The Lords disposed of her body in a funeral befitting someone of her status."

Simone sucked in a shocked breath. "Caelan. Her family—"

"She was murdered by a rogue Chimera who has since been... handled."

My Omega stared at me in horror. "They won't settle for that excuse."

I turned my attention toward her, letting her see in my face how little concerned me these days. "Then tell them to challenge me. I will burn their world down and dance on the ashes of their bones."

Simone dropped her eyes and swallowed hard. "Very well." She rose without another word and headed back inside.

Seymour made another warble and bumped me again. I stroked a hand over his trap. "You think she's still there, too, don't you?"

Seymour bumped me again.

CHAPTER
Thirty-Five

Time had become a true construct as I floated in a space of magic and unfathomable, ancient power. My father was the Fae King, and his magic felt like an ember compared to…whatever this was.

I'd lost myself for a while, no idea how long. But Ash had kept my heart protected in a cage of bramble and ironwood, and eventually I, or whatever was left of me, had awoken, floating in this strange never-ending place. I had no true body, or nothing I could see anyhow, nothing but my mind and my burning heart filled with grief and rage and love.

And so, I'd spent my time floating and thinking in the nothingness, wondering how I could possibly come back to myself when the tree had taken everything. My life, my friends, my magic, my…everything.

I had no greenery, no flowers or fauna, no friends or family, no Caelan, no love.

Nothing but the emptiness and a well of grief so profound I could drown inside it if I let myself.

Fury rose in me, an anger so vast I could set the world on fire. I had everything, and I'd gotten tangled up in politics I had no right to be involved in and look at me now.

Fae princess. Ha.

Just a girl made up of atoms and a thorn encased heart with nowhere to go floating in a sea of tree magic.

My memoir would be explosive.

I had nowhere to go and nothing to see and nothing but time on my…

Oh yeah. I had no hands.

This would be funny if it wasn't happening to me.

I rued the day I'd gotten caught up in the fae. I'd been too trusting, too open, too willing not to tell them to fuck right off and go play in the trees and mounds from whence they came.

But if I hadn't done the things I'd done, would I have met Caelan or realized my mom and dad had sacrificed so much to keep me safe?

Would I have known a tender touch from a lover or met Rowan and grown apples in the greenhouse?

Would I have made Seymour or laughed with Simone? Made a giant Jacaranda to piss off a Shifter Lord?

Accepted the parts of myself that terrified me and allowed me to become the person I needed to be to survive?

Granted, this wasn't technically surviving, but I was still conscious. And that meant there was still a way out. I just had to find it.

My thoughts wandered to Moira and how she'd healed me when nothing another fae had done. Was that the key? I wasn't in tune enough with my fae side to know what I could or couldn't do, but if my father couldn't counteract this magic, what hope did I have to do the same?

But I wasn't just fae, was I?

A thought occurred to me, something so outlandish and wild that I spent the next…

Sigh. Time. I could have been here for a hundred years, and I wouldn't know it, would I?

Let's just say I spent a long ass time working the plan out.

And you bet your ass, I had a plan.

Sometimes Hazel pissed me off. The witch was good at what she did, but the way she went about it made me want to chew my own arm off.

She was so goddamned slow. How many times did she have to mortar and pestle herbs to get the right consistency? Goddamn woman, get a food processor or a coffee grinder.

For fuck's sake.

I was barely keeping my shit together while Hazel was humming to herself as she set up the boundary surrounding the tree. Did all the candles have to be white? Couldn't we just go to the dollar store instead of ordering some stupid European beeswax candles 'soaked in the light of the first Monday's full moon.'

Witchcraft felt like being punked. Did any of this shit actually matter, or was there some massive conglomerate full of white dudes wearing suits and expensive cufflinks in the shape of dollar bills laughing their ass off while they tricked the masses into purchasing shit that didn't matter?

Power was inherent. Power was everywhere, all around us in the air and ground. We were made up of atoms for crying out loud, and the forces around us fueled those atoms. We could all become supernovas if we put our minds to it.

And Hazel was over here worried about spring water pulled from a virgin's tears.

Kill me now, please.

Even Caelan was twitchy. His claws kept retracting and sliding from his skin, and he looked like he wanted to bite Hazel's head off like the last part of a lollipop.

"Staring at me won't make me go any faster," Hazel said primly as she added a touch of probably something stupid to the cast iron bowl in the middle of her wooden table.

"How is this going to help?" Caelan asked, his voice barely understandable. Eyes of burnished gold cast a light over the area.

Ash was seated cross-legged on the ground, his eyes closed, though I could feel his amusement. He always thought it was funny when I got annoyed like this. The dryad had seen my temper and didn't flinch, so I wasn't afraid for him to see my annoyance.

I kept my temper mostly hidden from Evie, though when she got back, maybe I'd be more open about myself. She deserved it.

I was a shit for hiding myself from her for so long. All she'd ever done was love me.

"It may not," Hazel said. "This is merely a beacon to let her know where we are. If she's still conscious, it may lead her home."

"Her power is gone," I said. "How can she escape?"

Hazel's hands stilled. She turned to face me. "Never in my life have I met someone with her sheer will to live. All Evie wanted to do was overcome her challenges and try to carve out some semblance of a life, even after everything. I have to believe she is fighting to find a way to return to us." She buried her shaking hands in the folds of her skirt.

"It is the only thing I can believe if I don't want to fall to my knees and scream to the heavens."

I blinked in surprise as Hazel turned back around and finished up.

Okay. Maybe I'd been a little hasty in my judgment. If she needed virgin tear spring water, I'd stop being a bitch about it.

She finished up a few minutes later and stepped away, her sharp gaze taking everything in one last time.

"Step back," she commanded.

We all walked back a few feet.

Hazel lifted a hand and twisted it toward the circle. As one, every candle lit up. The brick of incense began to smoke before a sharp, pungent scent circled the area. I wrinkled my nose but stayed silent.

Hazel nodded once to herself.

"Now we wait."

Fear had no place here. There was nothing to be afraid of except for my thoughts.

Granted, those were terrifying on a good day, but right now, it was just me and my consciousness floating along like one of those long-lasting batteries.

The moment my metaphorical battery died, I'd be in deeper trouble, but I still possessed all my faculties, and I'd come up with a real dumb plan.

If it failed, no harm, no foul. I was basically a space rock so no big deal.

But if it succeeded…the fae were going to be real pissed off at me.

A tug to my left caught my attention. Nothing had tugged me since I'd been in this place. I sent my thoughts in that direction and let myself float along. But the thing, whatever it was, kept tugging, and I caught a hint of something familiar.

Something…someone who loved me.

Hazel. If I could cry, I would.

Hazel was calling me home.

And I would do my damnedest to answer her call.

I let go of everything fae. I let go of my first knowing of Cliona. I let go of my mother's eyes and cold demeanor and the later revelations that told me maybe she really did love me. I let go of my father, my plants, my roses, my shop, everything that connected me to the fae. My Floromancy was the hardest to let go, but I needed the burning fury of something else to save me.

When my mind was clear and I'd buried my heritage so far down I could no longer find it, I let the fiery rage of the Chimera fill my thorned heart. I thought about Finn and his hands and lips on me, and how I'd felt such hope only to be let down and wounded both in spirit and in body. Fury filled my missing bones, my veins, my heart. I let the anger drive me until I hurtled through the ancient magic like a rocket, heading straight for Hazel's summons.

I remembered my hurt and pain and confusion, and I remembered Finn's burning eyes when he savaged me. I remembered how hard I fought to come back to myself.

All I ever wanted was to be loved.

And someone had used that against me, sending me into a years'-long spiral of grief and self-recrimination.

No more.

Even when I'd worked so hard to overcome what happened to me, I still held the feeling so close to my heart that I was flawed.

Nothing.

No one.

I didn't deserve love or friendship or anything because I was fundamentally flawed.

Fuck that.

I was Evie godsdamned Quinn, and I would no longer be afraid of who I was, even if it scared the shit out of everyone else.

If I had to become the Chimera to find my way back to the people I loved, then I would. I'd gladly wear the crown of a savage monster if it put me back into Caelan's arms. If I could see my friends again. If I could touch the ground and feel the living earth between my fingers once more.

A jagged split tore through the never-ending nothingness, the color of my Chimera.

Red and gold, like a bleeding heart of fourteen karat gold.

Take that, fucker, I roared inside my thorned heart and hurtled toward the opening.

CHAPTER
Thirty~Eight
CAELAN

The sound of wood splitting plunged the Keep into absolute silence.

Moira rose to her feet, her eyes wide with shock.

Ash's expression tightened.

My breath caught and held, praying for something I knew I didn't deserve but wanted more than anything I'd ever wanted in my life.

Hazel bowed her head and brought her clasped hands up to her heart.

"Evie," I whispered. "Come home to me."

CHAPTER
Thirty~Nine

MOIRA

A scream of rage and defiance tore through the skies, the voice of the divine feminine clawing itself back home. Flowers sprung up beneath us, a carpet of riotous color underneath our feet.

Poe and Fee shot through the sky, their wings beating in glorious color as they circled the tree that had brought us so much misery. A jagged tear formed in the bark, the ragged edges the color of crimson and gold, a beacon of power shouting a challenge to anyone who might question its right to appear.

Tears sprang to my eyes.

A soft shuffle of wind and Cernunnos and Cliona appeared inside the Keep.

"Get back," the Fae King warned, his eyes trained on that crack. He said nothing else, only kept his attention on the tree.

We stepped back as a shield of silver and green rose around us.

The tear widened, the edges of it glowing with crimson fire.

A hand slid into mine. Ash. I squeezed his fingers, unable to form any words.

The Shifter Lord's posture was tight, his expression blank, but his eyes burned a fiery gold.

The leaves were the next to catch fire, a cheery crimson bonfire.

"Fuck yeah," I whispered. "Burn it all down."

We waited for I don't know how long, watching with held breaths as the tear slowly widened and fire consumed the World Tree.

None of us gave a shit about the fae at that moment, at the possible consequences this might bring.

I wasn't even sure Cernunnos or Cliona cared. They did nothing to stop what was happening, only provided a shield for us in case things worsened.

But when the wood began to groan, Cernunnos took a step back, his eyes widening. Cliona stepped closer to his side, her face a pale mask of worry.

He extended his shield to protect him and Evie's mother.

Seconds later, the world exploded into fire and knocked us all ass over teakettle.

A nude woman with burning skin and long ebony hair stood there, her naked back to us.

Her eyes glowed a furious crimson and gold. She opened her mouth and a vengeful scream tore from her lungs. Magic sparked at her palms as she raised her hands.

The ancient tree trembled under her gaze, its wood groaning as it tried to arch back from her fury, but it was too old, too rooted to the world to escape her rage.

Evie Quinn sent all her power at the remnants of the World Tree.

And a moment later, the world stood still as that all-consuming tree collapsed into a pile of crimson ash.

My best friend stared at it, her lips still curled with fiery anger. Her hands dropped a second later, and her eyes rolled back into her head.

Caelan, the Shifter Lord of Texas, and the shifter I suspected might become family soon, caught her before she hit the ground.

CHAPTER

Forty

TWO WEEKS LATER

We were all sitting around a campfire drinking hot chocolate when an odd shift in the air sent the hair on the back of my neck standing up. Things had changed exponentially in my life, my magic the main thing.

I was more sensitive to power than ever before, and I recognized this signature of power.

I rose and jerked my head to Moira and Ash. Without a word, they rose to follow.

We walked through Caelan's property until I found what I was looking for.

Ash sucked in a breath. "Tess!"

The banshee lay curled on her side, unconscious. I shrugged my jacket off and covered her up. Ash bent and scooped her up, cradling her close to his chest.

"Thank the gods," Moira breathed. She brushed a hand over Tess's hair and closed her eyes.

Caelan was there a second later. "She can have a room in the Keep. Simone is getting one ready right now. The Keep Healer will be down in a moment."

Ash nodded his thanks and took off running with Moira close on his heels.

Caelan slid his arm around my waist. "I was beginning to worry she'd never return."

"Mom said when a banshee inhabits a living body, it can take weeks for them to recover. But what Tess did..." My voice trailed off.

What the banshee had done was save a lot of lives. She might not have been fast enough to save me from that cursed crown, but I'd found my way back.

Just like she had.

"She destroyed Titania from the inside out," Caelan finished.

My mother had been shaken by Tess's act and the sheer power it must have taken to do so.

She had no idea how long it would take for Tess to regenerate but was confident she'd come back.

And she had.

I laid my head on his chest, soaking in his warmth. "We're complete."

"Mmm," he agreed. He turned to gather me in his arms. "Will you open the shop soon?"

I shrugged. "This extended vacation is kinda nice."

He smiled against my hair. "Joy Springs needs its Floromancer."

"And they'll get her," I agreed. "When she's ready." I tilted my head to watch the Shifter Lord. "Not a moment sooner."

He brushed my lips with his. "Any more visitors?"

There'd been a steady stream of angry fae outside my house over the last few weeks.

"Not after I fried the last one." I had no idea what kind of fae it'd been, but the woman with strange eyes had shown up outside my wards, demanding I answer for the tree's destruction.

I'd responded by giving her double middle fingers and turning her to ash, a cool new trick I'd learned how to do when I came hurtling out of that fucking tree.

The fiery talent had been coming in handy lately. There were a lot of pissed off fae demanding I pay for what I'd done to the World Tree.

Of course, they didn't give a shit what that stupid tree had done to me.

Typical fae logic.

Caelan's low chuckle sent shivers down my spine. "How about we go inside? Tess might be out for a while, and I have something I'd like to show you."

I snorted. "Is that something inside your pants?"

Caelan scooped me up and loped toward the house, ignoring my screams of laughter.

"I always want to show you what's inside my pants," he growled.

"And I always want to see it."

He stopped at the front door and kicked it open.

"Good news because I'm never going to stop showing you."

I laughed and twined my fingers through his hair, bringing his face down to mine to plant a searing kiss against his lips.

"Mine," I said quietly.

"Forever," Caelan swore.

Keep reading for a look at Book Five
Shifting Resolve

Shifting Resolve

BOOK 5, SHIFTER LORDS

Evie Quinn is a survivor, but she's tired of being a pawn in everyone else's game.

She never asked to be the heir to the fae throne, a walking, otherworldly bridge for the gods, or the hottest bachelorette in the supernatural realms. But here she is—dodging dozens of random marriage proposals and doing her best to keep Caelan from committing paranormal genocide.

Everyone wants a piece of Evie these days. The Council's patience has worn off, and they're ready to marry her off to the highest bidder. The gods want to use her for their own gain, and Caelan is growing ever frustrated with her attempts to keep things between them paused. But Evie still isn't ready to be a queen or a bride or a bridge, or anything forcing her to give up her autonomy.

But time has run out, and with Evie's inner monster dangerously unstable, her only hope might be to do the one thing no one expects—finally taking control of her world-shaking power, her fate, and most important of all, her heart.

Also by S.E. Babin

Shifter Lords

Shift of Heart

Shift of Morals

Power Shift

Shifting Winds

Shifting Resolve

Shift of Rule

Shift of the Wild

Goddess Shifting

Cocktails in Hell

A Twist of Demon

A Shake of Succubus

A Stir of Fairies

A Dash of Vampire

A Touch of Angel

A Whisper of Wolf

A Smidge of Voodoo

A Hint of Hero

OTHER SERIES

A Shelf Indulgence Cozy Mystery Series

Book of the Virago

Trailer Park Transylvania

Psychic Cleaner

About the Author

Sheryl likes cake too much and can be found hoarding it while hiding from her children in the pantry closet.

Follow her on Amazon at: https://www.amazon.com/S-E-Babin/e/B00J1J236A

A small press bound by the belief that every voice matters.

Sign up for our newsletter to learn about new releases and more.
https://oliver-heberbooks.com/subscribe/

Follow us on social media:

facebook.com/oliverheberbooks
instagram.com/oliverheberbooks
amazon.com/oliverheberbooks
youtube.com/@OliverHeberBooksPublisher